Jamestown Woman

By
Sue Allan

ISBN 978-1-906070-01-4

First published 2006 by domtom publishing ltd

Acknowledgements

The author would like to acknowledge:
her collaborator and researcher,
Roger Thomas Vorhauer

Printed and bound in the UK by
DPS Partnership Ltd
www.dpsltd.net

For my father

Chapter One

'A man must make his opportunity, as oft as find it'
- Francis Bacon

1623

They are nearing Martin's Hundred. One man sitting near the prow snatches up the line then, slipping chest-deep into the stinking green river, he hauls the boat up to the muddy bank. The rest, with jack coats on and muskets ready, quickly jump ashore like deer hurtling over a fallen tree. They are met by silence. An all-enveloping silence, rising up like the thick black ooze about their leaky leather boots. Not a bird rises up in alarm. No creature scampers off into the undergrowth. There is nothing. It is as if even the great mother-goddess herself is in hiding, too ashamed to let her presence be known in the wake of what her children have done.

Thomas can smell evil hanging on the air even before the soft breeze begins to ripple its way through the dense bed of reeds, teasing apart the cutting blades to mark out a pathway where recent feet have fleetingly trod. Despite the pounding in his chest and the tightening of his stomach, Thomas too begins to weave his way through with his comrades close at his heel. Tall grasses beyond wave and beckon on - in whispers they call – follow if you dare. He dares.

Soon he and his men are in a tobacco field by a small patch of dark, bare soil. It is only recently dug over and in it the teeth marks from a rake are still clear and crisply defined. Discarded, the implement lies at rest, prostrated headfirst down in the earth. Other tools are haphazardly strewn about. Nearby, a pouch full of precious tobacco seeds tumble out onto the ground. Some are crushed beneath the fresh imprint of a moccasin. Further along and in plain sight, a woman's abandoned shoe lays bereft of its partner. Yet, where is she? All this serves to heighten the dread.

It is not until then that Thomas notices the

blood. A red rivulet of it running down the dirt trodden pathway between the remnant rows of last years crop. It pools, tackily at his feet. He steps aside and, half crouching, tries to trace it back to source.

It leads him on towards a patch of weeping browned undergrowth. He pauses for a moment, lifts his head and listens again. Still nothing. He glances back across his shoulders to the others. They are fanning out silently making searches of their own, yet none beyond sight of another. Cautiously he follows on with his throat as dry as gunpowder. Leaning in amongst the debris, Thomas suddenly finds a familiar male face staring blankly up at him. Thomas half smiles back in relief before it registers. The head is on a spike. Beside it is the decapitated body of a nodding acquaintance he last spoke with in Jamestown only a few days before. Less than a yard further in, Thomas can see long, blonde tresses and the mutilated body of his wife slumped face down, tossed aside like a child's doll. It is too late. Thomas now fears that when they reach the plantation house they are going to find everybody dead.

The nightmare was shattered as Thomas woke up to thankfully find himself somewhere else. Beside him, his wife murmured in fear, as she too began to rouse from a deeper but none the less troubled sleep. Quickly Thomas's strong arms reached out to sweep aside her terrors and gathered her safely in to him.

'It is all right!' His once familiar voice reassured her. 'It is all right... I am here now!'
Bessie sat bolt upright and opened her eyes. Thomas's dark loving gaze met hers.

'Oh Thomas!' She cried in disbelief, 'I thought you were dead! They were coming to tell me you were dead!'

'It's all right, my darling,' he said. 'See? I am here. You were feverish again, that is all. 'Twas naught but a wicked dream.'

'It was a dream?' She murmured hesitantly. 'Or...am I dreaming still...a wishful dream where you are not dead... yet you are?'

'No. You are not dreaming now, Bessie. Feel me! I really am here.'

'Bessie'- it felt strange to Thomas calling his wife by that name. Almost as strange as it was for her to now hear it after so many long years of being known by her alias of 'Dorothy'. Stranger too was the realisation that, after almost three years, her 'dead' husband had inexplicably returned to her from beyond his grave. His loss, on the eve of the Separatist's departure from Old Plymouth, England, had been almost more than she could bear. Now, by some miracle, she was in recovery from a near fatal illness to find that God had returned him to her... but at what cost?

Bessie's head was still swimming as she began to take in her gently rocking surroundings and soon realised that she must be aboard a ship.

'Are we on the Mayflower?' She asked without really thinking. Yet, as soon as she had said it, she knew it could not be. The scale of this vessel was smaller and the smell too sweet to be of that floating death house.

'No.' Thomas answered. 'You are aboard the 'Delver'. Her Master let us have his quarters so that I could nurse you more privately.'

Bessie's head swirled with surreal and cruelly taunting images, though reality was swiftly taking hold as she began to focus her mind more clearly. Still upset and confused, Bessie braced her head with her hands. Her recollection of past events was very hazy but she did half recall being helped from her cottage in New Plimoth and down the main street. Then? Then she must have passed out for she could remember nothing after that.

'How can this be?' She said after a moment or two. 'I thought you were dead. We all thought you were dead! At least, that is what I was told...'

'I know,' Thomas replied, 'it has all been like some terrible, cruel conspiracy to keep us apart. But I am here with you now and everything shall be all right.... Here,' he said raising a bowl to her dry cracked lips 'try sipping some of this water. It will make you feel cooler.'

Bessie let go of her head and drank a little. The sweet water felt clean and good in her paper dry mouth.

'Good girl! That's better... isn't it?'

Bessie nodded weakly in agreement then handed back the bowl.

'Lie back down now, my love and rest...' Thomas said raising the flimsy cover back over his wife's waxen arms and chest. 'This must have all come as a terrible shock for you.'

'No!' Bessie immediately threw it off again. 'I don't want to... I don't want to sleep... I want to talk... I want to know what has happened!'

Thomas sighed and put down the bowl.

'Very well then,' he suggested gently, 'let us start with you telling me everything that you know about what supposedly happened in England...and then...I will try my best to explain what came about from my own recollection. Perhaps then, we will find firm ground to try to rebuild our lives after this dreadful mess.'

Bessie faltered with these words for she understood fully what her husband meant by his rather understated remark. This 'dreadful mess' was the fact that after all this time, Thomas had pitched up in New Plimoth, with ne'er a word of warning, to find that Bessie had gone through with a marriage to another man. Luckily, his long-time friend, Governor William Bradford, had intercepted him before anyone in the settlement had the chance to recognize him. Bradford had then set in action ways in which to limit the damage to all concerned, that the revelation of an act of bigamy might bring. The cataclysmic result of which, had led to Bessie being hastily spirited away from New Plimoth and aboard the Delver, to avoid the dreadful personal consequences, should her awful crime be discovered.

'Nothing,' Bessie replied lowering her eyes defensively. 'I was told nothing at first. The other women simply fell upon me and told me you were dead! I pleaded with them but they said I could not be taken to you because you were already buried. Then... only much later ...did it all come out. During the long nights aboard the Mayflower, as we tended to those who were dying by degrees, Mary Brewster told me... She fed my withering soul, piecemeal, the details of what had befallen you in Old Plymouth. That you had been found lying in the street, brained. She said how, that in her humble opinion, it had been 'a mercy' that you had been taken so swiftly and that I had been spared from the ordeal of watching you inch towards death like so many she and I saw out of this life. Gilbert Winslow, William Bradford and Stephen Hopkins ... they all saw you laid out in the mortuary... You were dead, Thomas!' Bessie recoiled from him in horror. 'You were dead! They were absolutely convinced it was you, Thomas!' she said. 'Were they deceived?'

Thomas remained steadfast in his composure and without a flicker of deceit on his face replied,

'No, Bessie. They were not deceived! Though I have no recollection of any of this at all, I was told much later about their attendance upon me. So I know your account is true.'

'Then...' her voice faltered with fear, 'did you come back from the dead?'

'Maybe so. Who can say? Where is a soul when it is not in life? It is as much a mystery to me as it is to you all. However, they do say that if I were in but a stupor, then it was the deepest, soundest of any ever witnessed for I showed no sign of breath or life at all. Please... please, Bessie!' He pleaded reaching out for her hand once more, 'Do not be afraid of me. Not you, of all people.'

Bessie steeled herself, trying hard not to flinch at his touch. She felt sickly faint and her heart was racing so. She asked Thomas for more water. He fetched some, leaving her relieved that she was free of his uneasy grip. She drank from the bowl slowly, all the while trying to conceal from this man that she was indeed afraid of him.

'The strangest thing,' Thomas resumed the subject, 'is that I have no recollection of what happened to me at all. All that I can remember is being dreadfully cold. So very cold and for so very long in some strange, far off shadowy place. I think I half remember snatches of conversation going on about me, but that is all. Then it was suddenly as if I were brought into a bright, bright light. Then, there was warmth. I remember being warm again and blankets wrapped about me and a fire burning somewhere close by.'

Thomas then went on to explain how, at the very edge of his intended grave, he had apparently let out a groan and briefly opened his eyes.

'The town bailiff saw and at once stepped in to intervene. After that, he oversaw my slow recovery for the month or two that it took.'

'A month or two?'

'Yes. My injuries were so severe at first that my speech was slurred and I could not even stand in balance. But before winter set in, I was almost my old self again. Though now I am often dogged by headaches and black bouts of melancholy yet I believe even these are subsiding now.'

'So what then?'

'What then?'

'Yes, Thomas!' Bessie pushed fiercely. 'What did you do then? You say you were well again by that winter but it's been almost three years since! Did you not think to try to find me?'

'Yes, of course I did!' Thomas snapped defensively. 'But it was not that easy! I went straight to the Virginia Company and explained what had happened. How I had paid for our passage and that from all accounts, you must have somehow gone on ahead despite of everything. They listened but at first dismissed me out of hand, refusing to refund me my investment. I was distraught! I did not know how I was going to get to you. I had no money to my name. Then, just as I was about to give up hope, an associate of the Company sought me out in private. He knew I was desperate and put to me a proposition that I would have been a fool to pass over. If I accepted, then he would arrange passage for me on the next ship bound for Virginia. Overtly, I was to work as if in the ordinary employ of The Virginia Company, in a privileged position he would procure for me. Yet, at the same time I was to act in secret, under his direction, for a quite separate entity and very wealthy benefactor. To that end, I came to be living in Jamestown ever since. As the result of which, I have acquired both the promise of a parcel of land and I have a cottage at my disposal.' Bessie rubbed her forehead. She had now the most splitting headache and this sudden pitch into the present was making it throb even harder.

'You mean to say that you have all of this in place? All of these fine arrangements yet...yet you left me...you left me to my fate in New Plimoth?' she said with anger fast usurping any fear she had before.

'Yes... but it is not quite like that,' Thomas was quick to jump to the defence. 'There is more to the story and it is far too involved for you to take in just now. You obviously need to be resting still, my dear...then...when you are better I will explain it all fully. For now...let's be content that we are together again and that nothing is ever going to part us!'
Bessie was not content to let it lie.

'I want to know now!' She insisted.

'Later! When you are stronger,' he said 'you are quite overwrought just now and I think it best for you to rest.'
Bessie glared at Thomas furiously, then leaning in, spoke straight into his eyes.

'You think you know me, but I warn you, you do not! I am not the Dorothy you knew before! She is dead...left behind...abandoned!'

'She is dead all right! Buried in a box up on burial hill and there she must remain if you are to live! What choice would you have had us make for you, Bessie? To send you back to England to stand trial as an adulterer? Knowing how that would end? What do you think your punishment would have been under Church law for bigamy? ...You would have been hung, Bessie. Mistake or no! Hanged by the neck until you were dead as an example to all women!'

'It is not fair! I did nothing wrong!' She insisted. 'I believed you were dead! I was so broken-hearted that I thought I would die from my grief! Yet, what was I supposed to do when I did not? Take my own life? Live out my days in a cave? ... I did as I thought you would have done... In fact as you once did! I entered into a marriage contract in order to help a child survive, that is all...I followed your example and I married out of necessity for all concerned. I am sorry if that hath offended you!'

'It was not quite the same when I married...'

'No ...you are right! It was not the same... you knew full well that I was still alive when you married!'

'Enough! Bessie! Enough!'

Thomas was taken aback by his newly-found wife's ferociousness. There was something very different about her, this woman he thought he had known. She had always had the capacity to be fiery, yet now there was some unknown quantity, something unrecognized, slipped in with the mix. For the present, Thomas was not certain if it was to his liking.

He had however, gleaned an insight into why this might be. Quite by accident, he had chanced across Bessie's leather bound journal when it slipped from her hurriedly wrapped bundle of possessions as he carried them onto the ship. Thinking it to be perhaps a volume of Shakespeare or such, he had later searched it out to while away his bedside vigil as his sick wife slept. He knew in all good conscience that he should have put it down once he had realised his error, but having started, he found himself compelled to read on. He soon came to appreciate just how much past events may have taken their toll upon the survivors of the Mayflower. Much less trauma, he reasoned, would have marred even the meekest of characters. His wife's heart-wrought words, as they scratched their miserable way in her delicate hand across the previously unblemished page, bore witness to the fact that she had been much affected. He knew exactly from reading them how much she had suffered and had already taken it into his mind, with anticipation, that there might well be occasions when he could be called on to make some allowance for this and to treat Bessie accordingly.

'I have been sitting with my feet in Hell's hearth these past few years' she ranted. 'I have tended to living corpses, watched them disintegrating into their graves in front of me. I have seen plump sweet children shrivel up and die like late September blackberries, spat on by the Devil then left to the mercy of the elements. I have borne witness to sights and lived through such horrors, as you cannot begin to imagine! SoThomas!' She warned. 'Do not dare chide me! I am well enough and I need to know everything!' She insisted. 'How else am I to ever come fully to my senses? I thought you had died, a long, long time ago. Then, no sooner than I am resolved to my grief and the loss of every dream and hope I had...then...suddenly...you are alive and I am in turn torn away from the hard earned way of life and its certainties that I have grown to accept.'

Thomas's patience was sorely being tested.

'I presume you mean by this 'life', that other husband of yours...Francis, wasn't it?'
Bessie was cut by that remark and immediately struck back in her defence.

'My marriage to him was made out of necessity, much as you claimed was yours to your Dutchwoman. Yet mine remained unconsummated as part of the bargain. We slept fully clothed and with a board between us in the bed. Did you?' She railed. 'But, yes...now you ask...Francis is a part of it...as is all I have left behind in New Plimoth! Now...now I no longer even have my identity. Come to that, how can I even be sure of yours? That you are my Thomas and not some devil's incubus sent in disguise?'

'What folly.' He roared. 'Of course it is me!'

'What happened then Thomas? Tell me now!' She demanded. 'What really kept you so long from coming back for me? Pray tell of this position that pressed you to be in Jamestown. In truth, why did you come for me at New Plimoth at all?'

9

Thomas checked his temper and tried to cool the conversation down by degrees.

'The undertaking I took in the Company employ was by way of my talents in drawing.' He explained calmly.

'A position with The Virginia Company? ... Drawing? And this is what kept you from me?'

'Yes. I needed to earn my passage before I could take leave to come in search of you!' Thomas took a deep breath then continued to explain. 'I was engaged by them to draw the virtues of the plantations of Virginia. To paint the colony in the most favourable of lights so as to help procure more investors and settlers into the venture. Then my presence in the colony became even more pressing and 'valuable' in the wake of recent events there last year. As I said, my appointment has proved very lucrative. Very lucrative indeed...'

'Lucrative? Yes, I expect they have good need of a man of your talents to lure poor unsuspecting souls to this God forsaken place.... then to abandon them to whatever fate befalls them. They left us to rot Thomas. Did you know that? Instead of sending us a shipload of good supplies, which we desperately needed, they sent us more people. Sick, hungry, people with little more than the clothes they stood up in...exploiting the knowledge that we would not turn them away, and could not do anything other than share our motley stake with them. And yet at the same time, the Company still pestered our Governor with spiteful letters, stuffed full with even more impossible demands to be met... whining reminders that we owed them a great debt that we should make shift to repay. Had it not been for intervention by the naturals at New Plimoth, we would have all but starved to death that first year. I tell you, countless wasted lives lay in the hands of those wicked Company men.'

'I can never defend them for their wretched dealings with would-be settlers, but you must be able see the business reasoning behind it?'

'Must I? What care they, Thomas? What care

these fine Company men? The most of them are safe in England, sleeping upon their feather beds at night like blameless babies...'

'You were pitched up here... you and your party...far off course from Virginia where the Company had need of new colonists for the expansion of their project. In Virginia, they are crying out for people to till the fertile soil and to clear land for new tobacco plantations.'

'Tobacco?'

'Yes, the profit is enormous. Ten... twenty fold, anything that your New Plimoth settlers can hope to procure by way of wood or skins. Our English explorers came to the New World in the expectation of finding gold mines yet instead they found a weed worth near as much as gold. Fortune indeed brings in some boats with nobody at the helm! The Mayflower was never intended to go to New England. When it did...and especially in view of recent events, it proved most inconvenient for the Company. Instead of immediately working for their profit, your party became a burden. It is like a small holder having two sows. One a lusty healthy beast and the other a weakly runt. The owner has feed for only one. What does he do? Split the resources equally between the two? Or feed up the strong sow, who is bound to grow quickly and multiply and bring in a goodly sum at market with her prodigy. Do you invest the majority of feed in that while dispensing the bare minimum to the runt, just enough to keep it alive so it might return at least something? New Plimoth is the runt and Jamestown a lusty pig of a town. The Company has been relying on New Plimoth's willpower to survive, knowing that if it were strong enough, then you would root about for your own food in order to keep alive! Which would you have done?'

'But at such a grave cost, Thomas! Such shameful days we live in when men's lives can be weighed up so short against that of a profit! You, better than any, knew how they cheated us in our dealings... how they used us easy. I cannot believe that, knowing this, you would contrive with them and cheat others?'

'No Bessie, I did not! This is what I cannot tell you....not yet ...not all I have been about... Besides, I believe the massacre of last year has brought up short many a man's faith in the Company's ventures and their handling of the colony and that they will shortly be called to book for it!'

'Massacre? I have not been told about any massacre in Virginia! Only that there had been some 'uneasiness' between the settlers and the naturals there ... but that was all.'

'Yes. I know. I had a long discussion with Messrs Brewster and Bradford about it and I understand that they wanted to avoid widespread panic amongst the rest of you. By all accounts, your colony has remained at peace with the naturals. However, both men agreed full heartedly with me that no matter how peaceable your relationship has been up until now, that is not to say that the status quo shall always remain. Attack by the 'naturals' of this New World was ever the gravest fear of our people and I understand much has been done of late in New Plimoth to maintain your security and safety should such an event happen there too. Standish 'et al' are well prepared in what course of action they need take. Unfortunately, when it happened in Virginia, we were not.'

'What happened there, Thomas?'
Thomas looked at his wife and wondered how best to describe this harrowing event. Should he tone down the awful things that had happened and risk being accused by her later of being dishonest or tell her all... even the most distressing details? He decided to try for the middle ground.

'By stealth, deceit and low cunning, those naturals in our part of the country perpetrated such a bloody carnage. It was quite unlike anything one might witness in the course of honourable combat in battle with Europeans.'

'How do you mean?'

'Well... one of the heirs to the Powhatan chiefdom,

12

is a contemptuous despot named Opechancanough. He has secretly long held a smouldering hatred for us. Yet, for many years, while his brothers each ruled in turn, he was powerless to act. However, when the old chief died, and the next brother proved too frail to rule, Opechancanough seized power and set about to rectify that. He devised a plan to employ his race to deliberately prey upon our goodwill and friendship towards them. He lulled us, like innocent infants, into a gentle complacency and ease with their increasing presence amongst us in Jamestown and upon our scattered plantations away from its immediate protection and aid. While they pretended to be our friends, all the time they were planning and conspiring to act as a whole but with one accord...to butcher we English to a man and so expunge us from the face of their earth... from our rightful colony.'

'Our rightful colony?' Bessie argued. 'Wasn't it their land to begin with and not some vacant lot to snatch from nature? This was their home first, was it not?'

'You are but a woman!' Thomas said in exasperation. 'You do not understand how we men are duty bound to aid progress.'

'No, you are right! I do not understand it...nor do I understand progress solely for the sake of progress. And what is it that you men would have us believe is progress? To build up this entire land into a new little England? If so, then tell me...what part in this new England would there be for the naturals?'

'Surely you cannot mean to defend them?' Thomas countered. 'This chief of theirs spoke of us in his talk of war as being like 'vermin' to be eradicated! He asked his followers what they would do if they had but one grain-store and found it full of rats devouring all? Would you not beat them out, he reasoned, then search for their nests and destroy their litters also? These rats are us!'

'And would they not be justified?' Bessie said defiantly. 'How is this any different from what you are doing to them?'

'You would not side so readily with these savages had you borne witness to the aftermath of their treachery!' Thomas rebuked his wife swiftly. 'We in Jamestown were warned of the plan to attack by some convert naturals who could not stomach their leader's intentions. Thus, we were able to save ourselves. Unfortunately our colony is scattered up and down the James and as for those furthest away, we had no way of raising the alarm in time. They never stood a chance! Nor could have dared to imagine the chilling horror which was about to unfold.'

Thomas went on to tell his wife, in no prettied-up way, how in the previous year, Friday, March 22nd, had started no differently than any other day that spring. Though most of these homesteads had palisades and were fortified well enough, should they ever have need to face an outright attack, the planters themselves were completely unprepared for the events of that day. Many of the plantation owners and workers had grown accustomed to morning visits from the 'friendly' naturals. Usually, these natives bought along poles laden with game and fish and often sought out the men folk in their workplace to trade and encouraged amicable chats. In consequence, the naturals were routinely then offered hospitality inside the homes. Even for them to be invited to join with the English at breakfast was not unusual.

'And this was their treachery!' Thomas seethed. 'That they would so viperously repay the kindness of their hosts in so vile a manner. For, at some prearranged point or signal, these natives went berserk. They struck out at our unwary settlers with table knives, hammers, scythes, axes...whatever came to their wicked hands ... They slaughtered our people like game. Then, to press home their point, when murder was done they made their way back to the corpses and hacked them about!' Bessie listened in shocked silence as her husband continued.

'I saw heads, Bessie...heads with their faces

sliced off like you or I would carve ham from a joint. The only thing remaining to identify their humanity were lifeless eyes...fixed in disbelief...staring out blankly until buzzards came later and set about pecking them out. There were women in bloodied aprons with their bodices ripped open and their breasts excised. At their side, small children laying dead in the dirt... even the babies had their heads staved in! I helped to bury countless corpses, many mutilated beyond all comprehension and left for carrion. In one mad frenzy, these devils destroyed hundreds of our people. They burnt down houses, destroyed crops and slaughtered any livestock that they could not carry away with them. So, do not ask me Bessie, to defend your savages!'

Bessie was horrified.

'And you saw all this?'

'Yes. I saw all this,' he replied coldly. 'Not only did I see it, but the Company made me go out and record as much as I could in my sketchbooks. That way, my work could bear witness to the attack and would serve to validate any reprisals that we made thereafter.'

'Reprisals?' Bessie tried to reason. 'What if you take an eye for an eye? Then they take out your other eye? Will you fall blindly then into a spiralling war of revenge?'

'There is a world of difference between unprovoked attack and reprisal! We do not fall on them and slaughter for the sake of slaughter! The day that we do, then that will be the day that I will concede to you...' Thomas snapped.

Bessie immediately stalled, fast realising that she may be provoking her husband to anger.

'It is the fact that you have an intellect,' Thomas continued with a renewed calmness to his voice, 'and ideas of your own that drew me to fall in love with you in the first place. Yet, it is also prudent for you to remember that I am your husband and that you should know your place. For it would be to no good for the tail to try to wag the dog! The worst of the matter is,' Thomas tried to explain, 'that despite the shortcomings of the Company, the colony was at last beginning to bear great promise. We had above a thousand settled people, for the most in good health and well fed. The plantations were prospering and with such promise of a good harvest of both tobacco and crops a plenty to follow that year. There were even vineyards due to come to fruit. The iron foundry, the glass works - all were flourishing until that day of the massacre. Then, at a stroke, the savages took away all that had been so hard fought for and reduced the colony to mayhem. Yet worse than they having slain so many of our friends was that they had managed, at the same time, to kill even those that remained alive. All of us died inside that day...'

Thomas reached over and held Bessie's hand gently in his. He looked longingly into her eyes and tried desperately to engage them with his.

'I had planned to come to you last summer,' he said 'but with such widespread carnage, it became impossible. Every man was needed to defend what was left of the colony from further attack. Every able hand was vital to work the land so we might replant as many crops as possible to replace at least a little of the multitude that had been destroyed. Even so, we barely had enough food to survive that following winter. Then, what with hunger and sickness, our number was so decimated that once more we were forced to bury our dead at night so the naturals could not reckon our remaining strength. When spring came and the Delver arrived, I leaped at the chance to join it. I dare not come right out and admit that I was in league with Separatists, so I instead volunteered to provide extra sketches and drawings to stand alongside the cartographers' work of refining the maps of the coastline and the fishing grounds up north in order to get a place on her though I hate being at sea. I knew I would be coming to you... that's if you were still alive. I did not know if you had survived or not...yet I clung desperately to the hope that you had.'

'And what now?' She asked hopefully. 'Are you

now done with Jamestown? Are we on our way back to England?'

'No,' Thomas replied regretfully. 'We are not going to England. The Delver is on its way back to Jamestown.'

Bessie immediately looked up in total astonishment. How could her husband even be considering such a dangerous thing after all he had just said!

'Jamestown? After all that has happened! What kind of family be you to me, Thomas? Have I fledged with a cuckoo that would now cast me from out of the nest and into the waiting clutches of a cat?'

'Trust me Bessie! I am the only true family you have. I have told you the truth of the situation when I could have so easily lied to you instead. Trust in this truth, Bessie! Even with all I have said about Jamestown, I believe we will be safe in Virginia. I promise you! Even as it stands, the colony has above ten times the population of New Plimoth. It is still in recovery, true, from such a dreadful catastrophe yet even so it is still much in advance of New Plimoth. If the naturals in New England decided to attack there, like the Powhatans did in Virginia, then they could be utterly obliterated... Believe me, Bessie...I am taking you to a far better prospect... Wait and see.'

'And the naturals?' She asked. 'How many more fold are the naturals in Virginia who brought about this massacre?'

'I will not lie...there are many! It is true. A whole nation of them in number against our pitiful hundreds. Yet, we have the advantage of them. Not by number, but by weaponry. Their bows and arrows are no match against our muskets and cannon. And how they fear our Englishman's thunder!'

'Yet, they managed to kill so many Englishmen despite their thunder?'

'Again that is true and I believe the Company has much to answer for in its neglect in providing enough guns and armaments to protect the colonists against such attack. Also for its poor dealings with those who

17

have come to Virginia under false pretences and their neglectfulness of the majority there after. As I said, Bessie, what I have done in secret is not at all for their benefit. Indeed quite the contrary.'

'What is it exactly, Thomas, that you have done? What is that look in your face that betrays to me that there is so much more you are not telling me?'

'Bessie, it was never my intention to take you away to Jamestown! Although I have collateral interest there, I am finished with it! My covert work was done there and I had hoped not to be in that place when the wings of doom I had set fly to England come back to Jamestown to roost. My plan was to be reunited with you in New England and to start out afresh in New Plimoth. I could have sent a message back with any one of a dozen excuses to the Company as to why I could not return with the ship! Now...now that is impossible. I have nowhere else to go but back.'

'But work for whom, Thomas...?'

'I cannot reveal my employer's confidences.... I cannot tell you Bessie and that is the truth! I am sworn to secrecy and besides, it is best for your safety's sake that you do not know the detail of what I am about. I am sorry... but do not press me upon this. In time, as circumstance dictates I may... no... I will tell you all. As it now stands, I have no other choice but to return to Jamestown as if ever the loyal Company man and you? You must be willing to play out your part as my equally loyal Company wife...It is imperative... You must heed to bide your tongue my love, no matter how sorely provoked to let it lose with honest thoughts. No one must suspect other than this, for in truth, if I am found out, there are some that might not hesitate to do me harm in return...and you!'

Bessie thought for a moment. What other choice did she have?

'Very well,' she said. 'If I am to take up my place as your wife, I must learn to trust my husband once more... and he I.'

'Good. Then we have an understanding.'

Bessie nodded in agreement that they did.

'And now... I think that you really must rest.'

'Yes, I think so too,' she said slipping back down upon the bed. 'There is so much for me to take in and now I am quite exhausted, although much easier in my mind now that most things are settled between us.'

'Let us both rest!' He said lying down beside her. 'Rest now and then when you are stronger we can try to begin this marriage anew...'

Soon Bessie slipped into a peaceable sleep. As she dreamed on, with all the stealth of a cat Thomas rose up from the bed. He stooped by the chair to pick up his wife's journal, hastily abandoned to the floor earlier. Such a gift, he thought to himself, as he quietly secreted it away amongst his own things. A dead woman's words; an evocative, first-hand account of human suffering of such epic proportion that none who read it could surely fail to be moved? Such a damning condemnation and one so eloquently put lay betwixt those battered leather bindings. A condemnation of the Virginia Company and its lust for profit above all else that might seal the fate of the accursed party, if only it should reach the hand and eyes of the King. This tale of an unknown woman might also serve, in the future, to cast suspicion away from Thomas...

Chapter Two

'The Quick and The Dead'
- Book of Common Prayer

The Delver made its way back down from New England, hugging the coastline for much of the way. As it did, Bessie only then began to appreciate the sheer beauty of this verdant unspoilt country. When she first arrived, in sixteen hundred and twenty, the only real New World landfall she had witnessed from the sea had been the winter-bleak, inhospitable coastline around Cape Cod. Now, completely redeemed from the illness that had almost claimed her life, the experience of the Delver's odyssey, along America's seemingly boundless shoreline, was enabling Bessie to comprehend the enormity of this newfound dominion.

Passing by the Delaware lands, Bessie wondered how much longer their journey would last.

'It will not be long now, my darling,' Thomas said slipping his arm around his wife's trim waistline. 'We are on the homeward leg of our journey.'

'How far is it to Jamestown?'

'That depends. I know we are due to drop anchor again shortly, but I understand that will be for the last time. There is a little cove, just clear of the mouth of Delaware Bay. The cartographers want to recheck it against their maps. Meanwhile the Master plans to send a party ashore to replenish the ship's water. He says there is a spot nearby where the water is sweet and crystal clear. After that, I would say we could be in Jamestown within the week or so, God Willing!'

While the Delver dropped anchor and the shore party were gone, Thomas relaxed on deck with his wife, making one or two last minute sketches to add to his already bulging portfolio.

'These are beautiful!' Bessie admired her husband's artistry. 'Really beautiful, Thomas.'

'Those are for me ...for my own private pleasure

and nothing to do with the Company. All they want are stilted views of thriving plantations... panoramas filled with impossibly bountiful game, or for this trip... easily identifiable landmarks! But yes, I agree ...these sketches are beautiful, even if I say so myself! Then again, it is a beautiful land!'

Suddenly a mariner cried out from his watch.

'Master! ... There...' he said pointing out to something in the distance, 'coming up from the south... it's a ship!'

'A Dutchman?' The Master exclaimed.

'I canst rightly tell...but she's well down in the water... Wait... Oh God! ...I think she's a Spaniard!'

Bessie sensed a sudden tension mount.

'Has she an escort?'

'Not that I can tell, Master.'

'Well! If she's a treasure ship heading home to Spain, then let's hope she'll not be so eager to lock horns with us in a hurry. That is, if she has not seen us yet.'

There was every possibility that she had not. For the Spaniard was well out to sea with the sun to her back, whereas the Delver had the advantage of being against the backdrop of the tree line and with her sheets dropped, quite possibly indistinguishable from the land.

'Well, here's hoping they have not!' said the mate. 'For loaded or not, she could be down on us before we'd a chance of getting underway and I'll wager she is armed to the gunnels ... not like us with naught but a couple of feeble murderers to defend ourselves! We couldn't even piss on her with the size of our cannon.'

'Better reason yet then, for all of us to stay still and to try not to attract her attention. For if we do, their Captain might well be wondering what an Englishman is doing with his anchor dropped in such a desolate bay. He needs only half a brain to string two thoughts together to realise that we are a mapper. Then, they will go all out to capture us for certain,' the Master warned gravely.

'Why?' Bessie asked Thomas. 'We have nothing

of value to them. Do we?'

'Yes, I am afraid we do!' He replied. 'We have a cargo worth a King's ransom...the maps! Not only that, we have the cartographers and navigators too, which means if we were captured alive we would be taken prisoner... Taken back to Spain, Bessie, and probably tortured until we'd given up every detail of the position of our settlements...our armaments...our numbers.'

The Delver and her crew waited patiently for what seemed to be an eternity. Waiting to see if the Spaniard would turn shoreward and make towards them. As good fortune would have it, luck was on their side that day. Eventually the Spaniard passed by, none the wiser to their existence. Evening was now falling fast and with the light beginning to fail and a difficult stretch of navigation ahead, the Delver remained at her anchor for the night.

With a magnificent dawn-break, the ship was soon under sail once more. It seemed that in no time they were approaching a ribbon of island the naturals called Assateague. Bessie thought it mysterious, half-hidden as it was in a fine shroud of sea mist. It was here that the Master changed course a little to follow an invisible path further out to sea.

'Tis a treacherous stretch near in,' he explained. 'A real wrecking ground for foolhardy ships that fail to pay these waters their due respect. For in places the draft beneath your keel can quickly vanish into nothing. Better we give the land a decent margin, from now on, until we near Cape Charles!'

Beyond the grasp of Assateague, a chain of pretty islands slipped by until eventually, the Delver was approaching the Chesapeake Bay. In near perfect weather and from the vantage of the ship, Virginia appeared a breathtaking prospect. Bessie was relieved to learn that their sea journey was almost at an end. Yet, at the same time, she was also extremely apprehensive about what the future might hold.

*   *   *

Soon the Delver slipped through the teeth of the

bay by Point Comfort and on into the mouth of the James River. Almost immediately, Bessie noticed the air begin to change from the fresh Atlantic breeze to suddenly becoming much more sullen and humid. Lumbering their way up river the blue-grey water soon dulled into a soupy, sludgy green-brown and the cloying smell of rotting vegetation began to permeate the heavy air. It put Bessie in mind of the farms of her childhood in Lincolnshire and how the labourers would periodically dig out the drainage ditches along the field edge. The resulting dredge of earth and weed would be piled up on to the sides of the bank and left to fester in whatever weather followed on. The smell on a hot sunny day, as decomposition set in amongst the displaced reeds and waterweed was every bit as rank as this.

Running the length of the riverbank, they passed by large areas of marshland, teaming with fine looking duck and wildfowl. Huge stands of mature trees with slinking creepers intertwined would suddenly open up into large swathes of cleared land given over to intensive cultivation. Once or twice Bessie glimpsed a heavily fortified building that she took to be a plantation house. Numerous jetties also slipped by, some with small boats tied up... others vacant and lifeless, yet most veiled in a haze of veracious flying insects swarming just above the water's reach.

Eventually the Delver arrived off Jamestown and a shock of gunfire ricocheted across the river with a tell-tale puff of smoke rising up from its fort.

'A rather extravagant welcome!' Thomas remarked aloud 'Do you think they mistake us for an English supply ship?'

'No welcome salute, I fear' replied the Master. 'An armed escort makes ready ashore. It looks like there has been trouble here again!'

Sure enough, a party of armoured men with guns and pikes had already emerged from the palisade and were half way down the pathway to the jetty to meet them. Good deep water mooring meant that the Delver could come straight to shore and throw across her lines for a rapid securing and swift disembarkation.

'Look lively' shouted the Master. 'All that needs to be ashore, take your belongings and go!'

Thomas grabbed his leather portfolio with straps still dangling loose and handed it to his wife while he hastily gathered up their bundles then made for the side.

'What is wrong?' Thomas asked one who was throwing up a gangplank to aid passage down onto the jetty.

'The naturals, what else?' He replied gruffly. 'They tried to raid a planter's boat here, two...three days since. Two servants had their throats slit as they slept aboard and then the savages went on to try to set fire to part of the palisade. But, thank God, they failed and were severely routed by our men! Still, all the same, the Governor has put us all on high alert in case they are thinking of striking again. He says we must show force at every opportunity and to act as if there are natives watching us at every turn so they might see that we mean to stay - regardless!'

As Bessie stepped from the Delver, she was helped by a gentleman in armour who quite put her in mind of Captain Miles Standish back in New Plimoth. It gave her comfort for a moment and she smiled. However, she was soon to discover that there would be precious little else in the near future that would do the same.

They made their way along the well-worn pathway towards the safety of the settlement and from without all seemed uncannily similar to Bessie's New England home and so offered her up some comfort to take from being thus so. Wringing posts stood hammered into the bank side like lonely sentinels beside abandoned drying lines and makeshift wood log benches, which had no doubt often witnessed a chatter of women as they gathered to do their washing. As far as Bessie's eye could determine, all around the outside of the palisade the forest had been cleared. There were little fenced-in fields in sight and pens for livestock, although they all looked to have been bereft of care for some time. In fact, at many places along the river, the lush green forest had also been cleared in part and enormous stacks of hewn trees trunks lay close by jetties waiting to be put to use. These areas too seemed mostly devoid of any activity that she could see.

As the great wooden gates creaked agape to gobble them up from the dangers without, Bessie realised, within a few fleet footsteps inside, that first impressions often set out to deceive. This was no New Plimoth.

Nothing Thomas had said during the voyage down could have prepared Bessie for the stark reality of Jamestown. It was a noisy, cramped habitation of little upward of twenty or so houses. Mostly they were of wattle and daub with not one that could honestly be described as being 'grand'. There was also a church and some stores. The mean buildings appeared to have been thoughtlessly thrown together, higgledy-piggledy, with cramped yards barely big enough to be deemed useful. The house timbers looked excessively warped with huge shakes opening them up and premature decay lent an overall impression of dwelling places that were as unkempt and uncared for as perhaps those who lived there.

Meanwhile, in the dirt street which belched up clouds of dust with every step that Bessie's still unsteady feet took, there appeared to be a deliberate planting of exotic-looking, fleshy weeds towering into the air above her head. They seemed to have been in receipt of some lavish attention while the scant planting of corn she had also noticed, parched in the yards alongside stunted gourd with withered leaves. Then, quite suddenly the overpowering stench hit her. It was more than reminiscent of the Gainsborough Mart Yard on a market day. A heady combination of the stale sweat of both man and beast mixed in with urine decaying in the dazzling afternoon sun. In all, Bessie perceived this to be a place low in spirit and devoid of any true direction.

As Thomas led on, leathery purse-faced men, dressed in little more than rags, hardly looked up as they sat about seeking shade from the murderous heat, smoking their pipes and swatting at the biting swarms of insects niggling at them. There seemed to be little industriousness from any quarter, save that of a lone man sat upon an upturned log busily at work as if immune to the heat that held so many low. Beside him stood 'Peg,' a most curious creature. It was a pale-coloured, three-legged greyhound bitch which wagged her tail profusely greeting all who passed by, friend and stranger alike. So much so that two men ambling by actually seemed to stop with the sole purpose of petting the animal and handing it some titbit or another from out of their pocket. Bessie thought how this poor damaged creature seemed to capture the whole ethos of this place.

The dog's gaunt-faced, yet sinewy master, looked up briefly from his labour to greet Thomas by name. Thomas reciprocated with a cheerful 'Good day to you Jack.'

Mad Jack they called him. Day in day out, he could be found sitting outside his canvas and wood shack, beside an enormous woodpile splitting logs for the settlement's use. Wood was one commodity there was never a shortage of for new land was being continually cleared for the soil hungry tobacco, even now in these uncertain times. It was valued, not just for building and for fuel, but more importantly it had been precious in the one processing skill the natives deeply envied yet had not mastered for themselves... smelting metal. For now though, the colony's thriving ironworks were as but a not so distant dream. It lay idle and weed covered. All its foundry men were dead.

Mad Jack had been in Jamestown for almost as long as it had existed and had come across from England as a clear-headed, young indentured servant. Against such doubtful odds, he had duly served out his time and had been offered land in his own right. Yet, while others chomped at the bit to get hold of property of their own, Jack steadfastly refused it. Some wondered if it was because of all that Mad Jack had suffered and seen in those early years. Having born witness to cannibalism by some in the face of starvation and having survived such other adversities which had killed most of his peer group, was enough to pitch any man into 'strange ways.' Whatever the reason, Jack seemed content in his present condition, preferring not to mix much but to remain at his 'post' near the gate, scratching out a pittance where he was free to sit and watch the comings and goings all day and answer to no-one. Thomas explained to Bessie how Mad Jack was especially interested in the newcomers and possessed an uncanny knack of summing up each one's chances of survival, seemingly with but one cursory glance no sooner had they stepped from the ship. He somehow knew, or could pick up on some tell-tale signs only he could read, as to who would live and who would succumb to the Jamestown curse.

'That one's quick...' Jack would say or 'him's not so quick...' and anyone overhearing would know exactly what Jack meant. This was a place for the quick.... the rest were merely walking dead. Or as Jack would say, 'them's that are only looking for a spot to be planted.'

'I do not think that Jack is so 'mad' as he makes out,' Thomas remarked to Bessie in a sideward whisper. 'In fact, of the entire party that came over with him, Jack turned out to be the only one who was destined to be quick! The rest are long dead.'

Looking around at the sorry state of some who passed by, Bessie could not but help thinking that here there were many awaiting planting still. For this country consumed human lives like a raging fire does logs.

Yet but a few yards on, in contrast to the foregone drab and rags, Thomas and Bessie were met by a lurid popinjay in boots if ever there was.

'Ah Thomas!' He squawked. 'You are back! Good man! I look forward to hearing all about your excursion later...Good day Mistress...' he added smiling broadly in Bessie's direction, 'and this must be...'

'Bessie, Sir George! This is my wife Bessie!'

'Good grief!' He exclaimed in surprise, 'I must be getting befuddled in this heat for I had quite got it into my head that you had said your wife's name was Dorothy...'

Neither Thomas nor Bessie offered any resistance to Sir George's presumption that the error was of his own making.

'So, Bessie! And from which family are you come over, my dear?' He said leaning in with a friendly yet leery grin. 'Maybe I know them!'

Without quite understanding the question, Bessie made an awkward reply.

'Sir...the Hickmans of Gainsborough Hall in Lincolnshire.'

'Ah! Yes! Of course, I know of them! Good merchant stock, hmm? And you would be what? A daughter... a niece?'

'No sir,' Bessie replied. 'I was their housekeeper.'

'A servant....' Sir George's eyes dropped away from her like a hand from a red-hot iron as his flushed face assumed the visage of a dog chewing at a wasp.

Bessie could almost read the thoughts buzzing through his mind yet were kept from reaching his tongue. A servant? Master Thomas, this fine gentleman's son, wasted on a servant? How old must she be... thirty and five if a day and barren no doubt...so why waste himself on her? Bessie was made to feel so uncomfortable that she wished the ground would open up and hide her away from his presence.

Thomas squeezed her hand.

'I am indeed lucky to have been able to prize her away from their bosom,' he said, ' so high in regard was she held by Sir William...'

'Hmm ...quite ... em...' Sir George cleared his throat and looking straight past Bessie towards her husband and continued. 'Your travels...as I was saying...we must talk together of them later. Good day Thomas ...Mistress...'

With that, he hurried on his way.

Thomas and Bessie soon reached their appointed

cottage. It was tiny but adequate for their needs, consisting of but one room with a dirt floor. At one end, it had been separated off with a partition thus creating an area for possibly keeping livestock - complete with a half-loft above and its own external door. Only, when Thomas took Bessie inside their new home, they found several gentlemen already ensconced there, one of which was sprawled prostrate on the large four-posted bed as drunk as could be. However, on recognising Thomas, two quickly gathered up their belongings and after profuse apologies, half dragged their comrade away with them to find alternate lodgings.

Bessie tried to set about cleaning up the mess but could scarcely muster any heart to put into it. She was tired, hungry and had little will to fight this place so instead Thomas went off to find some acquaintance that would lend them the makings of a cold meal.

That first night in Jamestown, sleep eluded Bessie. She lay upon the covers of the filthy bed and cursed the humidity that held her hot and wakeful when she yearned for nothing more than to escape from this place and into dreams. For in truth, she feared that from now on that this might be her only means of escape. Thomas slept though, stretched out beside her in just his britches and snoring loudly. She looked at him in the half-light and felt cheated out of a better life left behind in New England.

She was alone, at last with her husband. Yet, she had scarcely reacquainted herself with him and had come to doubt that he really loved her at all. Although there had been some pretty words and flowered sentiments spouted by him on the voyage down from New Plimoth, Bessie had yet found little evidence of such love in practice. It seemed to her as if she was entered again into some 'mutual arrangement' much the same as her marriage to Francis Eaton. For twice Thomas had come in search of her because of this profound 'love' he professed to hold in his heart yet, like her marriage to Francis, this one also had remained unconsummated.

Something else was missing from within her soul. Something she would never willingly have given up but rather that it was as if something had been sapped from out of her and yet, she could not fathom what it was. Only that she now felt empty and she longed to feel whole once more. Bessie watched Thomas sleeping and tried to remember how it was when they were together before. Yet, what are memories but the shards of a broken looking glass that's image no longer reflects the full truth.

*   *   *

It was next day, as Bessie sat beside the cottage, sewing in the gentle morning sunlight, that she suddenly realised how much she missed silence. Above all else, the stillness; the quietness of temperate old-world summer afternoons in the garden of England where silence was only gently broken into by birdsong; distinct, clearly audible and so pleasing on the ear. At this time of year, especially, there was no silence to be had in Jamestown. Not only because of the constant comings or goings of dozens of people, now tooth by jowl in such a tightly confined environment but also on the part of nature herself. In Virginia, the constant high chirring of legion insects continued all day, droning on into the night and a crescendo of slow, cruel torture to her ears. Yet, when she commented upon it to 'long time' colonists they would look puzzled by this and reply 'what noise?' It was as if their ears had grown immune to the sound or simply that their minds had somehow switched it off. Try as she might, though, Bessie could not. It only proved to serve as just one more constant reminder that this place could never become a home to her.

As she sat at her mending, Bessie thought of how much she missed her old home in ordered New Plimoth and the camaraderie she had enjoyed there. She regretted having to leave it without even a goodbye to her good and steadfast friends. Friends who had no doubt been led to believe that she now lay at rest in that coffin buried in the dapple shade of the hillside, high above the settlement looking out to sea. Though she was grateful to have been reunited once more with the only man she had ever loved, Bessie did not want to make a death with him in Virginia.

All of a sudden, Bessie found her thoughts broken as a sober young girl approached her and asked, 'Pardon me, but are you Mistress Bessie?' The girl had asked earnestly.

'Yes, I am,' Bessie replied rather amused. 'Why do you ask?'

'No offence, Mistress,' she replied hesitantly, proffering up a folded note. 'Just that I have never seen a gentlewoman sitting out in the sun doing her own mending, Mistress.'

The girl's observation quite took Bessie aback. In the New Plimoth settlement all the women sat and sewed and far more menial tasks than that, no matter what their former station back home. She, Mary Brewster and even Katherine Carver, bless her soul, had even hauled up their skirts and taken to the fields, in mud and rain, to help clear the land and to plant New Plimoth's first desperate crop and worse. Without the luxury of droves of servants, all hands had been pressed into work for the better of them all. Circumstances were quite different here in Virginia. No matter how quickly the serving class came to sicken and die, there always seemed the certainty that before too long there would be another shipment of poor willing wretches to take their places. If one were as wealthy as Sir George Yeardly, then they might even be able to afford a shipment of unwilling servants - black-a-moors. For this was the one difference between the old and the new worlds, above all else, that for Bessie set this place apart from any other and made her despise it so. It was the unnatural and utterly abhorrent to her mind, presence of enslaved African men and women.

Bessie opened up the message and quickly read its contents. It contained her first formal invitation as Thomas's wife into polite Jamestown society, such as it was. None less than the colony's unofficial first Lady

Temperance Yeardly, was inviting Bessie to 'call upon her' after church the following day while her husband and the men folk remained behind to conduct some discussion of security. Bessie accepted and at the duly appointed time presented herself at the Yeardly residence.

Standing outside this Jamestown house, Bessie was struck by how lowly a dwelling it was for a master of such wealth as Sir George. Back at the New Plimoth colony, basic amenities were understandable considering that the settlement was barely into its third year. However, Bessie had thought to expect something of better standing here, considering that this town had been in existence for more than sixteen.

Inside, it was clean with fine furniture yet no more opulent than one might expect from a yeoman farmer of good acreage back home. The house was unmistakably superior to the comfort of most in Jamestown yet, still no way was it befitting a lady of such high station. Yet, this was Jamestown and not England, a place where many envied the Yeardly household for having dried peas at their disposal when there were none to be had in the rest of the town.

Temperance Yeardly was a handsome-looking woman and despite her fine pale features, deceptively robust. During the past years in Virginia, she had also proved herself a strong one. For indeed 'survivor' was exactly what Lady Yeardly was. Having first come across on the Faulcon in sixteen hundred and nine, she had somehow survived the 'starving time' when eight out of every ten colonists had perished. Though she then went back to England, undaunted she returned to Jamestown with her new husband to endure yet more bouts of sickness and pestilence, food shortages, drought, hurricane, freezing winters and sweltering summers. (Though Bessie later came to the opinion that perhaps the advantages of her position rather than constitution had no doubt played a great part in this). However, truly remarkable was the fact that Lady Yeardly had fairly wagered her life in childbirth and had two living children to show for it and another child now clearly in prospect. Bessie quickly found herself picturing Lady Yeardly's arrival in her mind's eye. She could imagine her stepping ashore and with Mad Jack marking this lady out as being very 'quick' indeed.

Bessie was received in what passed for as her Ladyship's parlour where she was invited to sit and partake of some small measure of balderdash.

'I do so try to meet as many newcomers as I can but some are barely arrived before they depart again!' Lady Temperance said in a manner that might be construed that she considered such departures as a personal 'nuisance' to her. Yet barely had Bessie put such an interpretation upon the lady's words when she suddenly realised that in fact this was not the intention at all. She concluded instead that Lady Temperance's tone, constrained and lacking in deliberate emotion, was merely a defence against the awful realities of this place.

'This land uses both our sexes easy but disproportionally so,' she explained. 'My husband tells me that since our first coming to this Virginia, upward of some six thousand souls have been sent across. Do you know how many remain, Bessie?'

Bessie shook her head warily implying that she did not.

'Almost all remain!' She said sinisterly. 'Yet only above some scant twelve hundred or so are alive today. That is a mean of some three hundred odd souls, thus far, that have passed over for every year of our tenure here...'

Lady Yeardly paused in reflection for a moment, as if silently saying a prayer for those dead then continued in a solemn tone. 'We silent wait like stands of English wheat, in fear to watch at where next the scythe will reap....'

Bessie also reflected upon these awful statistics. It was true that her former New Plimoth colony had lost half their number that had come over aboard the Mayflower in those first dreadful six months. Yet the losses settled down into no more an exceptional death rate than could be expected back in the old country, what with winter hunger and spring fevers. Yet, approaching three hundred deaths in a year? She knew from Thomas that more than three hundred were murdered in the massacre yet what, she worried, was killing so many more beyond native attack even with the ague, brought on by the mosquitoes, it should never account for so many.

While Bessie's mind wandered, Lady Yeardly's young children ran into the parlour in search of their mother. Young Elizabeth, a beautiful child of around five years of age and her brother, Francis, probably younger by no more than a year, sat quietly at her skirts playing with a wooden ball while quite unmoved. Temperance continued to candidly chat away to her guest.

'You see, I have invited you today as I feel it is my duty, having lived here some while, to pass across any word of encouragement that I may. Any little advice that I feel might help increase your chances of surviving too. However, I trust that you will understand, I no longer allow myself the indulgence of forming attachments too closely, be that of servants, friends or...' Looking down at her little ones added, ' ... offspring. I warn you, if you do any other then it will break your heart else.'

Bessie felt a little shocked by this almost callous yet casual remark, all in full hearing of the children.

Unperturbed, Lady Yeardly then set about instructing Bessie upon the finer points of survival in the colony as if she were some gentlewoman, fresh from her sheltered English fireside chair and not as one already seasoned to the adversities of this new frontier. Bessie found it quite insulting and but for the sake of her husband, bided any counter remark she might have wanted to make.

'Do not go about this place early in the day or as evening draws on in summer ... and oftimes late into the autumn ... without a veil of muslin over your face and never leave off your stockings. No matter the heat and temptation to go without, you must keep at least past your knees covered up for there are monstrous biting insects here and it is my opinion that the welts that do rise up after doth cause much infection. Needless to add, such irritation too... And about your bed in those months, I suggest you hang a swag of muslin instead of the usual heavy curtain to likewise give you peaceful sleep away from their attention. We have muslin cloth by the bale fit for such purposes in the store at your disposal for a very modest price. If possible, before retiring and while there is still good light to see by, search about your room and seek out any of these spiteful devils and smite them dead. There are herb concoctions too, we have learnt from the naturals here about, that do both mute the attraction of human flesh for these praying insects and both ease their bites. I will send a servant to you tomorrow, to point out around the settlement where you might pick up the ingredients to make such a tincture for yourself.'

'Thank you, my lady,' Bessie replied politely.

'Temperance! You must call me Temperance when we ladies are in private. Neither my husband nor I was born to the peerage but of good merchant stock. Having proven his mettle here in this undertaking, he was elevated by our Sovereign. Though, 'she cautioned, 'when we meet with our menfolk or in public, my husband insists I am addressed by my full title of 'Lady Yeardly.' He says we must make such distinction for the sake of order and moral and that we have a duty to maintain courtly standards, even if we are in Virginia!'

The whole social structure of Jamestown was a worry to Bessie. She saw all as but a sorry attempt by these merchants as blindly replicating their version of the homeland left behind and its ingrained pecking order, without the vision to see that all this could instead be a God-given opportunity to build anew with equality. Instead, Jamestown creation by the elite was like the futile act of a pining child trying to recapture the substance of its dead Mother. Though to the lesser order of this New World, England was for all intents dead. For they thought that she might as well be, as they were the ones who had more readily come to consider that the chances of their living to see her again were but slight.

'When it rains,' Lady Temperance continued to advise, 'put outside as many pots and pans as you have to hand to catch as much rain water as possible. For what heaven sends, you can rely upon to be pure. Store it in a freshly steamed barrel, if possible and keep it covered at all times and better still, stored inside in the coolest part of the house. However, you will find many a time in the wretched summers, that this will be spent and you might then be tempted by thirst, to drink the brackish water of the James. I tell you, do not! It is as potent and as deadly as any poison taken straight! Even so, with cleansing it might be all there is to be had. Do you know how to cleanse such water?' She asked.

'Yes, I do!' Bessie replied confidently. 'I would pass it through a mess of Sphagnum moss set above a layer of sand and charcoal to filter out the bad. Then, I would choose to boil mine into an infusion with herbs or hips as it fogs the brain less than to be always drinking small beer!'

'I am impressed! But then I am forgetting that you have lived in this New World before here and that indeed we have a new northern colony!'

Bessie cared not one bit for this condescending treatment as if she were some naive child instead of a woman of mature years and so seized the opportunity to put forward one or two questions of her own.

'When, pray Temperance, may we women leave the compound to do our dirty washing? Only when my husband and I arrived at our designated house yesterday, there was a gentleman availing himself of our bed and had been so for some month past, it turns out. He made quick enough shift but the sheets smell rank and look as if his custom was to sleep with his boots on!"

'Ah.... yes,' she replied with embarrassment. '...I am sorry for that but it was only a temporary measure as there was nowhere else available to them...'

'And now?'

'Death has a habit of settling such matters... I will ask my servant to search through the company stores to try to procure more linen for you but I am afraid sheets are in short supply generally. For those who die in their bed are usually buried in them! As for washing, for the present we are not to! Our men are hard pressed enough to secure the safety of our work parties and as such have none to spare for such luxury...Maybe in a week or so, when things have settled down a bit, the Governor will be able to arrange something. After all, no one has ever died from dirt?'

'And may I ask? ...' Bessie pressed Lady Yeardly. '...In times of say...want? Should we exercise any privilege that we might enjoy in that instance?'

'Yes. Most assuredly, so! Above all else, in such circumstance, one must press every advantage in order to survive. We owe it to the Company shareholders to survive and to continue to prosper this colony for the King's sacred benefits. In fact, it is our duty! There is no need of me to tell you that! After all, you are a Company wife! Above all else, you must become accustomed to making decisions with one's head and not with one's heart. Suppose you had but a small cauldron of stew to share out among twenty hungry mouths? Would you dole out a scant portion to all that hungered, regardless? Or would you instead concentrate that resource upon the five or six that contributed to the pot? In times of need, it is a matter of the survival of those fittest to do so. The mongrel must sometimes be sacrificed in order to maintain the pedigree bloodline. My husband informs me that you were once a maidservant. Is that true?' Lady Temperance had the knack of firing off questions like a volley of lethal arrows.

'Yes... but I progressed to the position of housekeeper to the Hickman family of Gainsborough Hall and personal companion to Lady Frances.'

'You bear yourself well, Bessie. Had I not known differently I would have taken you as a natural born gentlewoman. Were you a foundling by chance?'

Bessie was quite at a loss as to why her Ladyship should have asked such a thing.

'Only… if you will forgive me for saying…You have intelligence far beyond being a mere peasant. Even a donkey with the most accomplished of grooms might never be expected to grow into a mare!' She then added, 'I have heard it rumoured often that some lady of noble birth or another, having been deceived by a man in some unsuitable tryst and proving with child, have entrusted the ensuing offspring into the care of simple peasant folk to raise. I would wager that is what you are… just such a foundling and nothing to raise the unnatural hopes of our servants here!'

Bessie replied, as politely but firmly as she could, that she had no recollection of ever overhearing her parents say a thing to suggest that they were anything other than that. Yet, Bessie also had the feeling that Lady Yeardly was steadfastly holding on to her own theory for the better of this fragile society.

'You say you were a companion to Lady Frances? Does that mean that you can read?'

'Yes, I can. I was taught by the then Dowager Lady Rose when Lady Frances was a little girl. Then in later years I used to read aloud Shakespeare's words for my Lady.'

'How very modern, not to add generous, of her to undertake such an indulgence. She must indeed have been very perceptive to have thought so highly of you and to have invested so much time and effort in your education.'

This last comment was added in a tone as to infer that Bessie should indeed doubt her parentage. Yet, before she could respond to it Lady Temperance had moved swiftly on.

'Excellent!' She exclaimed. 'Then you must visit me… often … and read aloud to me. In return, you may avail yourself of our fine collection of books. I must confess, I am finding this latest confinement most tiresome having to be away from our plantation house and so enjoy whatever diversion I can salvage from this cultural waste land!'

'Thank you, Temperance. You are most generous.' Bessie was uncertain as to whether she had just been insulted or complimented.

Inexplicably, Lady Yeardly's countenance suddenly altered and Bessie thought she noted an overtone of threat.

'My husband knew of your Lady Rose Hickman and her reputation. Excellent merchant family background ... admirable commercial practices yet...rather tainted by misplaced religious leanings in the past, I hear rumoured. I mean... of course...that it had been muted that they have in the past harboured some Separatist fanatics, but I suspect that was before your time there. In any case, I do expect none of those wayward ideas have rubbed off onto you, my dear! Have they?'

Bessie held her anger in restraint. 'No, my lady. I have no wayward ideas of which I can think of...'
'Good. I am so glad to hear of that. We have so much adversity to contend with here without the complication of any would be schism in matters spiritual. The naturals have done more than enough to try break our spirits of late!'

As a sign that Bessie's visitation was now all but played out, Lady Temperance called for a small hessian sack to be brought in and presented to her guest.
'Here, 'tis but a little something, but please do not show this to anyone else nor say where this was to be had.'

Bessie looked inside. It was about two quarts mixture of dried peas and beans.

'Your husband contributes greatly to the good of this place and I feel certain that you will too...' Were Lady Yeardly's parting words.

Back at the cottage, Bessie took up her bundle of possessions and threw it onto the bed and began a frantic search for her precious journal. She rummaged through the pile, checking and re-checking its contents but still could not find it anywhere. Bessie was so angry inside. She needed to vent her rage and opinion within the safety of its pages lest it burst out of her and she might scream out at the top of her lungs at the wretchedness of this place. Instead, she was left to sit brooding over the events of the day until Thomas finally arrived home much later.

'You have been gone a long time,' she said calmly. 'Yes! There was much to be discussed and considered. How has your visit been?' He asked.

'I am not certain,' Bessie replied. 'But it was very much like an inquisition honeyed with a bribe,' she said proffering up the small sack for Thomas's inspection. He unloosed the tie and looked inside.

'Peas and beans! My, but aren't you the favoured one?'

'They were a gift for you as much as for me, I believe,' she said curtly.

Even so, there are some who would not believe their eyes if they were to see these. As far as I know there are none to be had anywhere in town just now!'

'Rather like chickens then?'

'Chickens?' Thomas puzzled.

'Yes, have you not noticed? I have not seen even one since we arrived.'

'Ah! Yes! Chickens! You are quite correct. There are none in town but plenty at the plantations. So, I can assure you that you shall not go short of eggs for the planters come into town with them quite regularly to trade.'

'Then why not keep them here?'

'All eaten last winter...along with the chicken feed. Such was our want.'

'And since?'

'Well...thereby hangs a tale! But to cut a boring tale short I shall but say that they are no longer a welcome entity here in the town?'

'Why ever not?'

'After some interval without them...it was noted that in their absence there were no longer so many disputes and complaints, as in the past, of poultry roaming at will around the township... No more scratching up of precious seedlings in neighbouring yards ... or infestations of tiny foul mites being passed on to plague we humans, that it was decided by the council not to encourage the restocking of them.'

'Well, that is fair enough if the yards were not fenced in to protect the householders food crops, but they are.'

'The streets are not fenced in though, Bessie, and as you have seen, any spare patch or dirt about them or the houses is quickly taken up by spare tobacco seedlings after planting out the main crop, so as not to waste a single precious plant.'

'Tobacco!' Bessie said in utter exasperation. 'I might have guessed. This tobacco seems to take precedence above all else around here.'

'With the pretty price it fetches, can you blame the men abouts here from planting up a few plants where they may for their own consumption? Look about you and at how many smoke it to counteract the effects of this place?'

'Too many smoking too much, if you ask me. Surely it cannot do any good to perform so unnatural an act?'

'Some doctors say it opens up the lungs and sooths the chest and remedies much antagonism within the patient as to be quite a panacea for all that ails.'

Bessie remained unconvinced.

'Then would it not be just as well to sit in the hearth and breath in the wood smoke, if that be the case.'

'Maybe so, but you have to admit that there is something about smoking tobacco that affects the mood more than burning damp logs?'

'How did your meeting go, Thomas? You have not said much.'

'In truth there is very little new to know. We need to be vigilant against attack by the naturals. To even keep watchful eyes and a trained pistol upon those converted to Christianity that still come to trade with us outside the town palisade. How powder and shot is low and that we must be prudent with our use of it until

42

fresh supplies, promised by the Company, can arrive.'

'It was ever the same in New Plimoth. Never enough powder and shot for our pistols.'

'I own my own snaphance but many here have no weapons at all at their disposal, apart from swords and such. Worse still, even the ordinance, such as it is, is not serviceable though the Governor will vehemently deny that if pressed. Quite apart from the naturals, the master of the Delver joked how if he had been a Spanish barque idling up the James he would meet with very little resistance and most like would make it all the way here to Jamestown unchallenged. Perhaps even to be able to range his cannons on the fortress and fire before our guards even had a chance to respond.'

'And what of the naturals?'

'Well, there has been some escalation since my departure from here. Some taking of eyes, you might say. In April, more than twenty of our colonists were killed by the naturals. They had gone out on an expedition to try to trade with still friendly natives but they were attacked and the naturals got away with armour and guns. In a show of strength, the Governor sanctioned reprisals.'

'A counter attack?'

'A massacre of our own doing this time. William Tucker went to a Powhatan village with gifts on the pretence of negotiating a peace treaty with the naturals. They took along strong wine, knowing the naturals weakness for it and gave it to them to drink by way of sealing the pact. Then our men sat, watched and waited. For with the assistance of Doctor Pott, they had poisoned the naturals' barrel.

Bessie was utterly horrified.

'Oh my, but that is a dreadful low thing to do!'

'No worse than they did to us last year!' Thomas quickly defended the action. 'At least we did not torture and mutilate them!'

Bessie backed down. She was saddened by her husband continued support for that which she knew and believed to contravene the scriptures she thought they both held so dear. Yet how could this be? This madness for profit and land that had corrupted this God fearing people into accepting Christ's words on a Sunday yet moved them freely to murder the next?

'How many were killed?' She asked quietly.

'They think around two hundred from the effects of the poison and Tucker's men dispatched perhaps another fifty, at least.'

'Then they are set to come for the other eye in good time...'

'Yes, that is the consensus so we are reminded to keep extra vigilance. No more hunting parties without extra-armed men as backup. Trips in to town from the plantations are to be made only by river, and if possible using the cover of darkness... And any deaths...well... we are to bury our dead at night once more.'

'In short, we are to live our lives out as if under siege?'

'Yes. And in the case of further attacks, we are to strike back at them immediately with the aim of inflicting as much, if not more casualties upon them so that they might come to an understanding that we English are neither weak nor a force to be intimidated.'

'Then may the Lord have mercy us on...'

Chapter Three

'Tis a great ability to be able to conceal one's ability'
- Francois de La Rochefoucauld

Next morning, Thomas was out early for a further meeting with the Governor and some of the Company men due in from the plantations. There was a particular topic the Governor wished to discuss with his elite, as well as much by the way of Thomas's drawings and accounts to be readied for sending on to the Virginia Company back home. The Delver would be returning that day from its safe mooring off Fort Comfort. After that, it was bound for England.

When Thomas joined the meeting, the room was already in uproar. As a paper was hurriedly thrust in his hand, he unwillingly found himself set fair thick in the fray.

'Some puffed up nobody drops anchor here for a while and then sets himself up as self-appointed critic of our colony then tittle-tattles his way back to whisper lies and slander in His Majesty's ear!' Francis Wyatt slammed the table with his fist in culpable rage.

'Yes, yes, quite! Butler is a low snake,' Sir George conceded, 'who has no right to be spouting such venomous lies and meddling in our affairs. But meddle, he has! And now, my Dear Fellows, we are left to answer his charges...'

Captain Butler, Thomas recalled, had been out to Virginia the previous winter in the wake of the massacre. It appeared that on returning to England, he had presented a scathing report to the King about the Company's handling of the colony and the wretched plight of the people therein.

'He takes little note of all our achievements, now wiped out or put back by the Massacre, yet instead he spouts on about the number of deaths we encounter each year. Some at court are now openly joking that the only benefit we bring is to keep light the streets of

London of its unnatural number of youths by killing them off in our keeping!'

Thomas, like the others there, studied his copy of Butler's account and on reading through each of the charges, laughed off his remarks with utter contempt. Outwardly, he acted the Company's man like a true Shakespearian trooper. Yet, inwardly, his stomach sickened and clenched as he desperately searched for some memorable pro-Company sentiment to impart.

'Does this fool not realise that for such a great enterprise as this that some small sacrifice needs to be made for the sake of progress? All of life is but a gamble! Yet, what better game of chance could we offer these street-fodder than one in which they might get up and walk away from the table with wealth beyond their wildest expectations?'

'Exactly, Master Thomas!' Sir George exclaimed with obvious approval. 'You are a man after my own heart!'

'These indentured servants,' a planter spoke up, 'they are hardly worth their passage in any account. They are sickly from the off and much disadvantaged by their previous circumstance or else why would they die four or five to every gentleman? I say we should concentrate instead on buying in more Africans from the Dutch for they are a much sounder proposition and prove more adaptable to the conditions in this land.'

'I agree whole-heartedly with you, but supplies of that particular commodity is expensive and still difficult to come by. So, for the time being, I am afraid we are dependent on these fellows for our labour and therefore need to continue to attract them into our service.'

'Then how are we to counter this blast?' One of the others spoke up.

'By now, preparing this day, a document by way of reply to each of the charges set by Butler. After, I also would require of you independent planters that each man here set down a brief and glowing account of our own success and experience here in Virginia.

These, coupled with Master Thomas's most excellent representations, should vindicate us and scuttle these outrageous charges for good and all! Right gentlemen!' Sir Francis asked holding Butler's report up in front of him. 'So what say we to the first of the charges? That our plantations are sited on marshes, bogs and muddy creeks full of diseases and insects the like of which one might only find in the most unsound and unhealthiest parts of England...?'

*　　*　　*

Meanwhile at the cottage, as Bessie cleared away the breakfast things, Lady Yeardly's servant came to the door with her arms full of bed linen and the unexpected gift of a lavender plant and a small spray of its dried flowers.

'My lady grew that herself, Mistress,' the girl said proudly. 'It is from a single plant she had sent over from England. She has grown on dozens more now... only she didst tell me to relate how it is not to be planted in the dirt here in town. Oh! And how it will thrive much better if left in a pot of earth and sand and receives water only as soon as that gets dry to the touch.'

'Thank you...er...' Bessie struggled to recall the girl's name. She really wanted this young servant to know that, at least to her, it mattered.

'Susan... Mistress,' she replied proudly.

'Yes ... I remember now! Thank you Susan. Was that all?'

'Yes, Mistress... I mean no!' She said suddenly remembering that there was something else. 'My Lady also asks if you might make of use a sack full of feathers and some ticking she has spare, thinking you might like to sew some new pillows for your bed and if, in return and of no imposition, you would be kind enough to sew some into a mattress for her Ladyship's new baby's crib... Only I told her...Mistress...how fine and small a stitch I saw you make at your mending last time I called here.'

'Tell Lady Temperance that I am very thankful for the kind offer and that...yes...I would be most grateful for both and delighted to sew for her.'

'Very well, Mistress. I will go fetch them to you straight away.'

Bessie took the linen from the girl and laid it on the table with the spray of dried flowers on top. As she did, the lavender brushed against her sleeve releasing a heady rush of its fragrance into the air reminding her of romantic walks with Thomas in the garden at Gainsborough Hall. Then she recalled with some sadness, how much in love they had once been.

With the servant sent on her way, Bessie went over to the unkempt-looking bed and threw off its covers onto the floor. Then, she dragged off the putrid sheets and dropped them into a pile by the open doorway before setting about making the bed afresh. First, she struggled to heave the great straw mattress over. Having eventually succeeded in doing so, she set about beating it with a stick until the lumps had smoothed out and a shower of dislodged insects had fallen to the floor and quickly scuttled away. After that, she then left the unmade bed to air.

Meanwhile Susan returned with the promised feathers and the ticking, all neatly cut to size and ready for making up. Bessie plucked a few stems from the lavender plant, then carefully rolled and crushed them between her fingertips to release their scent, which she rubbed over her neck and wrists to deter any errant midges. Then, she settled down outside in the cool shade under the eaves of the cottage and began to sew in earnest. By midday, she had already stuffed the pillows and was over-stitching them closed. It had become hot and almost unbearably humid by then, making her all the more thankful as she cut the final thread free.

Bessie took the finished pillows inside and untied the bale of linen. As expected, the sheets were far from new but at least they were clean. She made up the bed and, tying the lavender flowers up into a piece of muslin cloth, she slipped them in between the bolster and two pillows to release their sweet perfume the next time she and Thomas were a-bed.

As she vigorously swept a heap of dust from the cottage floor out into the street, the air reverberated to a low moan of thunder some way off in the distance. She looked up. Overhead, a low-slung halo of shimmering overcast sky warned Bessie that, surely, this weather must soon break. She sighed in deeply and could smell the promise of rain.

Within in few minutes of going inside again, Jamestown shuddered under a terrifying clap of thunder followed by the heavy pitter-patter of rain drumming against its windows. Armed with pots and pans, Bessie dashed outside to collect rainwater. Then after, she ran back indoors to fetch the soiled sheets which she proceeded to hang on the line in the back yard. She may not have been able to go the river to wash, but at least she could harness the rain to refresh them.

By now, her hair and face were dripping wet. The rain felt so good against her parched skin that she found herself thinking how much better it would feel if only she could slip out of her clothes and stand in yard with the storm washing over her naked body. Then she let out a long sigh to herself as she realised how outrageous this flight of fancy was.

Making her way back indoors, Bessie was startled to find a young lad crouched against the cottage wall, sheltering from the rain. He looked ill and gaunt and so very young.

'Who are you?' She asked.

'I beg your pardon, Mistress,' he replied making to up and leave.

'No! ...It's all right...You look drenched! Come inside...out of the rain,' she said beckoning the bedraggled wretch inside.'

The lad followed her in like a lamb.

'I don't mind you staying here while the storm passes,' Bessie said drying her face with a makeshift towel. 'I just wanted to know who you were and that your parents will not be worrying after you.'

'James, Mistress. My name is James and I am a servant come here on the boat here from Martin's

Hundred.'

Bessie was surprised. He looked too young to be a servant.

'Martin's Hundred?' She said, handing him the towel so he could dry off too.

'It's a plantation, ten miles from here. We came in the night by river and in the early hours of this morning unloaded our boat. Yet, because we were not needed yet to load up ready for our return, our lieutenant told us to go wait in the town. Then the heavens opened up! Before we usually lay up in the boat but now we are forbidden to do so for fear of attack. So...I had nowhere to shelter. Nor hath there been provision made for my stay until we return tonight.'

'No provision? Do you mean, no food?'

'Yes, Mistress. I will not get any more food until we return. And when we do it is not enough to stop me feeling hungry...scarcely half of a penny loaf between two of us to last anything up to two days.'

'Two of you?'

'Yes, I have a friend...another fellow who came across from England on the same ship as me. He is a decent enough but some of the others we are set with are desperate indeed. They steal from anyone who is weaker than them and would snatch away even the meagre ration we have...but we stick together to fight them off.'

Bessie fixed up the lad with some cold meat and corn biscuits but he politely refused at first saying that he had not come to beg or impose upon the household but only to shelter from the rain. However, when Bessie persisted he took the food and quickly gobbled it down like a ravenous dog.

'Tell me about Martins Hundred, James. I have not been here long enough to see a plantation.'

'There's not much to tell...'

'Then tell me all about you.'

'I came here from London. From a place called Cheapside. It's a sour part of the city...noisy, crowded... but I would give anything to be back there with my mother and my family. When the Company men first came, they put it to my father that I would fare far better in the New World as a servant than on the streets of that city. They said how it was a wonderful place of plenty where I could expect food to drop into my mouth. Father listened and said that he would think well upon it before giving his answer. There were leaflets, freely handed out in our streets and alleyways advertising positions for young fit able lads as I was then. Company men would even come among us and read them aloud to entice us, for those which could not read. They said we would be coming to a sweet landscape of plenty and that we would live on the venison and game that abounded so plentifully that we would never be wanting or hunger. There were pictures of Eden waiting for us and, at the end of our service on a plantation; we would be rewarded with land of our own. For truth, none in my family could ever dream of owning land! But they were all foul lies Mistress, all lies. My father and mother would cry if they could only see me now. All this place has on offer for the likes of me is sickness and death. The land crawls with all sorts of insects that bite and give you the shivers and shakes and since I came from of that ship, all I have had to eat is loblolly water gruel, bread and sometimes a mouthful of beef ...never deer. It true there are wild duck and geese but we are forbidden to leave our work to go to try to catch any.'

'Why ever not?'

'Because from first light to dusk we have to work and the overseer is always at our back to see that we do. Even though we get sick from hunger, no one seems to care or to try to better our lot'.

'How many are there of you?'

'I do not know for certain, but of the twenty that I came with to the plantation, half are already dead. Of last year's twenty...there were five or six left when I arrived but now there are only three still alive...'

'What crops do they grow there for I cannot understand how there can be such a shortage of food on land that is farmed?'

'There is corn and beans and divers others... it's just not enough, for mainly the soil is given over to tobacco.'

'That wicked weed!'

'We feel that keenly too, Mistress, for in truth if they but put a few more acres over to food, even if we had a patch to cultivate to feed ourselves, there would be no wanting amongst us. Yet they do not and it is all down to the greed and madness that this cursed plant induces in the merchants.'

Bessie felt deeply saddened that this simple boy could see plainly, what his betters were blind to, or maybe it profited not to see. The cynical side of the woman's mind saw the advantage of bringing a fresh consignment of youths over each year in time for the crucial spring planting of the tobacco and the losses then could well be replenished by another shipment in time for the harvest. For youths of no consequence and too young to have heirs, who lived only as long as their usefulness negated any obligation on the Company for valuable land. If this were true, she reasoned, then why not save even more by limiting their rations?

'Where is this friend, Richard, of yours now?'

'He has a bolthole to go to. He boasts of a kindly couple who last time gave him some food but would find two of us a burden...'

'I understand. Then you too, on future trips, must look to me as your friend and I will help you as much as I can. Agreed?'

'Thank you Mistress, thank you,' he said with such gratitude in his face that Bessie reached out and hugged him. He seemed so desperately in need of that hug.

'Is there anything else I can do for you?' She asked reluctantly letting him go.

'Nothing Mistress...only pray for me at night if you would. It's the nights that I so dread above anything else.'

'Because of the naturals?...'

'Yes. Because of them,' he said nervously.

'Were you here during the...troubles?' Bessie could not bring herself to utter the word 'massacre' in case it troubled the lad more.

'No, I was not, but some of those that were do fill us up with dreadful stories. There are only about three dozen of us in all should they ever come again. And how many might come, we may not know...though our previous lieutenant, afore he died, did once say how there could be as many as three thousand of them hereabouts. Yet, also he said how afraid they are of our cannons and guns. Though they cannot know how very little we have in our armoury or they would surely have come for us by now! ...There were eighty, they say... eighty settlers murdered that day at Martins Hundred alone.'

'Yes, I know. My husband was sent thereafter.'

'They are all, mostly, buried in a pit out back from the shed where we sleep. At night, in the dark, I lay awake and sometimes I am so certain I can hear crying. Not just me, Mistress, others have said the same thing. We lie awake hungry wondering when we are going to die. It would be a comfort to know then, that you were saying a prayer for me to see me through till the morning...'

'How old are you, James?' Bessie asked.

'Fifteen, Mistress. I am fifteen.' He hesitated for a moment then told her the truth. 'Twelve, Mistress... the Company men told me to lie about my age. They said that a strapping lad like me could pass for fifteen easy and also I would get a piece of land of my own all the quicker.'

'Well James,' Bessie said holding back a lump in her throat, 'be certain that I will be saying a prayer for you every night from now on.'

With that, the gate bell rang out. The sun was shining once more and the rain over.

'That will be for us Mistress. Calling us back to start loading up. I best go.'

'Wait a moment,' Bessie said putting on her cap and wrapping the remaining bread in a cloth for the lad to take with him. 'Let me walk back to the gate with you. Let your friend see that you too have a friend.'

As they reached the gate and said their farewell until next time, Bessie noticed Mad Jack glance their way and give her a knowing nod. She already knew in her heart that without her help, James was not going to last very long.

When Thomas came home Bessie immediately told him all about James and begged him to help ease the boy's plight.

'Thomas, can't we do anything for him...he's only a child! Can we not buy him out from out of the merchant's service and instead take him on here as our houseboy? You have said before that we could do with some help of our own.'

'I cannot. I am sorry, Bessie,' he said bluntly.

'But I thought you said this position had proved lucrative and that you already had a tidy sum set aside?'

'Yes, I did have. But today I have been persuaded to purchase a parcel of land at a generous Company discount, so I am not in a position to do as you ask.'

'But you told me that your work was done here and that you wanted to get away from Jamestown?'

'That is true, Bessie. But now I have returned to Jamestown I cannot simply up and go back to England without the Company's express permission. And to do that I need a valid excuse so as not to arouse any suspicion. When one comes to hand, do not fear, we will be away from here as quickly as possible.'

'Is there nothing we can do for James?'

'The plantations are full of children like him, my dear...some even younger. What would you have done? Buy them all back?'

'Younger than twelve labouring on the land?'

'Yes, tobacco seedlings are very fragile. Small hands are best suited to the delicate task of transplanting them from the nursery beds out into the fields. That is one of the main advantages of using them. Tiny fingers are less lightly to bruise the stems of the plants. I know that the Company has been actively rounding up the excess children from the slums of London and other overcrowded cities and shipping them out here for just this purpose. Some are willingly given over by their parents in hope of giving their child a better prospect in life, while orphans and others are simply picked up and carried off. I know it is a distasteful practice...but there it is...the Company have not broken any laws.'

'Thomas! Have you no heart anymore? These children are being starved?'

'I have a heart...make no mistake of that! ...I just may not do anything outwardly to show my disgust at so much I have witnessed!' Thomas thought for a while and added. 'Perhaps we could do something for this boy...say...write a letter to his parents. Maybe they could come up with the money to buy him back. He told you his name and that they are in Cheapside. That is enough for me to get an earnest letter past the company scrutiny and to them via my contact.'

'Do you think that will do any good?'

'Yes. I think a letter like that could do a lot of good. You write down an account of all the lad told you as if it were he writing the letter. Then when you are done, pass it over to me and I will edit it and put it in my barrel with my own drawings and correspondence for England. But you must hurry! The Delver will be leaving on the morning tide.'

Bessie did as her husband suggested.

Later that evening, Thomas had walked with his wife down to the riverside to deliver his own special consignment into the safe keeping of the Delver's master. Amidst the flurry of activity that afternoon with the arrival of The Delver and the going of the plantation boat, Mad Jack's dog had slipped, unnoticed, out of the gate in pursuit of a possum. When finally Jack noticed Peg was missing, he called out to her but with no response. As Thomas and Bessie were stopped by the woodpile collecting up a few logs to take back with them, a voice from up high on the palisade called down cheerily.

'Tis all right, Jack. The dog is out here on the

other side of the palisade waiting to be let back in!'

With that, the gate was opened up just a crack to let Peg slip back into the settlement. She slunk through the opening, skulking past the gate man and back towards her master. Then, head slung low, the dog came to a halt some distance from Jack and refused to come any closer.

'Come on, you silly creature,' he called out, 'I's not going to scold you, girl?'

The dog pricked up her ears and slowly advanced once more.

As it passed by, Bessie gasped in horror as she noticed the edges of a large gape, low down in the dog's side, flap open as it moved along.

'It's been hurt!' She cried out.
At first, it looked like maybe the poor animal had come off worse in a tussle with some wild beast or another. It would not have been the first time one of the dogs had received a flesh wound that way. There was not much blood in evidence on Peg's pale coat so Jack did not get up to go over to his pet but instead stayed sitting and calling her on gently.

'Come on Peg. Come to Jack and lets be a-looking at you!'

Only then, as Peg came closer did it become clear that these were serious wounds instead.

Peg reached Jack and cowered a little in his shadow as if in atonement for running off. Then she rolled over submissively onto her back, nervously wagging her tail and looking straight up, with such pitiful eyes at her beloved master. As she did so, it was then with horror that all about there realised the barbarity of what had befallen the dog.

'It's been cut!' Someone cried out in shocked disbelief.

The dog had indeed been cut and in a precise and deliberate manner. Two parallel incisions had been skilfully made, probably with the dog forcibly held upright while a blade was sliced through its belly wall, shortly before being released again near to the gate. The result was a dreadful sight that would haunt many minds for the rest of their wretched days. For as Peg lay on her back, tail still wagging at her master's feet, her grey pulsing innards began to slip slowly out of her body and into the dirt below. Mad Jack sat, opened mouth and rooted to his seat in shock, unable to move or speak. Thomas pulled Bessie's face close into his chest to shield her from seeing anymore just as someone stepped forward, picked up Jack's axe from its block and cleaved the dog's head clean off. At least then it was put out of its suffering.

'Who would have done such a terrible thing?' Bessie sobbed into Thomas's strong shoulder as he led her away from the scene.

'The naturals,' he replied. 'I expect it's a warning.'

It was a warning. A warning that, even in broad daylight, the Powhatan could come at will right up the gates of Jamestown to deliver their gruesome message. None could expect mercy, not even the gentlest among the settlers would be spared if the English would not give up the naturals land. There would be no more negotiations or treaties. This was war. A war of attrition that would only cease once one or the other's culture and people had been completely annihilated and driven from Virginia's soil.

*   *   *

Bessie slid off her cap and shook out her hair from beneath it. The earlier drenching in the rain had softened it; beautifully defining the soft, dark curls now framing her ivory face and shoulders in the pale light of the flickering bedside candle. Thomas was already quietly in bed, with his back turned firmly on his wife. Silently, she undressed, taking off all her clothes before slipping gently between the sheets.

After such a day as this, and after weeks now of uncertainty, disillusionment and loss, Bessie desperately needed to be held that night. She craved the comfort of a husband and hungered, somewhere deep inside, for the love of a lover.

'Thomas...are you awake?' She whispered.

Her husband made no reply.

'Thomas...please...' she quietly pleaded, 'please hold me...'

Thomas immediately roused turned over.

'Oh, Bessie!' He said gently taking her in his arms. 'Of course, I will hold you...if you really want me to! My arms have been aching to hold you for so very... very...long,' he sighed.

'Then...why haven't you?'

'I did not think you wanted me,' he said. 'Then tonight, when I came to bed and smelt the lavender it almost drove me crazy. I was so filled with the hope that you had put it there as a sign...a remembrance of how we once were. I wanted to reach out to you and cover you in kisses and bring you into bed with me...but I was afraid...I was afraid of making a fool of myself...or by affronting you by making some unwelcome advance...'

'Unwelcome...?'

'Yes...I didn't want to upset you... I wasn't even certain if you still loved me... or if you could let me love you...so...instead I turned my back on you and pretended to be asleep. I also knew that if I did not, then I might not be able to keep my feelings under control any longer...'

'Oh Thomas! What fools we have been. I was not certain either if you still loved me...'

'I can't tell you how I have missed you...' he said. 'I thought you had gone...changed into another woman...after all I have put you through I could never have blamed you...and so I had resigned myself to it being so...'

Bessie silenced his doubts with her mouth upon his and with that, Thomas eased his wife back into womanhood.

*   *   *

In the quiet glow of dawn break, Bessie awoke with a start to find Thomas staring straight at her. 'What is wrong?' She asked.

'Nothing...' he replied, smiling. 'There is absolutely nothing wrong...I have just been lying here watching you sleep and thinking how wonderful life suddenly is!'

'Oh,Thomas!' She exclaimed softly reaching over and kissing him.

'I have something to tell you...'

'Really? What is it?'

'When you asked me about England... and my 'death'' he could now laugh at the word. 'There was something I did not tell you.'

'What didn't you tell me?' She said worriedly.

'The wretches that robbed me...they had followed me from the Goldsmith's shop in the town thinking I had something on me worth stealing.'

'Had you?'

'No, I had not.' He sighed. 'In fact I had taken something of value with me there and left it in their keeping...a ring.'

With that, he reached under his pillow and pulled out a leather thong. Secured to it hung a thick, burnished band of gold.

'I bought this ring,' he said holding it up to her eyes, 'when I first asked you to marry me all those years ago. I had planned to have it engraved for you as a keepsake as soon as we were wed in Holland. After.... after I kept it all these years under my shirt next to my heart...because...because I never stopped loving you or...hoping. This is what the robbers were really after, only I had left it behind with the Goldsmith to be engraved while I idled some time away around the town waiting for him to carry out the work.'

'What does it say?' She asked with tears welling up in her big dark eyes.

Thomas held it up to the light and showed her.

'To my beloved wife - 1620.'

He untied the ring and taking up Bessie's hand, he slipped it on her finger.

'Now you really are my wife,' he said.

'Yes Thomas,' she murmured. 'And you are truly my husband...'

Chapter Four

'The undiscovered country, from whose bourn.
No traveler returns....'
- William Shakespeare

The main disadvantage of being in love is the dawning awareness of the awful possibility of losing one's loved one. None now felt that more acutely than Thomas and Bessie. For after so many wasted years apart since first they pledged their love in the gardens of Gainsborough Hall, they were now in a place where they knew odds of survival were far from favourable. As soon as they could, Thomas resolved, the following year they would both leave for England – come what may.

The tobacco harvest that year was better than any had dared hope. The eager ships that came to greedily take on the countless barrels of cured tobacco leaves brought plenty of supplies across for the settlers, however, it was likely there would be still be food scarcities that winter. These shortages would not only affect the settlers. The naturals too had suffered from English attacks and the resulting loss of men and sickness had taken its toll upon them in these fevered months. Their heavy casualties meant that they too would have harvested fewer crops than usual. As a result, the Governor considered it quite likely that more raids from the naturals could be expected in a bid to steal the settlers' food.

With the prolonged hot summer of that year searing well into that October, the fall that swiftly followed was spectacular. Bessie had never witnessed such a sudden riot of crimson and gold, as there was that autumn. Yet, all too soon it was over. The leaves were fallen and trees left unclothed and shivering in the cold winds that followed on. The little cottage, that had once seemed quite sound to Bessie back in August, was now opening up like a sieve full of drafts. No matter how hard Thomas tried to patch up the daub, as soon as he did, the cold wheedled its way in from some other gap or another.

Each night as Bessie said her prayers, she had made one for James, just as she had promised. She often thought about the boy and watched out for him whenever a planter's boat was in town but he never came to the cottage again. She asked after him but no one seemed to know him or if they did, they did not care enough to be bothered. After a time, she supposed the worst and instead found herself praying for James's mother. Would she ever know what had happened to her son? Would anyone from the plantation, or the Company have considered writing and telling her? Or would she be left for years in cruel limbo, waiting in futile hope for him to return home to her as a grown-up man of fortune. Would every overheard snippet about Virginia burn in her ears? Bring back tortuous memories of that last parting as her little boy went bravely away into the great unknown? Or did she already know? Had she somehow sensed that her son was dead? Does a mother know when the mysterious, invisible bond between her and her child, in existence long before birth, has been abruptly cut? If so, then was James's mother mourning, even now as Bessie thought of her and prayed?

*   *   *

Poisoner Pott they had dubbed him and Bessie found that quite disconcerting, especially after Thomas had explained that they had both been invited to dine with him that evening. Yet, as she watched John Pott across the dinner table, as he engaged her husband in polite conversation, Bessie found very little outwardly, that was the least bit ominous about this rather mild mannered man. However, she did find his bright fascination with poisonous plants as harbingers of death rather off-putting in a man who had actually been engaged to preserve the lives of the colonists. So much so that, the longer this meal lasted the more unpalatable to her it became.

The walls of Doctor John Pott's cottage were

covered in shelves crammed full of bottles and vials of strangely named potions of various sorts. Life-saving remedies for curing a host of different illnesses jostled uneasily for position alongside those expressly designed to bring about sickness or death.

'This Virginia is brim full of new and potent plants and herbs totally unknown of in the Old World.' Pott explained to Thomas excitedly. 'A veritable treasure chest for the modern medic!'

On the other hand, as Bessie preferred to consider it, a veritable Pandora's box.

The gambit of Pott's treasured 'non-medicinal' varieties ranged from simple emetics, to those whose effect was hallucinogenic to others, which were outright, drop-dead lethal. In fact, Doctor Pott's newly walled yard had been lately given over to cultivating ready supplies of many of these wild specimens, like pokeweed, sassafras, crinkle weed, all of which were lovingly tended to by his equally devoted wife, Elizabeth.

Pott had learnt an incredible amount about many new drugs since his arrival a few years before, through either direct contact with the naturals' own medicine men or previously gleaned wisdom passed down by the old time colonists. His knowledge and expertise was by now most impressive.

'I find myself at a point in my career when I am now quite eager to catalogue my discoveries...' He explained to Thomas, wiping his plate scrupulously clean with a crust of bread. 'That is, one where I would most like to engage your talent for drawing, Thomas, in a sort of collaboration. I very much hope you might agree to make precise and detailed illustrations of all my specimens to sit alongside my notes... Pott's Herbal, my dear wife suggested I call it. It would be one of the most comprehensive volumes of its sort ever published and I envisage that it could easily prove a most lucrative prospect...for both of us. So? What do you say, Thomas.'

Thomas was flattered and immediately replied that he would be delighted to collaborate on the book.

'I need to write up each plants properties...that

is, its habitat...its preparation whether by distillation or infusion...the administration of the resulting drug...and... the dosage!' He sighed. 'Working out the optimum dosage has been the most difficult property to discover...'

'How do you achieve the right dose, then?' Thomas enquired.

'Ah! Trial and error...' he sighed again 'at the start it is all trial and error! Even the naturals have not quite mastered the correct dosages...then again...how could they be expected to? They are not in the least educated in scientific ways nor do they have accurate measures.'

'And this trial consists of...'

'Well...administering a precise dose of the particular drug in question and then carefully monitoring and meticulously recording the resultant effects... Not all lethal drugs, you see, are necessarily so from the outset...'

Bessie looked puzzled and John Pott noticed this.

'In other words...a drug deemed to be lethal may not actually cause death until it is administered in just the right quantity. For example, we know from classical literature that some past sages had actually dosed themselves up daily with small amounts of the poison of choice for that time...hemlock I do believe...then... over a period of time they gradually increased that dosage so that their body built up an 'immunity', if you like, to its effects. Thereby they might eventually reach the point where if they were then to be administered a normally fatal dose of that same poison, its effect would have been completely negated... In the same way, I like to presume, as should a viper accidentally biting itself! Its body being accustomed to the continued presence of its venom.'

Elizabeth laughed heartily at her husband's quip in a manner that Bessie found most unsavoury.

'So...I presume you used animals to conduct your experiments...' Thomas commented.

'At first...yes. But animals do not always react in

64

the same way as humans. Some substances can poison an animal yet appear harmless to humans...and vice versa...'

'So you have experimented on humans?' Bessie asked pointedly.

'Oh, yes. Of course! I have tried out some poisons on captive naturals.'

Bessie was quite horrified by the thought.

'You seem uncomfortable with that?' Pott continued.

'Yes, I am. These are human beings, are they not? Just the same as you and I?'

'Not quite like us.' Elizabeth Pott broke in. 'They are not in Christ...in fact they reject salvation in favour of their pagan gods. So their souls are lost in any case....'

'And you think that neither cruel nor barbaric?' Bessie persisted politely.

'Cruel? No!' Pott replied defensively. 'Cruel is to get the dosage so inadequate that instead of dispatching your enemy quickly and cleanly that you instead condemn them to a shamefully protracted and agonising death. I am a Doctor first and foremost. If instead of saving life I am required on occasion out of extraordinary circumstances to take it, then it is my God-given duty to inflict as little suffering as I can. Having said this, it was not we English who first took to poisoned warfare. These naturals have long been using drugs against each other. When our colonists first came, even as their chief Powhatan feigned friendship, he had his men 'experimenting' on us with their poisons. I take it you harbour some misplaced affection for these natives?'

There was an awkward silence as the conversation died on its legs. Bessie could feel her husband's anxiety and growing tension between her and her hosts, so quickly retorted, 'Why? Of course not! I am merely playing devil's advocate to your argument! And devils,' she feigned amusement, 'they truly be!'

With the situation defused, Bessie said no

more. She dare not though she was mindful to take up the argument against Pott's and Tucker's murderous poisoning of an entire village before. Instead, she smiled politely, followed Elizabeth's invitation to talk small and counted the minutes until she could decently ask Thomas if they might take their leave.

'What is it about this place?' She asked as they walked back to the cottage. 'What is it about Jamestown that seems to leach away at the hearts of people, who I am certain would be otherwise perfectly decent if only any other place than here?'

'Like Doctor Pott?'

'Yes. Exactly like Doctor Pott. I am certain that had he come over to New Plimoth instead of to here, he would be experimenting with plants and potions to cure instead of to kill.'

'I do not know. To be honest, I was not even any aware of it until I had you once more and my eyes began to open again. In this place, it is like we are all living in some parallel existence. England is reality. The reality that everyone here has left behind. It still exists on some distant plain while we are condemned to this place...to live out this dreadful fiction of our own making. Meanwhile, without even realising, Jamestown has us subtly changed. We are no longer the people we were back home. We think...we act...we react differently here. And so long as we remain, I am beginning to believe that we become as detached from reality as do dreamers walking through a nightmare. We try to convince ourselves that all will be well and that the horrors around us cannot really be happening because it goes against everything we know and believe in. Yet...knowing this does not help us break free... The nightmare continues to play out around us. There is nothing we can do until the dream is ended for us or until some gentle spirit like yours comes along and tries to rouse us from this awful mass delusion. You brought love to this place, Bessie. Maybe that is it. There is no love left in this place. Love and compassion for one's fellow human beings seems to have shrivelled up and died somewhere along the way.'

'Yes' Bessie said, 'love and compassion lay dead on the wayside while tobacco springs in its stead...'

*   *   *

November brought the first dusting of snow transforming Jamestown into a whited sepulchre. Too briefly, all looked clean and perfect before the filth and corruption seeped through once more with the melt. Winter bit and the fresh produce from the plantations had almost gone and even the supply of dried poor-jack fish was running low. Generously, Sir George gave over a head of cattle and two boars so all in the town might feast on meat to celebrate Christmas. After that though, most households in the town would be expected to look to their own resources to last through until the spring. So it came about that more each day, the men of the settlement turned their thoughts to survival and their skills to hunting.

Silence muffled the murmurs of a restless January dream like a thick white blanket smothering the sleeper. Bessie woke with a gasp and knew in an instant exactly where she was. She was still in the country that devoured souls.

Slowly she stirred her aching bones. Her nose was cold where her face had poked out from the bed covers as she slept and her still stockinged toes were frozen and numb. Rolling over, her out stretched arm foraged in vain under the sheet for her husband's warm body. He had gone – out hunting most probably with the others. Hunting and trapping for food had become a pressing pursuit of late. Supplies of food were low. The shortfall from some of the lost plantations, destroyed in the massacre, was still being keenly felt, so hunting was fast becoming necessary if they were to avoid the losses through hunger and sickness of the previous winter. Yet, this was also now a dangerous pursuit. One no longer to be enjoyed in ones or twos but endured in number and accompanied by a protective force.

Even under the layers of blanket and fur throw, Bessie still shivered with cold. The combination of chill and sleep had rendered her like a woman drugged. As a result, her body mutinied when commanded to rise and her unwilling stone-cold limbs refused, at first, to get her out of bed. So she sat on the edge of the mattress for a few moments, still draped in fur before hauling on her cumbersome boots.

A bright shaft of light from the tiny glazed window cut the gloom. In it, Bessie could see her pale breath expiring upwards into the chill cottage air. She glanced towards the hearth. There were a few damp logs lying in a white-edged stain of water. A can of snowmelt perched close by. Thomas had obviously fetched these in for her before he had left.

It was then that she realised that the fire was all but out. Bessie stood up and lumbered across the room. She crouched in the hearth beside the fire and tried vainly to breathe new life back into it. The embers responded by glowing brightly but she knew she needed to feed them quickly or else, they would soon die away and she had no dry kindling to relight it. Scrambling back over to her bed, she turned down the patchwork fur cover revealing a fine layer of dried grass, which had been added for extra warmth, between that and the top blanket. Bessie teased out a small handful, combined that with a few twigs and half-charred remnants she had found smouldering around the edge of the mound of ash, and managed to revive the fire enough to eventually risk placing a small log upon it. Although she had prized off the wet bark with her fingers, inside the wood was still a little too damp. As Bessie crouched by it, the fire spluttered and coughed, belching out thick heavy smoke that lay back down into the room instead of being drawn up the chimney and away. Her eyes were smarting so she quickly retreated from the hissing embers as they blackened the underbelly of the offering. Luckily, though, after a few minutes, unseen forces suddenly ignited and eager new flames began to lick at the wood.

Stiffly, Bessie rose up, grabbed her heavy shawl from the chair and threw it about her shoulders. By now she desperately needed a breath of fresh air so she went over to open to the cottage door. She lifted the latch and tugged hard at the metal handle but the door refused to budge. It had either warped or was frozen shut. Whichever, it made no difference. Bessie was unable to persuade it to move and so had to concede to being held a virtual prisoner indoors, at least until Thomas came home.

Undaunted, Bessie went over to the window but it too was frozen shut. She marvelled at the feathery frosted pattern newly etched upon the tiny glass panes by the cold. Curious to see how much snow had fallen, she tried to scratch away the thick ice with her fingernails to peep outside but so soon gave up. The opaque light shining in from beyond was so white that her dazzled eyes were forced to squint and water with pain. Bessie turned her back and struggled to readjust her sight to the gloomy surroundings inside once more. Is this what death is like, she thought? Standing in the darkness unable to face the bright countenance of heaven in the eye?

Bessie forlornly returned to the fireplace and set the black cast iron pan spidering across the red heat to warm the turkey stew inside. The leg had slowly bubbled away in the pot for hours until the dark flesh began to flake away from the bone like tender beefsteak. It was easy then for Bessie to lift it out onto a plate and then pick it over, separating out the meat from the gristle, sinewy tendons, feather shafts and bone. Once the meat was returned to the liquor, the resulting stew was extremely appetizing and filling. Walnuts, native corn and roots had all been cooked in with the turkey, making this a thick and hearty affair at first but now, after several re-heatings, it had become watered down into little more than a thin soup. Nourishing and welcome still, but not hunger stopping like it was before.

Hungrily tending the fire, Bessie could not help questioning in her mind the morality of some in that settlement having tens of head of cattle at their disposal knowing all the while that their neighbours hungered. Still, she knew she had also to be grateful for what she had. A few days before, Thomas had come home quite contently with the two fat turkey legs for the pot. Though at the time Bessie could not help but wonder as to which fine 'gentleman' had acquired the rest of the bird at the division of the 'spoils' from the hunt. Then again, she realised that they were extremely lucky in that Thomas was a favoured employee of the Company and an obvious favourite of Sir George Yeardly. Some lesser thought of, individual had no doubt only received the gizzards.

Stirring the pot, Bessie recalled the stews from long past at her time in the Old Hall at Gainsborough. Glorious thick pottages brimming with beautiful dried beans and lentils shipped over from Holland. Wonderful, plump, glistening beans from the continent, Italy and beyond with names she had long forgotten. Yet the taste, she had not forgotten the taste. She could almost savour them in her mouth as she thought on them.

When the soup was heated, Bessie ladled out a modest bowlful for herself. Not too much though. She needed to make certain there was enough left for the man of the house. Bessie needed to be prudent, just in case he came home with nothing at all. She mumbled a thankful prayer then quickly drank it down and then mopped out the wooden bowl with a scrap of cornbread left over from supper. Still tormented by pangs of hunger, Bessie set the can of water to heat for a brew of one of her comforting herbal infusions.

Drawing the metal poker through the ashes to tease up the flames more quickly, Bessie suddenly raked up a disturbing old memory. The ashes unexpectedly gave up some fragile white bones and the tiny top half of the skull of some past creature prepared for the pot. Only for one awful second, before disintegrating back into the mound, it had looked like the remains of a tiny infant. Bessie was deeply upset by the sight and quickly covered them over.

Once she had drunk down her herbal, time

began to drag heavy on her hands. The light was too gloomy inside to sew by, yet not dark enough to be improved by lighting a candle, so Bessie built up the logs to span across the mound of fine grey wood-ash like rafters in a church roof, then she sprinkled them with a little water to slow down their burn a little while she returned to her bed to rest. There was little else to do so she lay down and closed her eyes. She must have quickly fallen into a deep sleep for the next thing she knew she was awake with a start. Suddenly the room had gasped from a faint rush of breeze. Bessie's ears sensed the change in the air pressure and so she instinctively turned towards the door. It was still firmly shut.

'Then it must have been the other outside door...!' Bessie thought in silent alarm. 'Someone has just opened and closed it!'

Nervously, Bessie got to her feet and crept over to the wooden partition. Quietly peeping through a knothole in the planking, she could see nothing. Then, just as she was convinced that she must have been mistaken, she saw something in the darkness move on the other side. She shuddered as she realised someone was in there. Then an awful thought shot through her like an arrow. Maybe it was a natural. Jamestown could be under attack... just like during the massacre. The whole settlement could have been overrun by natives while she slept, for all she knew, trapped inside alone all day.

Then, all at once, she heard something knock over and sudden rush of daylight as the door must have been flung open, then left to bang in the wind. Heart pounding, Bessie left the partition and she raced over to the window but could see nothing. Then, a dark shadow loomed up and slowly passed by it.

Fearing the worst, Bessie quickly slunk back into the room and across to the far corner where Thomas kept his weapons in readiness. Frantically she searched for something to defend herself with. Thomas's loaded snaphance and Jack Coat were both missing. So was the hunting knife with its leather sheath that usually hung above from a nail. All that was left was a rapier with a broken off tip and a heavily rusted sword. Carefully she picked up the sword by the hilt and carried it, tip almost dragging along the dirt floor, over to the jammed-shut door. Then she stood beside it and waited. Footsteps slowly crunched in the frozen snow outside then came to an abrupt halt just the other side of the threshold. Heart pounding, Bessie raised up the sword up with all her strength, high above her head ready to split open the head of the intruder. Bravely poised she watched with dread as the latch slowly began to lift and the handle rattled. Suddenly there was an almighty crash against the door quickly followed by another. Then with the third, it gave way and fell open. A tall, fur clad man fell laughing into the cottage. It was Thomas.

'O my Goodness!' Bessie cried with relief, barely able to control the unwieldy weapon now swaying dangerously in her tentative grip. 'I was going to brain you! I thought you were a native!'

Thomas quickly reached up and steadied her arms to help her ease the sword back down to the safety of the floor.

'There!' He said. 'I am so proud of you, you brave thing!'
Bessie could not help but laugh off the tension.

Thomas reached back outside and brought in the sack he had discarded on the doorstep. With a cape of fur tied across his shoulders, topped off with a matching cap that extending well below his ears, he looked more like a wild bear than a man. This makeshift attire was absolutely necessary though to survive the extremes of the Virginia winter weather.

'Your face!' Bessie exclaimed. 'It's so red! It looks like you have just been scrubbed with a brush!'

'Yes. I know! It's freezing outside!' He teased as he grabbed a hold of her by the shoulders and rubbed his face into hers sending her shrieking into fits of laughter.

'You should see the James!' He exclaimed

persuading the door shut once more with his boot. 'It is frozen solid! Can you imagine that?'

Bessie could. She could remember the River Trent at Gainsborough freezing over and the Ancholme becoming ice when she was a child along with her father's grim warning not to try skating on it, even if the village boys were.

'There were a lad when I was about your age...' he had said, 'went out on to the ice to play. It were as solid as a plank of oak at the sides, so he ventured out farther thinking it must be just the same clean across to the other side. Only he gets out into the middle and the ice cracks...and down he falls, right the way through it into the freezing water beneath! By the time help could be fetched...he was dragged out dead and cold. Dead and cold, I tell you Bessie! So you heed me, my girl, and do not go skating on the ice!'

'Dead and cold'- Bessie remembered her father stressing those words.

'What have you there?' Bessie stared down at the sack.

'Wonderful things!' He said excitedly as his frozen hands fumbled to untie it. 'That is a brace of fat duck and just now I have hung in the store room such a hunk of fresh venison that would be fit for King James himself! We fell upon so much game such as I never witnessed before. We even had to cut down some branches to improvise a litter to drag it all home. I think the Lord must have been along with us today! Still...' he added solemnly, 'I pray spring does not come late... especially not this spring...'

With that, he gently ran his hand over Bessie's ripe expectant belly. Suddenly the bulge beneath his palm lurched and gave him quite a start.

'There!' Bessie said excitedly. 'Did you feel that?'

'Yes I certainly did!' Thomas grinned. 'My son has a fine kick!'

'Son? Who said it is not going to be a daughter?' Bessie teased.

'I did! I know he is going to be a son!' he said

wishfully. 'I just know it...'

The snow soon cleared and the weather turned milder for almost a month making Thomas think his wish had been granted. Then the weather picked up and veered in from the south dropping a mass of snow over the Jamestown area all but burying the homes and the fort. In its wake came a terrific ice storm, which brought down many trees across the trails the settlers usually used. It was freezing chaos.

Inside the cottage, drafts sprang up from out of nowhere and the cold was so cutting that there seemed no respite to be had from the chilling effect. Outside the snow splattered against the daubed exterior with the force of the gale and the wind bayed at the windows like angry wolves buffeting at the panes to get in. The need pressed even harder than before for Thomas and the others to go hunting again leaving Bessie alone in the house. Still, at least they both knew he would not be gone long and that Bessie was still more than a month and a half, at least, away from having her expected baby. So, when Thomas went away early that day, Bessie knew that he would be back before nightfall.

As usual, the door had warped shut again but Bessie was thankful that it had. For while it stretched in the damp cold weather, it did much to exclude the draft from coming in and besides, heavily pregnant Bessie had no reason to try venturing out in such diabolical conditions.

Bessie's sides stitched as she tried to shuffle down in position to tend to the fire and she hurt as she strained to get up again. Still, the regular little kicks from inside kept her company and helped her endure the long boring hours. By nightfall though, she began to worry. Thomas had not returned home and her 'stitch' was fast becoming stronger and more bothersome.

She curled up upon the bed to try to get some relief but the pain grew stronger as it came over her now in regular waves. Bessie looked at the candle stump and knew it must be getting late into the night yet still there was no sign of her husband. She dragged herself up and over to the fire to add a few more logs and set a pan of water to boil. She had not eaten for hours but was not hungry; instead, she wanted but a warming drink to ease her insides. Having boiled, she crouched down to pour the hot water over the herbs in a beaker only to suddenly realise that she was wet and warm below. Bessie's waters had broken. She was in labour ... and alone.

*   *   *

It was barely light when Thomas kicked open the door and came in. A wild, elsewhere look was in his eyes and the cuffs of his jerkin were red and matted with blood.

Bessie sprang up from the bed.

'What is it?' She cried.

He said nothing.

'What is it Thomas. What has happened?'

'Armageddon!' He said throwing aside his fur cape and hat. 'Armageddon is what has happened!'

'Another massacre?'

'Yes. Another massacre.'

'Oh My God! No! Where?'

'Beyond Smith's old abandoned fort...across the river...and southwest...four or five miles.'

'But I didn't think we had any homesteads out that far?'

'No,' Thomas said chillingly, 'we don't...'

'Then...I don't understand. Did the natives fall upon some of our men out hunting?'

'No...'

Thomas began to shake uncontrollably. Bessie tried to hold him but he would not let her. He could not even bear to look her in the eye.

'What is it Thomas...tell me...who was massacred?'

'They were...' he replied coldly, 'I think they were out hunting too...but they attacked us...they attacked us first...near the Chipokes...we retaliated...we followed them back into their campsite and we slaughtered them. We were ordered to... 'Take no prisoners'...they said...and that this was a reprisal...like for like...but then some of the men...some our men went berserk with the lust for blood. They struck out blindly with their swords or shot at anything that moved. There were women there ...children too...running amongst them was a young pregnant woman...caught up with a cutlass...her screams...the blood...it was...carnage...'

With that, Thomas broke down in tears and finally allowed his wife to comfort him.

'It's all right Thomas...' she whispered gently. 'It's all right...you are home now...'

'No!' He said pulling away from her. 'It is not all right! It can never be all right ...never again. I thought I was hardened to these people after Martin's Hundred. . When I had to scrape the blood off my boots after stepping over the corpses of friends with their innards hanging out...young children with their skulls caved in and their brains at my feet... I was so filled with hatred for the naturals back then that I thought they deserved nothing less than equal to be done to them... Yet now...now I feel sorrow for them. ...Sorry that they have had to live with the horror of what they did...With the tormented screams of the dying in their ears and the blood stained onto their hands that will never wash away. Please God, I never witness the like again.... never!'

With that, Thomas took something out from under his coat. It was a bloodied kerchief containing something limp and still. Thomas unwrapped the bundle.

'Lord have mercy!' Bessie cried in horror. 'It's a baby...it's a new born baby girl!'

He laid the child out on the bare wooden table. She was as still and as cold as ice. The small, silent face was contorted with her eyes tightly closed as if in an effort to blot out the cruel abomination playing out as she came into the world. Her tiny raised fists, clenched as if in outrage. The body, dark and wrinkled with the bloodied umbilical cord still dangling from where it had been wrenched from its mother, though Thomas had managed to tie it off a with thread pulled from out of his clothing.

'It was alive when I snatched it up to keep it safe... I heard it gasp... I was too late, too late, though.. wasn't I?' He wailed. 'I was too late to save it! ....It is dead...dead and cold! I will put it on the fire Bessie!' He sobbed. 'I can't bear to see it any longer!'

'No! Wait!' Bessie thrust out her hand to stop him. 'It is so very cold outside...It is so very cold and I remember my father telling me how the cold can do strange things to a body. He said once that, if you are dead from cold then you are never truly dead until you are warm and dead!'

'I don't understand...'

'No time Thomas, we must make haste...'

Frantically Bessie scooped up the child and ran to the fireside chair with it. She sat in the warmth of the flickering flames and with the infant laid out in her lap; she began to gently rub its tiny limbs. To massage warmth back into the icy flesh while Thomas looked on in deepest despair.

'Come on little one,' she said quietly, 'come on, you are not dead till you are warm and dead.'

As she rubbed, the child's face suddenly relaxed then contorted once more to let out a mew like a kitten. Then, the tiny lungs heaved to gasp in a life giving breath then exhaled it out into a full-fledged cry.

'Oh Thomas, it's alive. It's alive!'

With that, a second cry suddenly began to fill the tiny cottage. Thomas looked at Bessie in utter bewilderment.

'Go over to bed Thomas...' she said. 'Go over to the bed and see to your son while I tend to this little one...'

Thomas crossed the room in a daze, drew back the bed curtain to find another newly delivered baby nestled between the pillows swaddled in a piece cut off of sheets.

'Oh Bessie...' Gently Thomas picked the infant up and tenderly cradling its head in the nook of his arm, he took it over to its mother. Kneeling carefully down beside her, he said with tears of joy streaming down his face. 'He is beautiful...so beautiful, my love...'

'I want to call him James, Thomas,' Bessie said fighting back her own tears, 'I want us to call him James!'

'Yes Bessie,' Thomas agreed. 'Hello James...he said softly looking down lovingly at the baby still crying in his arms, 'I am your Father.'

'He is hungry.' Bessie unloosed the ties of her garment to reveal her full, round, engorged breasts. 'He needs feeding!'

She motioned to Thomas, who then passed his son over. Within moments, James was contentedly suckling at her right breast.

Bessie glanced down at the tiny natural nestled in her lap and now frantically trying to suckle at her skirt. Instinctively the baby rubbed her face back and forth across Bessie's knee in desperate search of her own mother's nipple to latch onto and feed. She must have been so very hungry and could smell Bessie's milk.

'This little one looks quite revived now,' Bessie said 'but we will have to keep her warm and fed...'

'Then there is hope,' Thomas said.

'Yes,' Bessie replied 'There is hope indeed!'

There was hope, so long as the baby breathed and thrived, but for that it would need nourishment. Yet, how was Bessie supposed to feed it? If she had milk from a goat or a cow, she might be able to soak a little up onto a rag and perhaps get the baby to suck upon that. That might just quieten the baby in the short term but it could never be enough though to keep the tiny creature alive. If there were a wet nurse in Jamestown, then Bessie could have hired her in but there was only one other woman she knew in the settlement who was in milk – Lady Temperance.

As the baby began to cry lustily, in frustration as much as hunger, Bessie felt her own milk letting down to flow freely from the vacant breast. Faced with the prospect of the child starving to death, Bessie did that, which if known by the other God-fearing Jamestown folk, would have horrified. Something that in future years would serve to enhance her later notoriety. Bessie raised the baby up to her left breast then offered up her nipple. She was an English woman daring to suckle a natural infant alongside her own white son...

Chapter Five

'Stony adversary... inhuman wretch'
- William Shakespeare

Bessie could not abide him at all. To her, this Rech was a vile man. He was not a planter nor did he ply any trade. By rights, she argued, he had no good reason to be in Jamestown at all.

However, Rech's wealthy step-father had already invested heavily in the Virginia Company and had recently been intensively wooed by them again to raise more finance for the revival of the much needed foundry and glassworks lost in the massacre. Having been seduced by the revised propaganda leaflets and the ultra-impressive returns on tobacco, Rech's father was about ready to invest the remains of the family fortunes in Virginia but decided to hold back until he could obtain a first hand, independent assessment of the Colony for himself.

Rech's step-brother and heir to the family estate was far too precious for his father to risk on such a venture. Rech, however, was not and carrying out this 'errand' for his step-father would possibly be the first useful thing Rech had managed to accomplish for him. For until now, Rech had been regarded by this parent as little more than lamentable baggage brought into the marriage by Rech's twice widowed mother. In short, he was expendable.

He was a weasily looking fellow with a pinched-in, pock-marked face whose age was hard to determine. His hair was fine and thin and rapidly receding back from his forehead leaving a large brown mole sitting evermore prominently in the middle of his extraordinarily dark beady eyes making it almost impossible for whoever was talking with him not to let their gaze constantly be drawn to it. His dress sense was almost as dull and drab as his monotone conversation.

To the Company, though, Rech was someone to

be courted. He was the calf of a much prized cash cow and therefore from his arrival in Virginia the Governor and his council had been at great pains to offer him every consideration during his stay. So it was that Rech suddenly found himself being generously entertained by the elite of Virginian society and unwittingly being shown only the better plantations. The troubles with the natives, whilst not denied, were played down whilst the wondrous profits of the tobacco leaves he had seen curing by the thousand in the tobacco sheds was greatly exalted. Thus leaving Rech to write home to his step-father with the most glowing report after barely a few weeks into his stay and urging him to invest all that he might into this most excellent prospect, including his own poultry inheritance expected from his mother.

Being unaccustomed to such treatment and spoilt by attention, Rech quickly came to revel in his own, new-found, self-importance and then to expect exceptional favour from all and sundry alike. Coupled with his 'Godlier than thou' attitude it came as no surprise when he quickly ingratiated himself upon the town's grateful new minister to such an extent that he soon became a self-appointed verger and then insisted on taking over the tedious task of writing up all the church records for the duration of his stay.

Despite all of his shortcomings though, Rech did have one unredeeming talent that should have made him eminently suitable for his father's task. Rech was a natural born snoop. While in Jamestown he ferreted his way into everybody's private business whenever the opportunity arose. He took in gossip at every turn yet never gave any of it out. In short, he had all the skills and traits of a blackmailer in the waiting.

*   *   *

There could be no going back. From the moment Bessie began to nurse Hope both Thomas and she were committed to living a lie. Had Thomas left the child be, she would have quickly died, either from the freezing cold or at the hands of one of the others in his party if they had come across her first. After the massacre in which their own women and children had been butchered and mutilated, not to mention the attack upon themselves earlier in the day, Thomas knew his hardened English cohorts were not about to show any compassion towards a mere native new-born. The only mercy they might have summoned up would have been to stamp upon her skull to hasten her demise. There was no longer any love left to be lost. Worse still, Thomas having been made fully aware of the explicit order against taking prisoners, his disobedient action could well be construed as mutinous. After all, could it not justly be argued that the colony was at that juncture in a state of war.

The problem now was how, in such a small community, were Thomas and Bessie going to keep Hope's existence a secret? Of course, they could never expect to. It would be impossible. Instead, they decided that their only option was to be actually quite open about the baby's existence. If only somehow they could succeed in passing Hope off as if she was Bessie's own daughter - a twin sister to their new born son. However, they were very well aware that this subterfuge could never be other than being short lived. While the two were still tiny and swaddled, Bessie and Thomas might just get away with the ruse but as the infants grew older, both knew it would be impossible to hide Hope's true identity from the other colonists. That is why they needed to get the child out of Virginia as soon as possible.

Though a thaw had set in, a furious gale outside still howled and buffeted down the chimney, rattling the pot stand below and fanning the flames ever higher. Bessie paid it no heed though as she was wrapped up warmly in a world of her own. As the snuggled-up logs glowed a comforting red in the firedog, she sat on the edge of the bed watching her babies at play. With the heavy bed curtains partly drawn around, Bessie had the infants already fed, and 'topped and tailed' with warm water. Instead of re-swaddling though, she had spread a thick shawl out upon the bed to let the pair kick about naked for a while. It was a freedom that they seemed to relish with gusto. Their excited little limbs flaying out in all directions as their frowned faces tensed as if with deep concentration at the effort. Bessie found watching them totally absorbing as she smiled on with awe and wonder. They were so different from each other in so many ways, she noticed, yet at the same time so very alike in others. Both reacted to outside stimuli like light or sound in exactly the same way yet even now, at such an early point in their tiny lives they were developing strong, clearly individual characters of their own. James, though at first the much smaller baby, was now steadily gaining weight. He would wake and mew gently to be fed, which he always did eagerly. As a result, he gulped down so much air that Bessie would have to spend a goodly amount of time with him sitting propped up upon her lap with his chin supported in the span of his mother's left hand while she gently rubbed his back with the other to bring up copious amounts of wind. After that, so long as he was clean, he would sleep long and deep, blissfully unaware of his sister's crying close by. And cry she did! Whereas James would rouse from his slumber slowly by degrees and was often content to just lie and look about the room, Hope always woke with an instantaneous cry. She was not so much a fretful child, as far as Bessie could work out, but rather a very alert one who reacted quickly to changes in her surroundings and who also knew exactly how to get a mother's attention. Once she had though, she would very quickly stop crying and settle down in Bessie's arms. Perhaps she felt safe there, Bessie thought. Maybe she needed the reassurance of that warm and comforting close contact after the trauma she must have undoubtedly suffered after being so brutally introduced into this life. Hope usually fed lazily and remained long and thin in appearance but nonetheless as equally robust as her now plumper brother. Though her bouts of wakefulness sometimes caused a problem, Bessie learnt to overcome this by securing the baby in a makeshift sling made from a shawl, and carrying Hope, native style, close to her body as she went about her daily chores.

Bessie reached over the bed and scooped her little son up in her arms and nuzzled him close to her face. His small arms reached out and brushed against her hair as his tiny lips mouthed her cheek. Bessie instantly took this to be a sign of love. The same all absorbing love that she was feeling for him. He was such a perfect little miracle and she thanked God for his safe arrival. After all the childless years of her womanhood, of caring and rearing other women's children, she at last had a baby of her own.

Then she looked down at Hope, and suddenly thought about the stillborn she had lost at Gainsborough Old Hall when she was only sixteen. The small, lifeless innocent should have been hers to love and cherish under happier circumstances. All the regret, all the guilt and the sadness she had carried with her throughout the years about that stillborn child now seemed to melt away with the snow outside. Hope, she began to conceive had been sent to her by God as a chance for some sort of redemption.

Gently Bessie placed James back down on the shawl and picked up Hope instead. She held the baby up to her face just as she had done with her son. It was then that Bessie realised that she felt as much love in her heart for this precious child as she did for her own.

While the recent snowfall had the town all but engulfed, the settlers had naturally kept themselves to themselves inside their dwellings in the warm. Come the thaw and the Sabbath though, everyone struggled to attend church regardless. Therefore, it was then, as Thomas mingled with his neighbours that he proudly announced the good news of the birth of Bessie's twin babies. For that and the following Sunday though, Bessie was thankfully excused church. She was a newly delivered mother. She was not expected to be seen out in public, not until after she had adhered to the custom of 'laying in'. However, on the fourteenth day she was expected to present her babies to the minister to have them 'churched'. A ceremony could not be avoided or delayed.

The problem as Bessie saw it was not so much how to disguise Hope's features but how to make the twins look more alike by blending their appearance. It was widely known that the naturals used dyes on their skins and in lotions to ward off mosquitoes so perhaps, Bessie thought, she might also be able to colour James's skin to blend in with his adopted sister's. Had it been autumn then she could have perhaps tinted it with berry juice but it was spring and all the berries in the woods were now long gone. Then again, what excuse could she make for doing so? There were no insects to ward off that at time of year. Bessie stared into the fire desperately hoping for inspiration. Then, it hit upon her like a slap. She pinched up a small amount of wood ash and rubbed it onto the back of her suntanned hand. Then she smeared a little onto the pale underside of her wrist. It seemed to work. The ash evened out the difference in appearance, lightening up the tanned skin whilst darkening down the light. However, the ash clearly did not fix well and would easily wipe off with contact or run with tears or drool. It also felt gritty and might cause irritation on a baby's delicate young skin. Besides, how could Bessie explain it away? Why would any sane mother want to cover her child's face with wood ash? Undaunted, Bessie took the idea one step further. She fetched out a clay pot of saved lard and scooped a small spoonful into a clean dish. Back and forth she beat it with the bowl of the spoon until it was soft and malleable then, she gradually added in finely sifted wood ash to make a smooth cream. This time when she repeated the experiment on her hand the mixture felt silky and strangely soothing. The coloured ash readily adhered to the skin and now had the added advantage of the fat content rendering it waterproof.

Excitedly, Bessie rushed over to the babies and smeared some onto their faces. It was perfect. Apart from repelling moisture, the greasy film served to further diffuse the light making the infants skin shimmer which in turn helped to lead the eye away from any difference in the two varying skin tones. It worked and Bessie felt relieved. It would buy them a little more time whilst Thomas worked upon securing them passage back to England.

With the addition of a little lavender oil, an emboldened Bessie openly hailed the concoction upon her babies faces as a remedy for all manner of skin ailments and a preventative for troublesome milk rash which might otherwise spoil her twins' precious complexion.

'This skin lotion of yours ...' Temperance Yeardly approached Bessie after church a few Sundays later, it really is extraordinarily good! It has cleared my little one's napkin rash admirably and proved so soothing on my own chapped skin. You really should let Doctor Pott have the recipe...'

*   *   *

It was a few days later and at the appointed time Bessie made certain she was ready. The house was clean. The babies were fed early and asleep in their crib. She sat and waited patiently. Within a few minutes there was a commotion at her door and it opened. Doctor Pott and his manservant led Thomas in and helped guide him over to the bed and lay him down. He looked flushed and confused and was barely able to coordinate his wayward limbs for himself.

'What on earth has happened?' Bessie asked anxiously as she rushed to her man's side.

'Your husband collapsed while sketching a specimen of Blood Wort for my catalogue,' Pott relayed as he carefully started to re-examine his patient.

'Has it poisoned him?'

'No! Of course not! What has happened to him is nothing to do with my drugs!'

'Then what ails him so? He looks half dead!'

'When I first heard him call out, I ran inside to find him in a state of collapse. He had vomited and his pupils were dilated. He was so incoherent that at first I wondered if he was simply drunk to the gills! However, I quickly ascertained that this was not the case. I noticed the erratic pulse in his neck so I examined his heart only to find it was seized by such palpitations and beating so rapidly that I feared it might burst! In fact, I am now pretty certain,' Pott said grimly, 'that he has had some sort of apoplectic fit. Mistress Bessie...I am afraid your husband's condition is most serious...'

'A fit? But why? He was perfectly well when he came to you this morning.'

'I think this has nothing to do with the present but more with what has happened in the past... He was taken with a bad headache not a week ago while working on some sketches. Thomas told me then that he had a bad head trauma some time before. Is this so?'

'Yes. He was beaten senseless and left for dead back in England but then he recovered...'

'In my medical opinion, one never fully recovers from such an insult to the brain. Damage deep within it may lie dormant for years only to be awakened by bad miasmas...' Pott looked into Thomas's eyes and held up a willowy finger. 'Follow this my friend,' he said moving it across the field of vision. 'How many fingers do you see?'

Thomas struggled to follow its path and slurred his reply badly.

'Itsshhtwo...'

'As I thought,' Pott observed, 'his vision is blurred and his speech impaired. And this weakness down the side of his body concerns me; the way his hand is clawed and will not flex. His drawing hand...it's almost useless.' The doctor shook his head. 'All these are certain signs that the brain is afflicted.'

'Can you cure him?'

'No, I am afraid I cannot. I expect he might make some sort of recovery in the short term but that is your best expectation. It is most certainly my opinion that sooner, more likely than later that, another such seizure will most certainly kill him. I think it would be best if the Company were to put his affairs in order and send you both back home so that you might be amongst family when...when you and your children most have need of them...'

Pott's man stepped forward to help his master prop his patient up more comfortably in the bed. Then the doctor made ready to hurry off to report Thomas's grave condition to the Governor. A very tearful Bessie saw both him and his servant out of the door then closed and bolted it firmly before racing back across the room and into her husband's arms as Thomas near leapt up out of bed to hug her.

'We did it!' he laughed.

'Shh!' She said. 'Someone might hear!' then she sighed deeply, 'you had me so worried when he first brought you in...you looked so...so ill!'

'I felt it!' He exclaimed fetching a small glass bottle from out of his pocket. 'This concentrate of sassafrass I took made my heart pound like crazy. I felt like I was going to pass out. I can assure you, after that it didn't take much playacting on my part to convince Pott that I was really ill!'

The two had concocted the whole charade in order to gain passage back to England. While working on Pott's proposed 'Herbal', Thomas had gained access to all of the doctor's research notes. Not only those about illnesses and their symptoms but also all of those relating to Pott's precious catalogue of native plants and the effects they had on the human body. The Doctor had noted that while common sassafrass had been credited with certain benefits when infused as a tea, if its oil was made in too great a concentrate that it caused heart palpitations. It had then been easy enough for Thomas to gather some wild sassafrass and make up just such a strong potion in private at home. Meanwhile, Bessie had seen first-hand the effects of dire palsy in both Lady Rose Hickman and Governor Carver in New Plimoth, both of whom she had closely nursed. Therefore, with her coaching it was not difficult for Thomas to first bring on the physical symptoms while then convincingly acting out other carefully rehearsed ones in order to completely fool Pott into diagnosing a potentially fatal complaint.

'There is a ship due in anytime, my darling.' Thomas smiled jubilantly 'And I fully expect you, me and the children to be on it when it leaves.'

Thomas did not have to feign illness for long. As an artist no longer able to draw, the Governor conceded that he was now of little use to the Company and so terminated his employment on their behalf and secured him passage on the next homeward voyage.

'Bessie...I have something to tell you.' Thomas said as they packed . 'I want to take you home to meet my parents...'

'Thomas...' Bessie knew how difficult this must be for him to bring up the subject. 'I know about the rift between you and your parents...'

'Then you know how wrong it is?' He looked at her with such sadness in his eyes.

'Wrong to be at odds with one's parents?' Bessie too had been scarred by such torment.

'No...for one's parents to be at odds with you over the woman you love and mean to honour. I just know that if only my father would agree to meet you in person then he would see why I would give up the world for you. I am certain that if only he could let himself be rid of his preconceptions and misplaced bigotry, he could learn to hold you in great affection... just as I know my mother will. Especially when she gets to meet her beautiful grandson. I was thinking that, with the money owed to me by the Virginia Company and the income I can expect from the tobacco sales next autumn from my land share, you and I could rent a small farm near by my parents and make a new life there.'

'Maybe you will find that he has mellowed with time,' Bessie encouraged. 'Maybe with your long absence he has found regret....'

'Maybe so,' Thomas said. 'All that I do know for certain is that for as long as I can remember, I have always been a failure in my father's eyes. And that in my later years, I contrived, either by error or design, that he should never find reason to change that view.

You see I took my revenge by beginning to live out my life so that I always would be at deliberate odds with him. Like a snapping dog baiting a grizzled old bear.'

'Yet, why was he like that with you to begin with?'

'For the life of me, I do not know. What can a child do, when too young to even have memory of it, to vex a father so that he is forever after the subject of parental scorn or derision? All I do know is that I spent the greater part of my formative years trying every way I could to please him. Always trying to earn his approval but then always failing. I did not know why then. I blamed myself, thinking that it was all my fault. That I was a stupid useless child. Then the more unhappy I became in myself the more I seemed to fail him.'

'And what of your mother? Did she think you a failure too?'

'No, she was ever the same towards me and my brother Stephen. Warm and loving and never divisive. She loved us both equally or, if she did not, then she kept it well hid. She would comfort me when I came to her crying over it but yet not once do I remember her interceding on my behalf with my father.'

'Perhaps there was problem between your mother and your father lying deep at the cause of this unhappiness and that you were an innocent party?'

'No! I am convinced that the problem lay somehow betwixt my father and I. However, as I grew older, I began to understand that I would never please him. I would never please him because he would not allow himself to be pleased by me.'

'And what of your brother? How was your father's affection towards him placed?'

'My older brother has always been everything to him. Stephen was his first born and his heir and I could never compete with that. My brother, for his part, played on this favour. He revelled in my father's attention as he stood at his side learning how to run our estate for the day when he would inherit everything. I felt left out...excluded. As a result Stephen and I would often quarrel and that only served to drive an even greater wedge between myself and my father. Then, like many a second son, I was sent away at fifteen to study for entry into the Church. I did not mind being sent to University. It was such a relief to be from out of my father's household and the cold cast of his shadow. At last I felt able to grow. I was free to express myself and my ideas without immediately being made to feel like a beetle being crushed under his heel. My confidence grew as I began to flourish intellectually. Then, in my second year at University, I began to reason that if my brother was going to inherit everything, leaving me to fend for myself and to make my own fortune in this world, then I should at least make a stand and choose my own path. I began to take art classes in between my religious studies which I had by then begun to find dry and lacking in spiritual substance. When I did attend my lectures, I found myself mixing with fellows who were deemed radical in their views by the establishment and myself becoming more and more in tune with their arguments than with those of my tutors. In the end, I was sent down. I was asked to leave altogether, much to my father's embarrassment. I had, however, already gained an excellent education of sorts in life!' Thomas said proudly.

'How was that?' Bessie asked.

'Rather than returning home for holidays, I had often crept south with my clique instead. There I graduated with honours from the University of Life. After all, I had studied the whole gambit of it within Shakespeare's plays, first hand in the playhouses of London and by listening intently as their virtues were discussed by actors, street philosophers and writers alike, long into the nights in the taverns.'

Bessie understood now.

'While I sat and listened I sketched. I drew little vignettes of the players on stage and found takers for these and other similar souvenirs amongst the richer play-goers. I was even commissioned to design some stage sets at The Globe for the Bard himself. The money I made during those 'excursions' far surpassed the miserable allowance provided by my father. It was then that I realised that I could make a living out of art. When my father eventually found out, he branded me a wastrel. Then, when I married a playwright's daughter he acted as if I had joined with the Devil. Had it not been for my mother's intervention, for she had always tried to take my side as far as she might without disobeying her husband outright, coupled with the untimely death of my bride, he might have disowned me outright for good. As it was, I returned to my father's house but our relationship remained never anything more than short of strained. And that is how it was when I first met you. I was making my living as a tutor to the offspring of prosperous and open-minded families in the county like the Hickmans. So you see, when I fell in love with you and told him of my intention to marry you, the die was already cast. It was never a personal slight against you, my love. Had you been a fine lady, I still think I would have struggled to have him accept you.'

'I understand...' Bessie said quietly in deep reflection. She thought back to the day that the other women waiting to sail on the Mayflower came to her to say that Thomas was dead. How she had told them that rather than sail, she intended to go back up to Lincolnshire to tell Thomas's parents of his death. Of how they had then told her that it was best if she did not and about the rift between her new husband and his father. It had hurt her deeply to think that she was somehow considered so cheaply. Now, she was truly beginning to understand why.

'I am so sorry Thomas. I never realised things had been so horrid for you.'

'It is alright, my lovely. All this hurt is behind me now.' 'Then,' she added quietly, 'I too have something I wish to tell you.'

Thomas listened.

'I also want to heal a rift. I would like to go back to see my mother and try and make my peace with her, that is if she is still alive. When I last saw her I was angry. I felt that she had betrayed me as her daughter. Now though, with the passage of time and all that I have come through these past years since, I see things differently now.'

'The more sand has escaped from the hourglass of our life, the clearer we should see through it.'

'Is that Shakespeare?'

'No. Niccolò Machiavelli.'

'Well...it is well said and exactly so! When my father died, I could not understand why my mother would so quickly take up with that beast of a man who became my stepfather. I was only young. All I could see was that my father was lying dead in his bed one moment and that she was remarrying the next. To me, it was as if she had never loved him at all, while I...I was completely devastated by his loss. In reality, I know now that she had little or no choice in what she did. Our cottage was tythed and with my father dead, we lost the right to stay there and that our home would be given over to another labourer. We would be made homeless unless the new man was single and agreed to take us on. If my stepfather had not come along, then we would have been turned out onto the street with nowhere to go. I did not understand then what a dreadful sacrifice my mother had made for us. She could never have loved this new husband. In fact, she hardly knew him. To have to marry a strange man and share his bed in order to keep us housed and fed must have been dreadful for her. Even more so when I now realise that she was still so obviously grieving for my father. I know she loved him. I can remember them together yet after...after she would not even speak his name.'

'As you say, she was clearly still grieving... Perhaps she was even angry with him...'

'Angry?'

'Yes. Grief does strange things, as we both know. Perhaps she was angry with him for dying and leaving the two of you to cope in such dreadful circumstances.'

'Yes, I can see that now. Perhaps that is so. I know that I was so angry at you when I thought you had died. I felt cheated that after we had set in motion such life-changing plans together that you had then suddenly gone and left me to go through with them alone.'

'Yes. I understand that Bessie. Well...I will make certain that you get the chance to go back to your village to put the past to rest.'

'We both shall. I am certain.'

'And on a happier note... talking of London and the playhouses as we were...'

'Yes?' Bessie smiled broadly in anticipation.

'When I have my money from the Governor and while we are in London, I fully intend to give you an education as well, my darling. I promise that I am going to take you to The Globe Playhouse to experience a Shakespeare play for yourself.'

'Oh Thomas, that would be so wonderful!'

'Not only that! I am going to buy you the most beautiful new gown in the City to wear to it!'

However, Thomas was not to receive his money from the Governor. When he went to collect it he was advised that Sir Francis Wyatt was 'unavailable' or so his clerk at the Company store had been instructed to tell callers. So were the other key figures in Jamestown on this day the ship was due to depart.

'Where is he?' Thomas asked. 'I must see him to collect the money I am owed...'

'They are all deep in conference, I fear, and gave orders not to be disturbed on any account. There is some commotion or another, I believe, over some important correspondence from England. As for your monies though, I have that all arranged for you Master Thomas,' he said checking through his bulky ledger. The clerk picked up his quill and curtly dunked it into his ink well and then set about scratching out something on a scrap of parchment. When he was done he casually handed across the grubby table to Thomas.

'What is this?'

'A promissory note on behalf of the Company.'

'But I don't understand. I need money now not a

note good only in London!'

'Do not take on so, now Master Thomas. 'Tis not a problem. This situation happens from time to time here in the colony. We have simply had a run on our available currency, that is all. A flurry of transactions all come at once! When you get to London, present this to the Virginia Company in the City and they will honour it for you. You may still buy anything you need for the voyage from me now, if you wish. I can deduct the cost from this...'

Thomas declined and walked away in muted anger. He was far from happy with the arrangement yet knew it was futile trying to pursue the matter any further. He could not force the fellow to hand over to him something which he did not have. Instead Thomas limped back to the cottage to start ferrying the family's belongings down to the harbour and aboard the ship. Nothing was going to prevent him from leaving on it with the morning tide.

'What are you doing, Bessie?' He asked on his return, curious to find his wife busily digging a hole in the dirt outside the cottage door.

'What does it look like I am doing?' She said mischievously. 'I am planting this before I leave!'
It was then Thomas looked down and saw the potted lavender bush.

'I don't understand... I thought Lady Temperance had expressly told you not to plant it out here?'

'Precisely!' Bessie picked up the clay pot and tapped out the root ball. She plunged it into the prepared hole which she started to quickly backfill. 'Besides... her ladyship has given out dozens of these plants over time with exactly the same instruction and do you know where the majority of them are now?'

'No...I do not.' Thomas was quite perplexed by now.

'I saw them last summer...in a neat line against the graveyard wall...and doing well enough outside while their mistresses smoulder nearby in their waterlogged graves. I made a vow to myself then...' she said defiantly, 'that my plant would not be joining them...that I would survive this place and do this very thing! There!' She said watering the plant in generously, 'now it has its freedom too...'

The crossing home was mercifully different to Bessie's previous crossing in The Mayflower. The weather was kind and the journey mostly uneventful despite the ever present tension should they encounter a Spanish Man 'o' war en route.

Mostly Bessie kept the babies below out of sight of the others. The days seemed long endless rounds of little else than struggling to care for her family under awkward conditions aboard ship. Conditions aboard were sparse but as comfortable as might be expected and far from cramped. There were few passengers aboard bound for England and Bessie was the only woman.

However, much was made more bearable for Bessie by the devoted attention both she and the babies received from her husband throughout those weeks of confinement. Bessie looked at her Thomas in a new light. How he would regularly cradle their son in the crook of his arm and speak to him gently about future plans he had for them both to share. How Bessie would sometimes awake after falling asleep exhausted to find him walking the room with young Hope, trying to keep her quietly amused so that she might get just a little more rest. He was so thoughtful, so loving towards both her and the children that she could clearly see that Thomas was nothing like this father he spoke of. He was his mother's son.

Throughout the voyage Bessie and Thomas tried to take the babies aloft at least once a day upon the deck to breathe fresh air into their tiny lungs. It was never without their bonnets though, covering their heads while Bessie's lotion disguised their faces. They need not have worried though as the sailors paid neither them nor the babies much heed as they went about their duties. The only real attention the children seemed to draw was that from the other notable passenger aboard

– a rather less than usually inquisitory Mister Rech, so full of himself instead of prying into the affairs of others. Though manifest in his own inimitable understated way, how excited he appeared at the prospect of returning jubilant to his family. At long last he could hold his head up and make his step-brother envious whenever he now spoke of his adventures in the New World in an authoritative manner. At long last, Rech could justify his existence by his usefulness all because of his recent service to his stepfather.

It seemed unbelievable to Bessie that after only a little more than a month at sea they had actually arrived off the English Channel and could see the shores of home once more. She cried more than a little. Bessie had never expected to live to see home again. Supplies were still good aboard so the Master saw no point in putting into Old Plymouth so instead made good use of the weather to press on to Dover and her magnificent white cliffs towering out of the water.

'Look Thomas!' Bessie said excitedly as they made to drop anchor in the harbour. 'I can see land in both directions.' She pointed across to a hazy landfall way off in the distance. 'It is land, isn't it?'

'Yes,' Thomas laughed. 'It is indeed land. That, my dear, is France.'

'I never realised France lay so close to England.'

'Well it does and that...' he said pointing up to the castle looming high above the port, 'is why Dover is so well defended!' A long boat was lowered over the side to row one solitary passenger and his belongings ashore. Rech was on his way back to his family and so the couple wished him a safe journey and farewell, grateful in the sound knowledge that thankfully their paths need never cross again. Soon the ship was hugging its way along the Kent coast as they made their way up towards the Thames estuary. The voyage was almost at an end...

Chapter Six

'A King of shreds and patches'
– William Shakespeare

Bessie cursed the Virginia Company. How dare they use her husband so easy? No sooner had the ship docked at Blackwall than the pair knew something was awry.

Curiously, no company representative came to meet it, even after being arrived for a day. There was further confusion and haggling at the dockside between the Master and the port official arguing as to who was going to the pay the harbour dues. Thomas sensed trouble. As soon as they were permitted to disembark, he sought out a carter for hire to transport his family and belongings. He thought it best if they all went directly into the City and to the offices of the Virginia Company to present themselves in person.

Away from its rank, uninviting dockyards, London was far larger than Bessie had appreciated from Thomas's description. It was a rambling, crowded, city of more than seventy-five thousand inhabitants with perhaps even twice that number sprawling out into the suburbs beyond its age-old walls. A mishmash of mostly wood framed houses cramped into a rat's maze of narrow streets and alleyways, which had mostly sprung up during its Elizabethan boom years and now threatened to swamp the impressive, ancient buildings of its more sedate eras. And dogs. There were dogs roaming everywhere.

Wattle and daub, tinderbox buildings were built so closely together that the thatched roofs of the overhung second stories often all but touched with those on the opposite side of the street. Bessie found this blotting out of the coal-choked sky up above oppressive, especially as she noted that at street level below all looked dark, dank and deprived of sunlight even in this, the height of summer. Cobble-stoned streets looked deliberately to be cambered inwards, forming open gullies running down the middle. Bessie assumed these were to drain away rainwater, much like the ditches and dykes in the country. Yet, the smell here was overpoweringly strong to be just stagnant water. Then she saw a woman's arm reach out from an upstairs window to casually tip the contents of a chamber down into the passage below. Bessie then realised to her horror that these were little more than open sewers, which hopefully in wet weather drained the water and waste down to the river. Yet now, in the height of summer, the filth lay stranded there, stinking and decomposing attracting swarms of flies by day and, as Bessie suspected, curious rats by night. No wonder Thomas had said that summer was the time of year that prudent Londoners of means chose to retreat to their country estates. He had also warned that summer in London regularly brought with it outbreaks of the plague.

At the Virginia Company office, the confused situation was not much better than at the quayside earlier. A large crowd of gentleman, more like a common rabble than a genteel gathering, had it besieged and were clamouring to be let in through its substantial yet firmly locked doors. It occurred to Thomas that they were all after but one thing...money. Though the Company had often before been in financial difficulties, with the phenomenal and continuing boom in tobacco over the past few years, no one had really considered that their investments might not be safe after all. However, since the King had recently ordered the Virginia Company to be dissolved, ever more desperate shareholders had gathered there daily, trying to find out what effect this would mean for their investments and when or if they were likely to get back their money. Thomas too now was beginning to worry that he might not see the salary owed to him either. He had now become just one more creditor caught up in the mêlée. Things did not bode well.

'This is madness...' he moaned. 'That conniving clerk back in Jamestown must have known about this when he passed me off with a promissory note!'

'Is there no one inside?' Bessie asked.

'Most likely there is, but I doubt that they would want to open their doors up to this! Would you?'

'What shall we do now?' Bessie tried to settle down Hope's crying by slipping her little finger into the hungry baby's mouth while the kindly carter awkwardly cradled still sleeping James. Both were past feed time and needed changing.

'I will have to come back later when it's quiet and post a letter under their door.' Thomas said none too confidently. 'And hope that word of where I am, will reach my contact there. But for now, we need to find somewhere to stay. I have only a little ready money, Bessie,' Thomas sighed despondently. 'It is not much for the City... it's too expensive here... but it is enough for cheap lodgings at an inn for a week or two if we cross over the Thames to Southwark. I know that area very well...'

Thomas had been so excited by the prospect of stopping over in the capital once the monies owed him from the Virginia Company were made ready. While there, he had relished the thought of being able to reacquaint himself with all the old familiar haunts of his misspent youth. During the breaks from University, he and his jolly band of young blades would regularly migrate south to the bright lure of London to indulge in the seedier side of its life. This thrived on the disreputable south bank of the Thames, especially around Southwark. The district was notorious for corrupting young gentlemen with its brothels and gambling dens, and above all else, its playhouses and Bear Garden. Thomas had been determined to take his wife to experience the thrill of seeing a performance of one of Shakespeare's plays but now he could barely afford to keep her sheltered and fed.

The family scrambled back onto the cart and were soon crossing over the Thames by London's only bridge; a great stone structure consisting of numerous arches spanning across the sluggish grey river below.

To the east, Bessie spotted the numerous masts and sheets of sea-going ships moored as far up river as they could reach while on the west, were a legion of boats and barges, small enough to be able to slip unhindered through the archways to ply their trade. Bessie was curious and impressed to find even London Bridge was crammed with shops and small buildings and heaving with people.

Once across the Thames, the family was in Southwark and passing by the former Catholic Cathedral of St Mary's Ovaries, an impressive church only lately saved from demolition. It was there, in the high street, that they found an inn, cheap and willing enough to take in the two fretful infants too, so they took a room and quickly settled in.

While Bessie fed Hope and James, Thomas composed a letter to the Company and decided that at first light next morning, he would set out to walk into the City and deliver it himself. He was optimistic that if someone was still attending the office, then at least Thomas's secret contact might be alerted of his plight and learn of his whereabouts.

He came back late in the morning looking rather forlorn.

'I have been walking along Bankside. It has all changed,' he groaned. 'None of it is as I remember. The Swan Theatre is closed and the Rose has gone. Not even The Globe is the same anymore.'

'Oh, Thomas!' Bessie tried to console. 'That's progress! How long is it anyway since last you were here? Twenty years or more?'

Thomas sighed deeply. Where had all that time gone?

'Never mind Thomas...' Bessie smiled, 'you can still take the children and me there for an airing after lunch. You can show me around and tell me how it used to be and my imagination will do the rest...'

Thomas laughed away his disappointment.

'I so love you, my Bessie...'

*   *   *

On their return that afternoon, a messenger arrived at the inn with a letter which greatly lightened Thomas's mood.

'Is it from the Company?' Bessie asked.

'No... But someone must have read my letter to pass on the details of our whereabouts. It is an invitation to call at eleven o'clock tomorrow upon ... Captain John Smith...'

Smith was a name that Bessie had rarely heard mentioned in Jamestown. Surprising really, considering that the town, if not the entire colony, owed its existence to the extraordinary efforts of this man. Then again, only a handful of the original settlers that came over with Captain John Smith now remained in Virginia and those that did had mostly betrayed him in one way or another.

Captain Smith's elderly housekeeper showed Thomas and Bessie into his 'study'. It was a rambling room; probably the largest in the otherwise modest, rented house yet it had been given over entirely to books, maps and other items appertaining to his one all-absorbing passion – the New World. Pressed for space as it was, nonetheless, all was neatly ordered and precise as one might expect from a soldier yet, curiously, it had the air of a place of retreat. A place of temporary withdrawal from the battles of life, where a military man like Smith might well reconsider past tactics, learn from his mistakes and plan for some future campaign.

Either he had not heard them enter or it was that he was so deeply distracted, studying the aspects of a vast globe of the world with the dark, young boy beside him, that it was quite some moments before Smith looked up and acknowledged the couple standing there. As he did though, Bessie was taken aback. For in those fleeting seconds of his ignorant bliss of her presence, Bessie had watched Smith at discourse with the lad and was immediately struck by how handsome he looked, in profile and picked out by the muted sunlight streaming in from the leaded lights beyond. It was as he stood up though, to greet them, that she noticed the limp.

That and the way in which Smith was obliged to rub his thigh briskly in order to coax it into action. Only then, as he stood full on, did Bessie spot the faint lick of scar creeping up from his salt and pepper beard-line and on into his worn traveller's face. The sort of face that took but a glance to know that it belonged to one who had seen places and done things that most men could only dream of.

'Ah! My apologies, Master Thomas!' Smith exploded into animation. 'I did not hear you come in, although I was, of course, expecting you to call at this hour! And you,' he said proffering a teeth-bearing smile of welcome, 'you must be Mistress Bessie?' He bowed gallantly and beckoned them in.

Bessie and Thomas returned the greetings. To be in London and yet hear Captain Smith speaking in a broad Lincolnshire accent was as easing for Bessie and her husband, as it must have been for their fellow county man to hear theirs. Although the couple were invited to sit and talk, Bessie soon found herself relegated to 'listener' in most of that which followed. She did not mind in the least. On the contrary, she found the whole experience quite fascinating, getting to know Smith by observing him in his own surroundings and by how he interacted with both her husband and the boy.

The captain opened his desk and produced a large portfolio of pen and ink drawings, which Bessie immediately recognised as her husband's work. As Smith pawed over them, Bessie assumed that this must be the mysterious patron Thomas had been working for all along.

'It is so good to meet you after all this time, Thomas,' he said. 'And might I add, even more pleasing to do so in person. I have, over the course of time, employed many an agent to work for me in Virginia, but how often have I struck up a regular correspondence with one only to learn, a few letters in, they are too soon gone from this world...'

Bessie gathered from this that Smith and her husband had obviously shared contact through a mutual and highly trustworthy source. This made sense. After all, Smith was a man who had so obviously been put at odds with the Virginia Company. He would have needed someone like Thomas to be his 'presence by proxy' to gather fresh input from the colony to sustain his now well-known writing of books on America. Knowing the Company's animosity towards the captain, no wonder her husband had wanted to keep his 'sideline activities' a secret. Yet, why could he not have trusted her?

Smith's young protégée tugged gently at the captain's sleeve as if to remind his elder that he was none too happy with being overlooked.

'How remiss of me....?' Smith responded generously by ushering forward the youngster. 'May I introduce my dear friend...Master Tom Rolfe.'

Master Rolfe, dressed in a blue silk suit and ornate lace collar, bowed deeply. He was the epitome of an English gentleman in all but stature and age, and of course for one other thing – his obvious exotic colouring.

Smith was hungry for information from Thomas about the state of Jamestown and the Virginia colony. So much so, that he took up a pen and jotted down copious notes during their long conversation that was to follow. Bessie had hoped to engage young Master Rolfe in play while the two men talked but was soon to be disappointed. Instead, this serious-faced child too had focussed his attention upon the intensive exchange, hanging on every word of his mentor and Thomas equally. For here too was a soul thirsting to drink from the cup of America and one with a much stronger claim to it than even Captain John Smith. For there could be few left in London who had not heard of his late mother, Rebecca Rolfe or Pocahontas, the native name that she was more famously known by.

The one thing that really struck Bessie during that visit was Smith's deep disappointment, which was glaringly evident during their meeting. He longed to get back to Virginia. Even more, he longed to be instrumental in founding a new English Colony, just as he had been with Jamestown. In truth, his only raison d'être these days seemed to lay in the repeatedly dashed hope of returning once more to his cherished mistress - America.

'I feel like a lover,' he explained to Thomas. 'The very marrow in my bones pines to be back in her beguiling embrace. Yet, I find myself cut off from the love of my life by an Ocean of indifference to my plight!'

Bessie knew Smith was jointly referring to the Virginia Company and the King. After all, he had been dismissed from Jamestown by the first amid a torrent of accusation from far lesser men than he, but men of higher monetary ambition and nobler birth. Men who had plotted to both remove and disgrace Smith even though he had been instrumental in saving their lives and that of the colony on more than several occasions. Men who looked down on him as coming from lowly stock instead of a being born a gentleman as they were. Men who treated him with blind contempt despite the fact that he had proved himself unrivalled as military tactician, explorer, survivalist, but most of all, as an extraordinarily well respected negotiator with the otherwise suspicious and dangerous Powhatan naturals. On the other hand, the King ignored Smith's pleas to be put to some good purpose by the Sovereign. It was cold waiting in the shadow of past exploits and lonely.

'Did you know my father?' Young Rolfe suddenly asked Thomas.

'Yes, Tom. I did briefly before...' Thomas glanced towards Smith; uncertain of how much the boy had been told.

'Before the massacre?' Tom had obviously not been shielded from the truth

'Yes...I knew him before that...'

'I am not in the least over taken by surprise at these happenings.' Smith snapped up the subject. 'I could see it coming one day, from our first landing. It is the same as here. You enter unannounced into a stranger's house at your own peril. You should expect that the owner's dogs would try to bite you! So, it is with the naturals.... We came to Virginia unannounced and they defended their homes and their culture. Had they pitched up here in England and started taking our houses and land, would we have settled back and simply allowed it? No, we would have defended our country with our lives. However, when you call at a stranger's house and your intent is peaceful, then is it not acceptable to shake the stranger's dogs off or kick out in defence in order to put your case.'

'And if you should enter that stranger's house and straight away both the stranger and the dogs make to kill you?' Thomas theorised.

'Then you quite rightly shoot them both dead.' Smith answered without hesitation then grinned broadly. 'For if not, then they will have the better of you and will do the same to all of your kind that comes after... The Powhatan only give way to those stronger than they. That is why you must never show your weakness to these people. Just as you should never turn your back on a strange dog...'

Bessie suddenly felt compelled to join in.

'Yet in New Plimoth we lived in peace with the naturals. One came to us who even spoke English. He came to live among us and he taught us how to plant the crops needed to sustain us!'

'Maybe so,' Smith answered. 'Maybe the Algonquin and other tribes living there are innately more placid in nature than the Powhatans of Virginia. Maybe it is because you had only taken enough land to feed yourselves and not the hundreds of acres at a stroke we have cleared to feed the demands of tobacco. Maybe... maybe New Plimoth's time is just not yet at hand! The trouble with Powhatans, all naturals come to that, is that everything with them is fluid. Making any sort of pact with them is like writing in sand...some or all may change depending on which way the wind blows or it can suddenly be obliterated with little or no warning. Your New Plimoth settlers did well to make any length of peace with the naturals so early on. The fact that you lost no men to them during that time speaks well of your methods for peace making.'

'We had a good man to liaise with them who was familiar with their customs.'

Captain Smith seemed surprised for where would one have come by such knowledge unless already a veteran of the New World.

'Was he an Englishman?' Curiosity had him.

'Yes,' Bessie replied. 'And he had your book as a reference to guide him. His name was Hopkins... Stephen Hopkins. Do you know of him?'
Smith smiled wryly.

'Yes, I know all about Mr. Hopkins and am heartened to learn that he had learned valuable lessons from his earlier ways.'

'He explained to me about his time in Jamestown. Of how he had barely escaped hanging and you are right, Captain, he indeed expressed deep regret at having learnt such a hard lesson. He paid the price by losing his wife and daughter.'

She thought back to Stephen and their walk together along the beach together soon after first reaching New Plimoth. They had all endured such a dreadful voyage upon the Mayflower and Bessie was then still mourning the loss of her husband and so many others only recently dead. She realised now how perhaps he had remoulded the truth about their chances of survival so as not to dash her remaining hope. He, above all others on the Mayflower must have known full well at that moment how much more dire things could turn ahead of them. Perhaps he had indeed learnt lessons from Jamestown and not just from his own mistakes. Maybe he saw the errors that had provoked the naturals into attacks from the early days and was determined not to fall into the same traps as the Virginians. Maybe Hopkins with this borrowed knowledge of the naturals ways would, unbeknown to the others, turn out to be the unsung saviour of that colony.

Thankfully, at that juncture, a servant knocked

on the study door. She entered holding a struggling Hope who was bawling at the top of her lungs and vigorously kicking her heels.

'Begging your pardon, Mistress,' she said trying to make herself heard over the child, 'but I just cannot get this little one to stop fretting for you! Your son is as good as a little lamb, but I cannot do a thing to stop this one from a-crying!'

'It's alright' Bessie said reassuringly, 'Give her to me and I am certain she will settle, if you have no objections, Captain Smith.'

'No, none at all' he replied. 'I may be a bachelor but I am not afraid of infants!'

Hope was handed to Bessie and she immediately stopped crying. It was then that the shawl slipped away to reveal her dusky features. Smith's eyes widened as he suddenly noticed the child.

'Good Lord! I had no idea,' he said, clearly noting her unmistakable natural features. 'How on earth did you come by this child?'

'There was a raid...' Thomas jumped in and began to explain, 'it was in retaliation...and we were told, on no account, to take prisoners. But there was this woman...and she was killed and I had to rescue her child. I just could not bring myself to see such an innocent die.'

'So I take it that the Company knows nothing about this?'

'No...Nothing... We passed her off as a twin to our own son who was born that very same day.'
Smith leaned in towards the baby who immediately responded to his rugged smiling face with a huge one-toothed grin of her own.

'My, but she's a beauty,' he said and for a moment Bessie noticed his eyes glaze over a little before adding, 'she so puts me in mind of the boy's mother.'

'What was she like?' Bessie really wanted to know and had been praying for such a chance as this to bring the subject around to Pocahontas.

'Spirited, just like I suspect this little one will be...

Fearless too...even as a child when first encountering we English. Most Powhatan children would have run away in fear...but not her. She crossed her arms and stood her ground. She was simply quite extraordinary. Had it not been for her direct help, I might never have succeeded in hammering out some sort of 'relative peace' and understanding with her father, the chief of the Powhatans. Not so much by her favour with him but by the information she passed on to me, even at his detriment. It proved crucial in helping us to ultimately survive in that place...'

Smith seemed to go away for a moment. His face changed and Bessie's womanly intuition sensed something unresolved on his part that still troubled him.

'You were close then?' she asked softly.

'We were as opposites in ways as any can be,' the captain replied candidly. 'Opposites in sex culture and age. Yet...yes! In an uncomplicated fashion, we were very close. We were two like spirits with an almost insatiable curiosity about each other. Though she ventured on to take that most dangerous of paths... one step further than I was prepared to. Where I had balked, she crossed over from her own culture and into ours. Much the same as I had almost once considered doing myself...'

'What really happened to make you leave Jamestown, Captain?' Thomas re-joined the conversation and Bessie lost her chance to probe further. 'I heard only bits and pieces...mostly from an eccentric fellow named Jack. No one else wanted to say much when drawn upon the subject, apart from to hint that you left under a cloud. In the end, I backed off in order not to arouse too much attention.'

'Life happened, Thomas ...' he replied matter-of-factly. 'My relationship with my fellow council members in Jamestown became...shall we say... strained. I had witnessed many bad dealings on the part of men who should have known better and so they began to fear I might expose their petty corruptions. So much so that I am almost certain there had been attempts made upon my life. Then, not long before my term in office was nearing its end, I suffered a dreadful accident.'

'An accident?'

'My powder pouch somehow caught a spark as I slept in my boat...I was almost burnt to death...I had to jump into the river to put out the flames. With the shock of it all, I almost drowned. As it was, my injuries were severe. A greater part of the flesh on my thigh was destroyed, not to mention burns right the way up my side where my clothes caught alight. My beard and hair too. I cannot begin to describe the abject misery I then suffered. I was demented through the agonising pain, mad from the lack of sleep and at one point I even begged the doctor to put an end to me... Instead, he drugged me up as much as he dared to and tried to heal the wounds. Then... from where I do not know...I found some fight left in me and knew that if I were going to live after all then I must get out of Jamestown and back to England. I was more dead than alive and my thigh was heaving with maggots. Yet even then in this grave condition, the remaining good gentlemen of the council set about to stop me from leaving Jamestown... Afraid I suspect of what I might say about them in England in the unlikely outcome that I should survive the voyage back. Eventually they let me go, but not after concocting a pack of lies against me in order to so blacken my character that if I should live, then there would always be a taint against my name. So, I vowed then, as Jamestown barely slipped out of sight, that I would live on in spite of them all and try to set the record straight. Hence...my writings...'

'So our late lamented bard was right then...' Thomas quipped, '...the pen is mightier than the sword?'

'It can be...' Smith smiled mischievously. 'But only if you are able to get your words published...and then escape being censored!'

His gaze fell away to young Rolfe, happily looking through the portfolio of pictures over again.

'Tis such a pity he does not remember his

mother anymore.' Smith remarked. 'Nor soon his father, I imagine. Both are gone now and I am his only real link with them and to the land of his birth. That is why young Tom comes here to visit...to try to confirm his own place in this world. His guardians are Englishmen who have never travelled to the New World so what do they know of his Powhatan family and their ways or how to prepare him, God willing, for the day he will one day grow into a man and return there to reclaim his birthright. He is the first truly recognisable hybrid of our two warring cultures in Virginia. 'Tis not a position I would envy him. For he is an heir of both bloodlines yet I fear will never fully enjoy acceptance by either. It is a pity he favours his father's ways rather than those of his mother else I would not fear for him so. This New World we have founded holds old prejudices, while this old one has discovered new.'

Bessie smiled down at Hope now happily mouthing her mother's bead necklace.

'Then you think it will be so for this little one of mine?' She asked.

'Maybe not to the same extent,' Smith surmised. 'For you have only weaned the child from out of the country, and I trust, not the country from out of the child. To the naturals and English alike, she will always be a natural, even if dressed and schooled as a lady. However, for young Rolfe, he will always be but half white and half Powhatan. That is a world of difference. There is a proverb I heard once on my travels to the East, 'a fish might marrying a bird...but where do they build a nest for their offspring? For an Englishman to take a native wife is just about palatable to our peers. Their offspring may, perhaps, be grudgingly accepted as something approaching English. But for a natural to take an English woman...that would be a wholly different matter. The offspring from such a union would never be accepted. And if you go one step further and were led to surmise that just such a union could be made under duress... Do they not say that the sins of the father fall upon the child?'

Bessie knew exactly what Smith was getting at. He was talking of an earlier attempt to colonise Virginia.

'Is that what happened at Roanoke? To the lost colony?' She boldly asked.

The Roanoke colony had been a group of mainly well to do settlers that were first brought over by Sir Walter Raleigh in the reign of Queen Elizabeth. Part of the party was later retrieved whilst a remnant remained behind. However, due to every available ship then being commandeered to fight off the Spanish Armada, there was no supply vessel left able to relieve them. By the time one was, the colonists had simply vanished without trace. Well, almost without trace.

'Who can say what happened to them for certain? Our Sovereign James commanded Raleigh to go search for them and to report his findings. Officially, Raleigh was later imprisoned in the Tower for failing to find them. Unofficially, rumour has it that he did in fact find traccs of the colonists but that an outraged James wanted this information suppressed. So, he had him executed under the guise of appeasing the Spanish for 'past crimes'.

'Why? To silence him?' Bessie was puzzled.

'As I said before...who can say. All I know for a fact is, that during our early explorations along the James River, some of our party came across a natural boy hunting in the forest near Port Cottage. He was about ten years old and had a head of perfectly yellow hair and a reasonably white skin yet, was in all other ways every inch a native. You must appreciate that the trade in women is commonplace amongst the naturals. They barter them between the tribes like any other commodity. Especially those captured in raids. Hardly the sort of propaganda a King would want leaching out when desperate to people a dominion which, if left unpopulated, might be snatched away by another nation who can...'
It was a sobering thought.

'That is the reason behind the standing order in the colony...' Smith threw in casually.

'Standing order?' Bessie had not heard of it before.

She looked at her husband and saw at once that he had. In the event of overwhelming attack by the naturals, each man knew that the unwritten standing order from the King decreed that on no account was one single white woman ever to be taken alive. Bessie thought about the women she had left behind in Jamestown. Did they know this? That in the event of say another attempted massacre, should their men folk perceive imminent defeat that they would turn to their women and put a musket ball in their brains...

The money Smith gave Thomas as they left that day was a godsend. Though only a small down payment against future sales of Smith's upcoming books, it was enough to tide the family over and pay their way back to the Midlands. With the dawning of this new day, Thomas was now more determined than ever to return to his parents and force them to acknowledge his choice of Bessie as his wife. More than this, he did not want his mother deprived of the undoubted joy she would find in a grandson. He was not so certain, though, how she would react to young Hope.

*   *   *

Thomas had been away for only a few minutes. He had gone downstairs to the kitchen of the inn to ask the maid to fetch up a kettle of hot water for his wife. Bessie was stood over by the window and happened to glance down to the stable yard below. What had caught her attention to do so, Bessie could not latterly recall, yet as she did, she saw a man stride in. She thought it odd that such an obviously important gentleman would have arrived there alone and on foot. He was very officious-looking, dressed all in black and was shortly joined by two armed blue coats. Though the window was ajar, Bessie could not catch the words of this unsmiling stranger as he approached the landlord who had scurried outside to meet him. However, Bessie could see that as they formed on the man's lips they did so with menace. The innkeeper listened nervously then retreated inside, only to reappear a moment or two later with...

'Oh My Word, it's Thomas.' Bessie gasped aloud trying to let out the window further.

With that, the stranger vigorously exchanged words with her husband. She saw Thomas shake his head and then he uttered something back before glancing up and catching sight of his worried wife's expression. He smiled back briefly as if to reassure her then...then he was hurriedly led away by the guards.

Bessie flew down the stairs like a scalded cat and out into the courtyard but it was too late. A carriage on the thoroughfare was already speeding away, taking her husband from sight. Distraught, she turned back and made to go inside, only to bump straight into the waiting innkeeper.

'What's your man been about then, Mistress?' he said.

'I am sure I do not know what you mean...'

'Those men...they were the King's men and they have taken your husband away!'

'Taken him where?' She pleaded.

'They did not say. Only I heard Master Thomas ask them if he might come back inside to bid you good-bye. But the official told him that his Majesty was awaiting his pleasure at Whitehall and how it was always wisest not to make the King wait! But do not worry Mistress,' he added with a cruel grin, 'both the Clink and the Fleet Prison are nice and close by...'

Bessie's heart sank. The Fleet Prison! That was the hellhole where Lady Rose Hickman had been incarcerated. What could the King want with Thomas unless...unless there were outstanding warrants to do with his past involvement with the Separatists?

She sat in her room sick with worry until her babies awoke and needed her divided attention. Bessie fed and cleaned them. Then she played and sang to them the best she could with the tears that kept welling up in her eyes and the lump in her throat that near silenced her lullaby. Eventually Bessie settled them back to sleep again. Then she sat, silently waiting until her children woke again and the relentless cycle of their care started over. At least it kept her occupied elsewhere than with the dreaded thoughts pounding in her brain.

As shadows crept across the room and darkness began to fall, the maid came up to light the candles and ask Bessie if she wanted some dinner. Bessie declined saying that she was not hungry so the girl went away again. All Bessie could bring herself to do was to care for the little ones and pray that Thomas would return...

*   *   *

Throughout the short journey to wherever he was being taken, Thomas could neither curry hint nor clue from his escorts as to what was going on. He was simply told that they were 'obeying instructions from a higher source' and 'not at liberty to discuss their orders,' only adding that all would become clear upon their arrival. Once the carriage did stop, he was hustled out of it so quickly that he barely had time to take in his surrounding before finding himself inside a rather large, grand building.

Thomas was shown into what was obviously some sort of antechamber and the door firmly shut behind him. He turned but within moments a second door opened up on the opposite wall and a figure swiftly stepped though, turned and closed it again. Thomas recognised the immaculately dressed man immediately. It was his Virginia Company contact that had first approached him with his Jamestown mission. A hitherto completely trusted Company man yet one who had felt much maligned by them in some distant past dealings and had savoured this, his revenge, cold by waiting patiently to become the instrument of their downfall.

'Sir...' The other man urgently cut in stopping Thomas from completing this greeting.

'Thomas, my man!' He spurted. 'I had no idea you were even due back in the country until my clerk brought your note to my attention! Still, no time for pleasantries now, my good fellow! We dare not keep the King waiting. His personal attendant warns me that although his demeanour is presently good it could change at any minute. King James's mood can be infinitely volatile when the gout is rampant upon him!'

'The King?' Thomas thought to himself. 'What on earth am I doing about to see the King?'

'Listen carefully!' The other man said hurriedly. 'Do exactly as I do and only speak when directly spoken to. Do not try to initiate any conversation of your own. We enter in already at a low bow and advance towards His Majesty with eyes cast downwards. Only when His Majesty talks to you directly may you look up, and do so straight into his eye. His Majesty does not trust anyone who cannot make eye contact when he is in conversation. Having said that mind, immediately after you have finished speaking, lower your eyes again. If you do not, then the King is known to interpret that as confrontational. When you are required to look up whatever you do, do not stare at his Majesty. Nor show any disgust or disdain in any way at any strange odours or sounds or sights that you might encounter. Have you got all that?'

Thomas nodded worriedly.

'Right! Then in we go!'

Stepping through the doorway as if they were removing some imaginary hat and lowering it down to their side with a flourish, the two entered stooped from the waist and with bended knees. It was a most uncomfortable posture to maintain. The two approached the dais and paused, waiting for what seemed to be an age for the sovereign's attention.

He sat amid the opulence of this Whitehall abode like a vagrant wandered in from the storm. His clothes were dirt-shined, ragged and threadbare whilst his body odour smelt so repugnant that it betrayed him as a stranger to bathing. When a servant brought in a silver salver of food, he savaged it like a half-starved, near toothless dog, swallowing down large mouthfuls without even bothering to chew. Yet, reason said that this man could not really be starving, for he was as corpulent as a market-day hog. Then, after gulping back a large mouthful of wine, he belched loudly before wiping his mouth on his already filthy sleeve. Could the man, Thomas now found himself stooped before, really be the King of England, he thought to himself?

Thomas was finding it difficult to stay poised and stooped for so long.

'So, you are our spy from Jamestown?' King James finally looked up, snorted and asked in a broad Scottish lilt.

Thomas looked up and straight into the King's eyes and was just about to reply that he was when His Majesty's thin balding sidekick snapped in to reply. 'Yes Sire!' As if Thomas was some sort of mute unable to speak for himself. He then stared towards Thomas, with the look of a bear-trainer and an expression that warned 'eyes down and let me do the talking...and all will be well'.

Thomas complied and quickly dropped his gaze into a sideward squint towards this attendant.

'Are you a smoker?' The King enquired with a stony gaze throwing Thomas completely off guard.
The attendant frowned and shook his head, urgently gesturing Thomas to reply in the negative.

'No, Sir.' Thomas replied looking into the Kings waiting countenance.

'Er hmm...' the King cleared his throat noisily before embarking on a tirade against the shortcomings of Virginia and the use of tobacco in general. '... It pollutes a man's inward parts, you know?' The King continued to rail. 'My physician has showed me... heavy smokers...cut open after death...full of an unctuous, oily kind of soot... Smoking is harmful to the brain and dangerous to the lungs...and a most loathsome custom to observe amongst one's subjects... But, so my Lord Chancellor reliably informs me, it proves an invaluable one by way of revenue for my exchequer... So what is a Sovereign to do?'

Luckily, Thomas took this to be a rhetorical question and said nothing.

'My physician tells me that even though this dread weed obviously causes damage to the health, one's subjects are equally likely to die from the pox or the plague, or from drinking the water before being poisoned by tobacco, so that the Exchequer might as well profit from the latter as the former only ever brings in a deficit! Er mm... But enough of this I am deviating from the point at hand...the Virginia Company. Your enclosures and correspondence from that colony have gone far in aiding my attempts to bring that insolent pack to heel...and for that you find your Sovereign most grateful.'

The royal advisor beckoned Thomas to come much closer still to the King. Maintaining his uncomfortable bow, he cautiously obeyed not quite knowing what to expect next.

'Be so good as to kneel, Master Thomas.' The sidekick commanded in a hushed voice.

Thomas did and was swiftly rewarded with the glint of something silver flash quickly by his head and on to his shoulder. Before he could take in what was happening, it was all over.

'Kiss your Sovereign's ring.' Another hushed cue was proffered.

Thomas immediately did as commanded.

'Arise Sir Thomas, good and faithful subject!' The King said barely acknowledging the man before him further as he made haste to return to his waiting wine. Thomas arose, as signalled, bowed low to King James as did his companion before retreating, backwards away from the audience suite and out into the antechamber once more.

'You have done your Sovereign's commissioners a great service, Sir Thomas.'

His companion's eyes brightened as he smiled in relief. 'Your disclosures and correspondence made all the difference against our move to expose the malpractice of the Virginia Company and our success in having it dissolved. The heart-rending account of the dead woman from New Plimoth was a masterly stroke.

As was the letter from that poor wretch of a servant in Jamestown...they were a very clever touch, Thomas. Both proved extremely moving and damning testament. In all, it made for compelling evidence during the enquiry. As a result, his Majesty expressly wishes that you be rewarded for your invaluable services...'

With that, he handed over a small wooden casket and a wax-sealed document. The one contained gold sovereigns and the other, the deeds to a modest manor in Lincolnshire.

'I wouldn't get too overly excited, I am afraid!' He warned. 'You surely know of our sovereign's Scottish leaning towards being prudent when it comes to money. Though being prudent with money is no mean quality in a King as well as a rare one! This estate came to him by way of forfeiture. There were ultimately no heirs left to claim it but of course, these matters are lengthy to resolve. In the meantime, a rundown estate only further declines in the waiting. Still, land is land and a title is a title! I am certain a talented man like yourself will be able to press both to their full advantage.' His demeanour darkened a little before he added solemnly. 'You will though,' he warned 'never feel occasion to divulge our 'relationship', I trust, Sir Thomas?'

'No sir. I can assure you...never.'

'Good! As you must surely now realise that along the way some two hundred thousand pounds of investments in the Company have been wiped out at a stroke. That is two hundred thousand reasons for revenge. More than enough for us both to wish our involvement in this matter to remain secret.'

It was a serious point to consider, but for now one that Thomas could afford to put out of his mind. All he could think about was that at last he could take his family home in style...

Chapter Seven

'All the world is a stage'
- William Shakespeare

Silently Bessie smoothed her hand across the slight creases in the emerald green skirt spread out across the bed in all its glory. Beside it, the saffron linen jacket, heavily embroidered with coloured silks, silver gilt threads and fastened at the front with bows of salmon pink ribbon was breathtakingly exquisite. She picked up the buff leather gloves. Bessie gently slipped one onto her still slender hand. It fitted perfectly and looked divine with its delicately worked gauntlet cuff, decorated with gold thread, seed pearls and gilt spangles. At the wrist seam they were trimmed off again with salmon pink ribbon but this time threaded through gold lace. She was quite lost for words.

'Say something then?' Thomas urged 'Are they the right colour, right cut? Only I was assured by a royal seamstress that this was quite the latest fashion from France!'

'It's all beautiful! Simply beautiful,' his wife sighed.

'The shoes were more difficult!' Thomas frowned and stroked his chin anxiously. 'I was not completely certain of the size but I can always send the carriage back to exchange them.'

Bessie held up the shoes by their pink ribbon laces and eyed them with some trepidation. She trusted that they would be easier to wear than they looked to the eye. It was not that she disliked them, more that she had always been used to wearing serviceable boots, not these fancy platform creations. Then again, this was London and from what she had seen of the streets, this type of footwear was necessary to avoid ruining one's finery by dragging the hems through the dirt and wet.

'My concern is more for the cost, Thomas! You must have paid a small fortune for all this!'

'And if I did, it was a small price to pay for the look on your face when you first saw them. Besides, I want to show off my beautiful wife when I take her out to the Playhouse this afternoon.'

'Today? We are going to a play today?'

'Yes. To see one of the late Bard's best!'

'But what about the children?'

'That is all in hand. The landlord seems unable to do enough for us now... Hence the clean counterpane and linen,' he said gesturing towards the freshly made up bed. 'And he says he knows where to get a wet nurse available for our immediate disposal.'

'No wet nurse, Thomas!' His wife pleaded. 'A maid is all they need. I will feed the babies before we leave and rather they hungered a little, or sucked on a honeyed-knot should they wake before my return.'

'Very well, my love. I will leave you to give the instructions...'

It was early afternoon as Bessie sat brushing out her long brown hair and dressing it high with two fancy bone combs Thomas had thoughtfully bought. Soon they were out in the thoroughfare making their way to join with the merry throng heading towards the Playhouse.

'Tis a fitting homage to the Bard himself!' Thomas quipped. 'That we still in life may make pilgrimage to revel in his wit and word though he is cast off this mortal coil! What better tribute than to be but two caught up in this midsummer madness! Tripping out together in happy procession to watch his play?'

Bessie could not fail to agree.

As they drew near, a whole host of jabbering playgoers suddenly converged on this great round wooden building like a pool of ale waiting to be sucked into its gaping mouth. Above, a large colourful flag slapped noisily from its pole as it danced in the warm breeze on high. Below, glowing ladies like a dazzling bouquet of colourful blooms, fanned themselves furiously in the near stifling heat or sniffed heartily the brightly coloured nosegays purchased from the waiting flower girls by their beaus.

However, not all was congeniality amongst the host. Here and there outside a small group of drabs stood and jeered, expounding the sinfulness of the playhouse and deriding its plays as works as being those of the Devil. Undeterred, the mischievously happy rabble jeered back defiantly at the Puritan dissenters as they pushed and jostled their way inside, each hell-bent on securing themselves the best advantage points for the show.

Inside heaved with theatregoers and peddlers alike, all in one noisy, sweaty clamour. Holding tightly onto his wife's hand, Thomas forced a way through unyielding bodies and edged their way towards the box man, paid over some coins and proceeded upstairs to the gallery to join the other nobler patrons and away from the common riff-raff. From the first landing, a few coins more took them even higher to bench with a stunning view overlooking the stage and protected from the open elements above should it chance to rain mid performance.

Bessie stared down in disappointment at the stage. It was not as she had imagined. She expected to see it painted up with at least with some sort of scenery. Instead the backdrop was bare and the stage open to the audience on three sides. Bessie wondered how the actors expected their audience to be transported away from this minimalist void and into the extraordinary realms of make believe with so sparse a setting? All was open. What chance of then of even employing sleight of hand or 'magic'.

'You wait and see...' Thomas smiled. 'With words alone you will see the scenes dramatically set and believe utterly that they do truly exist before your pretty eyes...'
Bessie still doubted.

The pit below, to the front of the stage area was now shoulder-to-shoulder packed full with hundreds. Standing, herded closely together they reminded Bessie of sheep waiting for dipping and nonetheless sweet smelling.

'How hard that must be on their legs,' Bessie uttered, grateful for the comfort of their seats.

'No. 'Tis no great hardship!' Thomas reminisced. 'Many are the times I have stood in that pit with good fellows of my youth. Aye and sometimes with rain lashing down upon our faces! Yet, I never was once tempted for a moment to wend my way from out of the crush in return for a seat outside! Yet,' he added, 'I must admit with age that I no longer think my shins and calves are up for the long stand!'

Suddenly, there was movement from the curtained recess at the back of the stage. Boys scurried out and a prop or two was quickly positioned out front. Then, from out of a rising curtain of tobacco smoke, the master of ceremonies stepped forward to speak and a hush swiftly descended to muffle the horde. The atmosphere was at once electric with anticipation for the play was about to begin.

Bessie soon found her husband's words to be coming true. Within moments, she and indeed all were transported to some far off place as if hypnotised. Disbelief was suspended as they fell headlong into a parallel world, spellbound by the power of suggestion infused in Shakespeare's every word. Aided by hidden musicians, sound effects and the sweet strains of fairy music filtered up from below the player's feet giving the impression of as if out of nowhere. Actor's entrances and exits were accompanied by a great deal of dramatic gesture and with the players dashing, here and there, sometimes to the very edge of the stage to cast asides to the audience. Against the backdrop of an oblivious cast, the one would flourish an open hand to their cheeks, as if to shield the words from the others on stage. This actor would then share thoughts with such intimacy that the hushed audience would be lulled into thinking that only they were aware of the words parting from that person's mouth. At other times, players ranted their lines like madmen yet strangely seemed none the less real in their sincerity than if they had been overheard in the natural course of conversation.

Then there was the impossibly beautiful Titania. Bessie refused to believe that she could be but a boy. With her long silken tresses, rouged cheeks and lips and convincingly delicate movement of limb it was impossible to imagine her as being anything else than a born woman. 'Twas all in all a surreal concoction yet an utterly captivating world where even Bottom, in his outrageous garb and an ass's head, flip flapped his pointy shoes across the hollow stage seeming as real a character to her as any met in life. It was quite unlike anything Bessie had ever experienced before. Puck's words at the close of play did summon up all she had experienced that day.

'Think this...that you have but slumbered here while these visions did appear...'

*   *   *

Soon they were on their way back home to Lincolnshire by a direct ship to the inland port of Gainsborough. To be sailing into the mouth of the Humber and then filtering into the Trent was joy enough but to be finally moored up in Gainsborough, within sight of The Hall where she and Thomas had first met, was like coming to the end of a long night beset with bad dreams.

A short carriage ride further on and Thomas's home looked as sweet as ever it had in the countless memories that had flitted in and out of his private dreams these five years past. The last time he had seen the village of Stowe-in-Lindsey was on his failed attempt at reconciliation with his father during his brief return from Leiden before he had left for the New World. That had failed dismally. In fact, his father's scathing put down of his intentions towards Bessie and the Separatist movement had left Thomas galloping off swearing that never would he speak with his father again. From that point on, the son was determined on disowning the father. However, despite all, here Thomas stood once more in the shadow of his home, willing to re-engage in peace making for the sake of his wife and his mother.

Blackthorn farmhouse was a goodly size; Bessie remembered thinking that as their carriage drew up. A sturdy stone and brick faced house with a newly thatched roof and plenty of out buildings dotted round and about. Everything looked well maintained and in fine fettle, all signs of a prosperous farmstead. Thomas knocked on the door and bided. Nobody came, so he knocked again. Still nothing.

'Perhaps they are all busy out in the fields,' Thomas said.

'Even your Mother?'

'You do not know my Mother. She prefers to be out amongst life rather than shut up inside the house all day. She is probably out the back tending to her beloved kitchen garden! Stay here and I will go look!'

'No! I want to come with you!' She said stepping down from the carriage. 'The children are sleeping soundly and will be perfectly safe here for a few minutes. You,' she said instructing the driver, 'you will come fetch me if they should start crying, won't you?'

'Yes, My Lady,' he replied respectfully.

Bessie still found it strange to be addressed so grandly

'Very well!' Thomas conceded. 'I suppose I have learnt that there is safety in numbers...'

As they skirted the sidewall of the house, the rear opened up into a large cobbled courtyard. On the far side lay a stone built stable block where a scatter of dirty straw was escaping out from the doorways and across into the yard. A scurry of curious chickens was busily scratching through it. Over to the left, there was a large blackthorn hedge covered with freshly washed linen, its corners tucked into the thorny branches to stop it from blowing away in the warm morning breeze. Then, to the right lay a low walled garden with a woman bent over double, her back was towards them busily working away. Thomas called out but the wind whipped away his words and carried them off.

'It's no good! She can't hear me!' He exclaimed impatiently. 'Wait here a moment Bessie, while I go fetch her.'

Bessie watched as Thomas quickly made his way over to the woman, who remained oblivious to him until the last. On reaching the small breach in the wall, where a narrow pathway began to weave through the burgeoning beds, Thomas suddenly seemed hesitant. As if he were but a trespasser intruding upon someone else's property. Then, he must have called out again because the woman suddenly straightened up and turned towards him. She stood motionless for a moment, not appearing to say or do anything. Bessie watched as Thomas advanced to within a few paces of her. He took off his hat and the woman's body immediately juddered as she suddenly crumpled forward and into his outstretched arms. Thomas embraced his mother so tightly and she him that Bessie suddenly felt like an intruder herself into this most intimate and emotional of reunion. She turned her back on them and made her way back to the carriage. As she did, she felt her own tears begin to well up into her eyes and a lump in her throat as thought about the possibility of just such a reunion with her own mother. Then she thought again and knew it could never be that warm an affair.

It was quite some time before Thomas appeared around the side of the house, arm in arm with his mother. Their faces were aglow with an absolute shared delight. So much must have been said during that initial conversation between mother and son yet Bessie never did pry into exactly what. It was enough for Bessie to see the unmistakable joy on their faces as Thomas proudly introduced Bessie as his wife. It was enough for her to be received with such a reassuringly warm and motherly kiss from the other most important woman in her husband's life.

'Mistress...' Bessie wasn't certain what to call her new mother in law.

'Mother...' she replied. 'You must call me 'mother' and look upon me as such, Bessie my dear. Just as I shall look upon you as my daughter.'

'What's all this then?' Thomas,' mother

exclaimed as the sound of a baby's cry shrilled forth from inside the carriage.

For once, James had awoken while Hope remained unstirred. Thomas reached into the basket, lifted him out and then proudly presented him to his mother.

'This is your grandson, James,' he said gently handing the child over to the old lady's eager hands.

'Oh my!' She cried, as her eyes widened with delight. 'He looks so much like you did when you were a babe!' With that, she nuzzled up to him and tenderly added. 'You both must be so proud of him!' She said turning to Bessie. 'He is absolutely adorable.'

Suddenly another weaker cry started up and Bessie scrambled back into the carriage to go to Hope.

'Oh my, but you are hot!' She exclaimed picking the little one up. 'You are not at all well, are you?'

Thomas's mother had heard.

'Is that another baby?'

'Yes...' but before Thomas could explain further Bessie had already fetched Hope out into full view.

'Oh my word, she must be ill to be that flushed,' the old lady exclaimed. 'You best bring them both out of this wind and into the house directly!'

With that the old lady made her way inside to the kitchen with James while Thomas led the way for Bessie and Hope.

Hope really was not her usual self. She grizzled away in her mother's arms as if too listless to be bothered to summon up a full-bodied cry.

'There,' Thomas' mother handed James back to her son, 'you take a hold of this little one while I fetch a nice cold compress for...

'Hope. Her name is Hope,' Bessie prompted.

'Yes. I will fetch you a nice cold compress to sooth Hope's forehead. I am certain that will help to bring her temperature down!'

Bessie thanked her gratefully as she continued to try to tend to the fretful child.

'She is certainly a strange colour...' the old lady

remarked handing the compress to her daughter in law. 'Is there anything else I can do?'

'No!' Bessie replied gratefully. 'I am certain it is but something over nothing...as it often is with these little ones!'

'But her colour...'

'It is alright, Mother.' Thomas broke in. 'Hope is not our own born child...rather she is a foundling. An American native foundling.'

As Thomas proceeded to explain about Hope, Bessie waited anxiously to see how his mother was going to react to this news. However, she need not have worried for Thomas's mother fully supported their actions in rescuing the child from death.

'Poor little mite!' She exclaimed in horror. 'What a wicked way for anyone to be brought into the world! She is such a dear little thing as well. 'Tis naught but sinful for any Christian folk to set about to hurt such an innocent baby? What is this wicked world coming to?'

'We...we smuggled her into the country and we are not certain what the authorities will do if she is discovered here,' Thomas explained.

'Then just do as Bessie has today. Do not try to hide Hope away because prying eyes will seek her out some day. Instead, I have a suggestion...'

'What is it?' Bessie asked.

'Well...it's all very fine to be looking out for a goat in a valley full of sheep...' Thomas's mother explained. 'That is so long as you know what a goat looks like! You might happen across one and know at once that is not a sheep but unless you have seen a goat to compare it with then...you will not rightly know what you have found! Hope's raven hair and dark eyes truly mark her out as being different. Even more than her skin, which might otherwise be explained away. However, I am thinking that there cannot be that many souls in this country that could look upon her countenance and immediately recognise her as being a native of America. Therefore, why not tell people outright that she is a poor motherless foundling whom you have taken upon yourselves to adopt as your Christian duty! Tell them she is of Spanish stock, if anyone asks and that you are bringing her up as a good protestant! Who would know the difference?'

'Mother!' Bessie exclaimed. 'That is an inspired suggestion.'

Something else was occupying Thomas's mind. All this talk of the babies and their travels but what of his father? Where was he and why no mention of him up until now from his Mother?

'Mother?' Thomas needed to ask. 'Where is my father?'

Her face suddenly turned ashen as it dawned on her that her son did not know.

'Your father? God Lord, did you not you receive my letter? I wrote to you care of the Virginia Company?'

'No. I have received no correspondence in America from any of my family. Why? What has happened?'

'Your father is dead, Thomas. So is Stephen. I assumed that you knew. In fact, I have been half expecting you to return to claim your inheritance and take over the farm.'

'Both dead?' Thomas could not comprehend it. 'How? What happened?'

'They were on their way into town. It was a filthy day and I begged them not to go but your father had insisted. Stephen was driving the wagon when the axle snapped and it rolled down into a steep ditch. Your father was thrown clear but Stephen was trapped under it, in the water and screaming for help. The horse had been dragged down the bank with it and broke a leg, leaving your father to try to lift the wagon over to free your brother. His fingers were all but skinned and bloodied when they found him. He was lying besides the wagon weeping. He managed to tell his rescuers what had happened then he collapsed and died. They think he had a heart attack brought on by trying to get to Stephen...'

'And Stephen?'

'Drowned. When they lifted the wagon over, they told me that he was lying face down in the water dead. The rain had drained down off the fields, you see and soon flooded the ditch. As the water rose up he was helpless to resist it...'

'Oh Mother. I am so sorry.' Thomas was quite distraught. 'If only I had known I would have returned immediately.'

'I am not sorry. I was at the time for the death of your brother...for the waste of a child corrupted, but I am resigned to that now. As a mercy from God. For had he lived he would have only brought misery to some poor unsuspecting woman as happened to me. As for your Father...I may sound cruel...but I felt enormous relief at his death. You see I never loved him. I was never allowed to. Our families arranged our marriage and he always treated me more like one of his livestock than a wife and companion. The only good thing I ever got from out of our marriage was you children. But he even had to spoil that. He was such a controlling man. Hard and bitter like a September sloe. And I could never forgive him for taking Stephen and moulding him just like himself. He was already very much like his father but after you were sent away to study, he began to leach away the few decent bits of Stephen and filled him instead with his own vile course manners. But I thank God that you were different. Yet, I am afraid your father hated you for it. He saw love and compassion as a weakness. He saw that in you from the moment you were born and wanted to crush it. He wanted to break you of your gentle spirit and instead make you more of the man he was. But you were blessed with the strength to resist him. Even though it angered him, you would not let your father break you of that spirit. At first, I tried to shield you from him. Yet I quickly learnt that if I hid you in my skirts when you came crying he would pick on you all the more, for he began to see how much it hurt me too. I came to realise it better for us both, if I did not step in. If I did not rise to his bait then he would quickly lose interest in trying to goad me further, by getting at me through you. It was hard for me at times to stand by and watch you cry over his loveless treatment but better that than for me to defy him and him end up beating us both instead. I was so relieved when he decided to send you away. I pleaded with him not to, knowing all along that if I did, then he would be even more determined to do so. I knew that at University, at least you would be free of him. Even if it broke my heart to be parted from you for so long.'

'I had no idea, Mother... No idea at all that things were so bad between you...'

'How could you expect to...you were but an innocent child without a malice thought inside your head. As you grew...I hid it even more from you, knowing that if you began to understand, you might make your move too early in life to retaliate, by trying to defend me instead of yourself. I do not know how he would have reacted to that. What rage he might have flown into and which dire consequence might have followed. As he was...he reaped what he had sewn and you and I have survived to tell the tale...'

It was a lot for Thomas to take in. He felt a strange overpowering mixture of grief, guilt and regret. He also felt anger. Anger that he had gone so many years thinking that himself was to blame for his father's attitude towards him. That he had wasted so much time trying to live up to his father's empty expectations in some futile hope of reconciliation. Now he was dead. Thomas was successful and he was not here to see it. Perhaps it was for the best after all.

'Thomas, can you ever forgive me for failing you as a mother?'

'I never felt that you had failed me mother. And now I see what you went through to protect me, I love you even more for it.' He leaned over and kissed her gently on the cheek. As he withdrew, with a voice all a-trembles she asked, 'Will you be staying here now? Will you be coming back here to live?'

Thomas's silence lasted but a moment.

'No' he said resolutely. 'I think I will not. I have

other land of my own to attend to now.'

'Land of your own? In America.' Her expression fell at the thought that after returning to her at last, her son might be about to say he was returning to the New World for good.

'Yes.' Thomas replied, 'but also land here. The King has granted me a title...'

'A title?'

'Yes, mother! You are in the company of none other than Sir Thomas and Lady Elizabeth. 'Thomas bowed over theatrically to his mother with all the flourish he had come to expect from Jamestown Rech and none of the subtlety shown by the likes of Smith.

'Bless me, my lord!' She laughed in amazement.

'He has also granted me a vacant manor not a short trot from here. I understand that it is much wanting by way of repair and maintenance and so we should be grateful of accommodation here with you for the interim, that is if you have no objection, Mother?'

'Objection? Why should I object? You are the only surviving heir to this place. This house is rightfully yours and I...I am only your tenant!'

'Maybe so by law, but I will always consider this house to be yours. For as long as you live this is your home and I am your respectful guest?'

'Nothing would please me more than to have my family here with me. But what about once you have repaired this other house? What are your plans then, Thomas?' His mother looked towards him forlornly. Thomas's gaze in turn sought out his wife who quickly smiled back in return.

'Naturally, Mother,' Bessie broke in, 'I sincerely hope that when that time comes you might find it agreeable to come live in with us...what do you say?'
The old lady smiled with tears in her eyes.

'I say that I should be most agreeable indeed, dear daughter...'

*   *   *

It should not have come as any surprise. Even Thomas had heard rumours of how miserly King James was even when presuming to be generous. Snype Hall was more than in a state of disrepair. It was practically derelict. It was a typical middle Tudor, two storey manor house, timber framed and thatched roof with several reception rooms on the ground floor and am impressive carved oak staircase set in a double height hallway to above. Yet, however splendid the house might have been in the past it was now sadly too far into decay to be restored. The thatch was breached in several places where some of the roof beams had rotted and fallen inwards. Its timbers were worm ridden and rainwater had slowly seeped unhindered into the heart of the house causing mayhem to the now disintegrating larthern plaster ceilings. There was even a show of fine grass beginning to sprout from out of the cracks between the red and black diamond patterned floor tiles in the entrance hall. Deeply disappointed, Thomas and Bessie reluctantly agreed that it would be financial suicide to try to attempt to restore the manor. Instead, they would have no option other than to pull it down knowing that they might never be able to afford to rebuild it. However, the land on the other hand was exceedingly good and well worked still by the tenant farmers under the guidance of the previous owner's steward. With continued good management and improvements, it would bring in enough revenue to allow the family to live comfortably at Stowe and perhaps extend the house there.

*   *   *

Thomas's mother was in the dairy when Bessie heard the clatter of something metal hitting the hard stone floor. A mild curse was uttered aloud as the old lady emerged with the broken utensil in her wizened hands.

'Tis my own silly fault,' she said raising her hands to the heavens. 'I was paying no heed to what I was doing when I turned about and knocked this from its hook. What I'll do now for making cheese, I do not know!'

It was the old lady's favourite ladle and the bowl had

snapped clean off at the neck as it hit the ground hard.

'I could have done that very same thing a hundred times and not have that happen! 'Tis such a nuisance,' she muttered sadly. 'Tis the most useful sized one I have and has done me good service for more than twenty years! I shall be utterly lost without it.'

'It can be easily mended, I am certain, 'Bessie said picking it up to inspect the damage. 'You have a smithy in the village, don't you?'

'Yes we do... Master Hill... His forge is not far from the inn. I could send Ned down with it tomorrow only I had all this milk ready in the dairy to be made into cheese.'

Ned was the farm's most trusted worker and linchpin to all that went on there.

'Why? 'Tis a pity to draw Ned away from his all his work over a broken ladle! Why not let me walk it down to the blacksmith. The babies are sleeping and I would love the opportunity for a look around for myself.'

'Why of course you would! How thoughtless of me. And if you don't mind running the errand then I will keep a keen ear out for the little ones waking.'

With that, Bessie put on her straw bonnet over her cap and set off up the lane for the short walk into the village.

The poppy scattered corn was standing so high that it was almost tumbling out from the edges of the fields. It was so hot and dry that day, as she lazily made her way by, that she could hear it crackle in the bright sunlight. All was boding well for an extra good harvest. It was a comforting sight to witness after the years of want and lacking she had so recently experienced in the New World. Bessie was truly grateful to be back amongst the fertile lands of her home and her thoughts turned to those she knew still there. What would some of those give to be here once more, walking England's green and pleasant land as she?

'I can do it mistress, but not until I have finished shoeing this here horse!' Master Hill wiped his face on his huge forearm. 'Twas a face flushed as red as strawberries. Red strawberries left out in the rain. Beads of sweat rolled down his face, neck and probably down his naked chest hidden beneath his thick hide apron too if only Bessie could see it. It must be hellish, she conceded, standing beside a furnace and hammering out red hot metal on such a day as this. 'If you want to leave it with me for an hour or so, I could send the boy up with it to the farm?'

'Tis no bother, Master Hill,' she replied with a grateful smile. 'I will leave it here whilst I go for a walk about the village and return for it later when you are done.'

This agreed, Bessie made her way towards the one building that dominated the Stowe landscape. When she reached the village whipping post she stopped, turned and stared up in quiet admiration. Until she had been to America, she had not yet learned to appreciate the age-old buildings all about her. Nor to realise the comfort to be found in such centuries old continuity. In America, everything was newly made, transient, harsh and un-softened by age. Unproven and lacking in the confidence that centuries old buildings inspire.

The ancient church of St. Mary sat upon a small grassy mount like a banquet's golden crusted, raised pie on a bed of fresh picked parsley. The walls, in places topped with a decoration that looked like pinched pastry, were so tall that it made Bessie feel quite giddy tilting her head back to look at them soaring upward into the cloudless blue sky. They were much higher than any other village church Bessie had seen in her travels. The large central square tower, decorated with four strange beasts jutting out from the stone work had in turn four distinct arms reaching out from it to form one large stony cross. Such a grand and impressive building, she thought, for such a quiet backwater as this. It was more like a Cathedral than a simple parish church.

Bessie made her way around the outside of the building to the south noticing the subtle differences in the styles of the stone work until she reached the richly carved door way to the south with its multiple false pillars and zigzag patterned Norman arches. The heavy wooden door was ajar so Bessie slipped silently in.

It took some moments for her eyes to adjust from the harsh brilliant sunshine to the delicately muted interior within. When they did though, she found the building no less beautiful inside than she had without. She was standing in the nave, dominated by a great arch of the tower and a large perpendicular window through which light gently filtered in projecting dancing shadows of trees onto the painted wall above the pews. Walking around the stone font, supported on plain carved pillars, Bessie noted how curious the effigies upon it were. Among them was clearly the head of the green man and a pentangle; both unashamedly of the old pagan religion yet set here to witness baptisms into the newer Christian faith.

Bessie turned east and walked towards the crossing under the tower, to see what lay beyond the screens obscuring her view of the rest of the church. The crossing was crammed full of high backed pews, as this was where most of the church services took place. It felt a little oppressive being enclosed by the screens to the sides and the low-slung roof of the ringing gallery above. With no clergy in evidence and not knowing if she was somehow trespassing into this holy of holies, Bessie dared herself on and into the chancel. It was the most beautiful part of the church and so peaceful that she felt the overpowering need to stop for reflection, so knelt silently for a few moments in prayer. It was then, as she opened her eyes and rose to her feet once more that Bessie noticed the two stone effigies rising out from the cold grey floor. Two almost identical recumbent ladies, their hands clasped in prayer, so much like the effigy of Molly Grimes she remembered from the church of her childhood. Fascinated, Bessie drew closer to inspect them. Their faces were smooth and their features worn away by time or mayhap ceremony. Perhaps they too had been ritually washed, just like Molly Grimes was each spring?

Then Bessie noticed the inscription on the southernmost one. She crouched down over it to try to make out the words. It was just about legible although some of it had been inscribed as if the stone carver had been gazing through a looking glass.

"Alle men that ben in lyf prai for Emme was Fulk wyf"

'All men that been in life pray for Emme who was Fulk's wife. How curious?' Bessie thought to herself. 'What on earth does this rhyme mean?' The inscription teased and tantalised her imagination. Why did the stonemason carve out part of the lettering so strangely, as if to disguise the true meaning of the epitaph? 'What if 'lyf' did not mean life? Could it not also be read as 'love'? Bessie thought it over to herself and decided that she found this interpretation to be the much more interesting of the two. Perhaps Emme Fulk was so beautiful that all the men in the village aspired to find a lover exactly like her? What if some had? What if her favours flowed a little more freely than a lady's ought? Perhaps when she married, many a secretly admiring heart was broken in the process? Maybe her husband was a horrid man like Thomas's father and the village men could not help but feel quietly sorry for her, powerless to intervene in her married misery? Or maybe Emme Fulk was simply such a good Christian matriarch that having departed after a life-full of good works, her family wanted to inspire all to pray to her example by writing such a glowing tribute? If so, Bessie continued to argue with herself, again why attempt to mask part of the script by employing mirror writing? Whichever the true meaning, Bessie concluded that this Emme must have been quite a woman to have such a touching, if not intriguing, epitaph written upon her tomb.

'They are most fascinating, are they not?'

The woman caught Bessie off guard. She had been so deep in thought that she had been unaware she had company.

'Yes, they most certainly are.' She said rapidly rising to her feet and shaking out her dusted skirts.

'I am sorry. We have not yet been acquainted,' the woman said in a slow broad accent that Bessie half remembered hearing once before. 'I am Amy Burgh,' she said quite haughtily. 'My family is descended from that of Lord Burgh, Baron of Gainsborough. And you?'

'I am Bessie...of Blackthorn Farm... I am only newly arrived.'

'Then you are Lady Elizabeth? Sir Thomas's wife?' Amy seemed impressed. ''Tis but a small village and gossip spreads abroad as quickly as weeds here!'

'Yes, I am,' Bessie replied. 'I was in the village upon an errand and thought to acquaint myself with the church before Sabbath. I apologize for not noticing you were also here or I would have introduced myself earlier.'

'No mind, I too was in reflective mood and did not notice you come in either. You see, I like to come here sometimes to think and to be close by my husband.' She looked down towards the floor. 'You see he is buried here right beneath our feet. As I hope I shall also be one day...'

'Your accent...you are not born around these parts...'

Amy Burgh acted as if offended by Bessie's remark and snapped back abruptly, 'No. I am from the far south.'

It was enough clue for Bessie.

'From around the Solent... Southampton perhaps?'

'No.' Amy replied looking rather bemused that this Lincolnshire woman should have come so close to the root of her dialect. 'But you are not so far astray of the mark. I come from the Isle of Wight. Have you heard of it?'

'Yes! Not only have I heard of it but I have also sailed past it. It looked beautiful.'

'It is,' Amy said with a wishful look in her sad blue eyes. 'My father owned a manor there, Knighton Gorges, near Newchurch. He always said that the island was the very garden of England, and we be privileged to work in it as husbandmen...'

'You sound as though you miss it...'

'Yes, I do. Whenever I felt sad on the island, I knew I could always climb up to some high point and look out and see the blue waters all about and safe in the knowledge that the English mainland with all its trouble lay just across the strait. Living on the Island was like being in our own little world...and it was, until I grew up. The problem with little worlds is that there is often a surplus of people to populate it. When I came of age, there were not enough vacant bachelors to match up to the number of eligible brides...'

'And so you ended up marrying a Lincolnshire man...'

'Yes. And now I am a widow and never once in all these years returned to see my island...nor am I ever likely too...'

'You should never say never, Amy. I have been a far greater distance, never daring to hope that I might find my way home once more. Yet, I have. Why should it not be so for you? If you have a mind to, I am certain you can make it happen...'

Amy sighed deeply and smiled.

'I think I like you, Lady Elizabeth. You and I should become friends...'

Back at Blackthorn Farm, Thomas's mother was so pleased to see the ladle mended. Now she could make her favourite cheese from her childhood village in Nottingham. Time was getting on, so as Bessie started to feed her hungry infants, their grandmother set about heating up a gallon of new milk in her largest pan until it sang to her that it was ready. 'Twas an almost whispered song and one only known to those of many years' experience in cheese making. Bessie had just put James down in his basket as the milk came to the ready. She quickly got up and aided the old lady in lifting it out from the hearth and away into the dairy. There, Thomas's mother quickly prepared seventeen drops of rennet in three times its bulk of cooled boiled water, then she quickly added this into the hot milk. As she stirred the two together, she sang her favourite song to judge just the right passage of time at the end of which she snuggly covered the vessel in a blanket to keep the heat in. While Bessie continued to pace the kitchen floor with a lingering Hope, she watched through the open dairy door as her mother-in-law arranged two cheese moulds upon the sloping draining table and lined each with a large butter muslin square. While she waited the good hour or more for the coagulation to progress, she re-joined Bessie in the kitchen for a bite of lunch.

'Shall we have a nice bit of that ham I've been curing, Bessie?' She said reaching up high into the chimney side to unhook a fine looking joint that had been set to slowly smoke there.

'I would like that very much indeed!' She said hungrily. 'This morning's walk to the village has given me quite an appetite!'

'And suckling two greedy babies too, I should say! You should consider easing some boiled goats milk into them too so you are not so tied. Also that way they do not sap too much of your strength away and 'twill bring them both along nicely. 'Tis gentler for a babies innards than cow's and I have a milk horn put somewhere about I could use.'

Bessie agreed that this sounded good sense and promised to give it a trial.

The two sat with their pleasant repast of meat, pickles and bread and a glass of refreshing elderflower and honey cordial. After, and taking full advantage of the babies still sleeping, Bessie and her mother-in law went into the cool of the dairy to finish making the cheese. In this task, the newly mended ladle proved its worth by taking large clean-cut slices from out of the curd and filling the waiting moulds. After being left to drain of its own accord, about a quarter of an hour, they took the corners of the muslin cloths and folded them over the top of the curd. By doing this, the curd would fall inwards as it continued to drain for the final quarter hour more. After this, they were free to get on with the dinner while the cheese continued to firm up.

As soon as it had, they could remove it from the cloth and place it on the cool dairy shelf until needed.

Thomas would be returned before long and no doubt hungry after the ride for one of his favourite home-cooked dishes. As his mother drew the fresh suet and flour mix together with a good sprinkling of water into a dough, Bessie chopped vegetables and finally talked about the new friend she had made earlier at the church.

'Tis not natural, if you ask me!' Thomas's mother said to Bessie as she stood over the floured kitchen table tying a freshly made kidney and beef pudding in a boiling cloth ready for the pot. 'When I die, I want to be buried out in the south side of the churchyard where I can warm my bones on a sunny day with the birds singing in the trees up above. I would rest content knowing that I was putting back a little goodness into the land from which I'd sprung. I would not want to die thinking that I was to end up buried beneath some cold stone floor doing no good at all! Where is the peace or the good in that, with all and sundry walking over your coffin?'

With that, she took up the pudding by the knotted cloth and went across to the great arched fireplace where a big black cauldron was already bubbling furiously over the fire. Carefully she leaned in, almost gobbled up in the great mouth in the brickwork as she gingerly pitched the pudding into the boiling water.

'There! I shall give that a few minutes then it will be time for that net full of vegetables to go in, Bessie!' She turned back towards her daughter in law to be met by a wry smile on the face of the younger woman.

'Come on! Out with it!' She said with a laugh. 'What has you about to go all hissy on me?'

'Tis your face,' Bessie grinned 'Here you are talking of your death and your face is covered in flour. You look as white as a ghost!'

The old lady laughed and plunged her face into her apron to wipe away the flour.

'Better?'

'Much better! Though your hair still looks much greyer than before!'

The two women joked together in complete comfort, each having quickly come to revel in the company of the other.

'What is this? Some sort of wicked plotting going on behind my back?' Thomas had arrived home and seemed well pleased to find the two women in his life on such friendly terms.

'No Thomas,' his mother put on her solemn face. 'We are having a very serious discussion about death...'

'Death indeed.' He wasn't quite certain if he should believe that. 'And what brought this about?'

'Twas my meeting with Amy Burgh this afternoon in the church.' Bessie replied.

'Amy Burgh! I am surprised she gave you the time of day for as long as I can remember, I do not believe she has said a word to a single member of our family.'

'Tis true, Thomas. But none of us was ever a 'Sir' before! I do suspect that is the only reason why. Our star is ascending whilst hers is sadly heading into decline...' his mother mused.

'I expect, as ever, Mother, you are right.'

'Why in decline? Who is she anyway?' Bessie wanted to know.

'The first lady of Stowe Hall....the entire county, or so she would have it,' her mother-in law sighed. 'In truth she is but one, more a sad and lonely widow now and one must pity her for that. Yet, she does precious little to inspire pity. Did she not tell you about her illustrious family connections?'

'Yes she did mention the Burgh family of Gainsborough Hall but not how she was exactly related. I know of The Lord Burghs from my time in service there. They were the Barons of Gainsborough who built and owned the Hall before Sir William purchased it.'

'There you have it, the very same. Amy Burgh reminds everyone that her husband was descended from the very same family. She also flaunts it abroad that he was the next male heir of that noble and ancient family...before he died, that is. Though now he is dead, she has little more than her children for comfort. Her son John does well for himself though. He is a high-ranking officer in the King's army so at least she has his reflective glory still to bathe in. Other than that, I am afraid she clings onto the past.'

Bessie thought this all so very sad especially as she had taken a strong liking to Amy. She realised how difficult it must have been for her losing her husband in the prime of life and feeling so isolated amongst the community as so obviously she did. Even more so, in the light of what had happened to bring about the fall of this ancient and much respected Gainsborough family. Sir William Hickman had purchased the Hall from the near bankrupt Burghs in the same year Sir Thomas Burgh died aged just thirty-nine. Then his only surviving son Robert, the sixth Baron Gainsborough and last direct male heir, passed away at the tender age of seven, leaving his remaining family with little more than grief to inherit.

How strangely, Bessie thought, does the world revolve in such small circles that she should be so connected thus to all the events spinning on about her yet, by the most tenuous of threads at times.

Chapter Eight

'Doubt thou the stars are fire...
Doubt truth to be a liar...'
- William Shakespeare

It felt almost surreal to Bessie walking through the gates of Gainsborough Hall and across the cobbled courtyard to its great oak doors. When she had just started her employ there as a young maid, she had often wondered what it felt like to do just that. She and her fellow maid, the mischievous Comfort, had often wandered away from their chores to peek out of the upstairs windows at the grand ladies in all their finery calling upon the family.

'Your Ladyship!' Comfort had once bowed so deeply to Bessie in mock greeting that her cap had slid straight off and into the filthy ash bucket and sent Bessie reeling into fits of hysterical laughter. Bessie remembered it and smiled to herself. It had been such a long time since she had thought about her dead friend. Of course, in later years as she rose to the position of Housekeeper and Lady's Companion, Bessie had often walked into the Hall through the front entrance, but only ever in the company of Lady Frances or more rarely, her mother, Lady Elizabeth and never of her own accord. It was not her station to do so.

'Good Morning Sir Thomas, Lady Elizabeth...if you will come this way please, the Master is expecting you...' The servant respectfully showed them in and led on, not up to the formal Great Chamber as Bessie had first expected, but instead to the garden room where she had so often spent a pleasant afternoon chatting with the younger Lady Frances. As they entered in, Bessie suddenly felt butterflies flutter up inside her as she recalled her last meeting with Willoughby some four years earlier. It had been in that very same room that Lady Frances had urged Bessie to leave the Old Hall in pursuit of a new life with Thomas. It was also there that a very angry sixteen year old Willoughby had warned her, 'if you go with this dubious fellow, then there is no coming back! That is all. I will not allow it and as I am in charge of this estate, de facto, my word is final on that matter...'

Bessie could still hear his smiting tone as clearly as if it had been yesterday.

She wondered if the passing of the years and growing maturity had softened his viewpoint at all. Too soon, she was about to find out.

'Thomas!' A fine looking Willoughby strode forward with arms extended. 'Or should I now call you Sir Thomas?' The greeting seemed genuinely friendly. Then his countenance clouded like a storm about to break as he turned his attentions towards Bessie.

'I warned you of the consequences of going off with this fellow...'

Bessie swallowed hard, uncertain how to respond.

'Well I am exceedingly happy that you paid me no heed...' a smile burst across Willoughby's face and he embraced her warmly. 'I was arrogant and foolish and I sincerely beg your forgiveness Lady Dorothy...'

'Elizabeth!' Thomas corrected politely. 'My wife has reverted to her given name of Elizabeth...but Bessie to friends and family.'

'A new name for a new life then? Well in that case I sincerely beg your forgiveness, Lady Elizabeth,' he laughed.

'And how goes life with you since we have been away?' Thomas enquired.

'Life goes...' he sighed philosophically. 'You know I lost my Mother the year before last?'

'No!' Bessie exclaimed sadly. 'I am so sorry...'

'Yes. So was I. It was all very sad,' he explained quietly. 'She thought the world of you though. Both my parents did. She was so upset when Frances told her what I had said to you. As I said before, I was young and angry. I hardly remembered Thomas. I was only three or four when he left for Holland. When he suddenly came back after all those years and wanted to take you away with him, well...in truth, I did not want you to leave. You had always been here since I was born. It was almost like losing part of the family...'

'I am sorry...'

'Do not be Dor... Bessie... may I be considered a friend and call you Bessie?'

'No... You may be considered as family...'

Willoughby let out a huge huff and smiled appreciatively.

'And Lady Frances?' Bessie was worried by her obvious absence and prayed that she had not died too during the ensuing years.

'My sister is well and will be so pleased to hear that you are returned?'

'Is she here?'

'At this moment...No! ... Unfortunately not! Her husband brings her to visit far too infrequently for our liking! Still, it is a good match. She married into the Rokebys... Yet next time she comes I shall send you word, I promise. In the meantime, do write to her. I know she has missed you deeply...as has my father.'

'Your father? I assumed...'

'Assumed that he was dead? No. He seems to have inherited my grandmother Rose's constitution and knack for longevity though I am afraid I do not think for much longer. His mind is still sharp but he is very frail these days. He bore the loss of my mother very heavily and since then has been in a sorry decline. I will take you to see him before you leave. He will appreciate that!'

'And what about you Willoughby? Are you married yet?'

'Good Lord! No, Thomas! I am not yet twenty-one! There is plenty of time for me to get an heir, especially if I take after my father! No, I am far too busy running the Gainsborough estate and overseeing the myriad of businesses my father has accumulated over the years. Anyhow, enough of me! Bessie,' he said turning to her with a rakish smile, 'would you mind if I spirit your husband away for a little. I have some interesting business propositions to go over in my chamber and would welcome the aid a fresh pair of eyes and an unbiased second opinion. I will send someone along shortly to take you up to my father. Are you agreeable?'

'Why, certainly Willoughby!'

'Good. Then we will see you anon. Now then Thomas,' Willoughby placed a friendly hand upon her husband's shoulder, 'tell me about your business ventures in America and your plans for the future. I hear a rumour that you have invested in tobacco...'

Bessie sat down on the deeply cushioned settle and watched the sunlight filtering in from the leaded lights, bathing the bright plumage of the painted peacocks on the far wall. Soon she was in deep thought and happy memories of her past life at the Hall. So deep in thought that she barely registered the door clicking open.

'Lady, Elizabeth, I believe...'

Bessie jolted back to reality. As she looked around the sweetest of sights met her eyes.

'Frances? Frances!' She dare not believe her eyes. 'You are here! But Willoughby...'

'Willoughby will have his tease!' Frances laughed as she raced across the stark tiled floor to embrace her dearest friend.

'My! Let me look at you!' Bessie clucked like a mother hen as they parted. Frances twirled for her former nursemaid just as she would after Bessie had dressed her for formal occasions before being presented to Lady Rose for 'inspection'. 'How beautiful you have grown! And you look so elegant in your fine gown and accessories!'

'And so do you, Dor...' Frances checked herself. Old habits proved hard to discard. Willoughby explained but...it feels so odd! You were always my 'Dorothy'! What do I call you now? Elizabeth?'

'No! Bessie. Call me Bessie.'

'Bessie. I like that. It's warm and cosy. Just like you!'

'So tell me all about you!' Bessie was so excited

and eager to learn all of her young familiar's news. 'I hear from Willoughby that you are married!'

'Yes, I am.'

'And are you happy?' Bessie needed to know that she was. She rightly suspected that it had not been a love match but more likely a sound business arrangement hammered out between the two families.

'Yes, I very much think that I am. Happier than beyond my initial expectations when the match was first proposed. I must admit though, that looking back it was much more difficult than I had imagined marrying with a virtual stranger.'

'I have come to think that we all marry with strangers. The one that you think you know and then choose to lay down with is often not the man with which you arise...' Bessie noted cryptically.

'Those are rather dark sentiments coming from one who eloped halfway across the world with the man she loved... What is it Bessie?' Frances sensed some regret in her friend's words. 'What has happened between you two?'

Bessie was not certain she wanted to burden Lady Frances with the story yet perhaps it was long overdue for her to confide all in another trusted woman.

'Well, for one...' she explained, 'we did not set sail for The New World together.'

'You did not?' This was completely unexpected and left Frances wondering why not.

'No, I ended up going alone.'

'Going to America by yourself? Why? What happened? Did you argue?'

'No... Thomas...he died...'

'He died? But I don't understand! How can he have died when I have just seen him with my own eyes walking with my brother?'

'It is a very long and unsettling story... Perhaps this had not been such a good idea.'

'Then tell me...after all, we have the time. Besides, you cannot start such a revelation as this without completing it!'

Lady Frances listened intently as Bessie gave her account of the events surrounding Thomas's disappearance in Old Plymouth. She carefully pieced together all the bits of the story she had since been able to gather in her mind and faithfully began recounting them. How, after Thomas had failed to return to the Mayflower at Old Plymouth, his friends, Gilbert Winslow and William Bradford, along with Stephen Hopkins, as a 'good measure in case of trouble', had gone searching for him in the town.

'Hopkins? Winslow? I have heard you speak of a Willie Bradford. He was here, wasn't he? He was part of your congregation when you tried to escape from Boston...'

'Yes, he was... Gilbert Winslow was a good friend to Thomas in Leiden. Hopkins is a fine fellow of the New Plimoth settlement, but I do not think then that Thomas was particularly acquainted with him...'

'No matter then...pray to continue. Bessie.'

'Well, Thomas's absence had us all greatly concerned, especially as he had known full well that the Mayflower was ready to set out on the morning tide. Some mean-mouthed strangers even put it about that Thomas had got cold feet and simply thought better of going to the New World and abandoned me to my fare. Nevertheless, I knew that could not be true... More importantly, his friends knew that Thomas would never have deserted me like that. As I said, they sent out a search party to try to find him. Then...much, much later Bradford and the other two came back to the ship without him...While scouring the rougher quarter of town, the three had happened across a black-toothed old ale sop. He seemed eager to pass on what information that he had...but at a price. This informant told how he knew of a stranger answering to Thomas's description... and that he'd been found slumped by a rowdy house in the alleyway.' Bessie was quite moved to tears as she continued her account.

'Goodness, Bessie! It wasn't him, was it?'

'Well, without seeing for themselves the others

had no way of telling. Anyway, the sop told William how this 'stranger' had fallen prey to some vicious robbery, or so it was thought. You see his purse had been cut and he had been stripped of his boots and coat.'

Bessie thought back to her later time aboard the Mayflower. Of how animated Mary Brewster had been while conveying the facts surrounding Thomas's 'death' as William Bradford himself had described them to her in detail. How Mary's face had hideously contorted as she had told how the old drunkard had described to the three, quite mawkishly, how he had seen Thomas's 'body' shortly after the attack, before it was then taken away by the authorities.

'Like a dead dog,' Bessie exclaimed, taking on some of Mary's gesture. 'Thomas was left lying in the street, with no more dignity than a dead dog! For quite some hour it appears...with a chattering rabble crowded in around him gaping at the blood running down the cobbles from his battered in head.'

Frances flinched at the awful image Bessie had conjured up in her mind.

'Someone had come across him quite quickly,' Bessie explained. 'They had even called for a doctor... from out of a more respectable alehouse not a stone's throw away... When, that is, the doctor could finally be persuaded to attend, he immediately pronounced Thomas's life extinguished. Even though he only examined him from afar. Probably for fear of bloodying his fine clothes, I expect. All he had wanted to know was had Thomas moved at all during that past hour? On hearing that he had not...or moaned or groaned...and had not been seen to take breath in all that time...the doctor simply added that Thomas must quite clearly be dead, just from the amount of blood he had lost and the obvious severity of the beating received. After making his pronouncement, the quack turned tail straight back to his drink. It was then that the sop held out his hand again to William for more money. He, said how he could show them where the body had been taken.'

'And did he?'

'Yes, but only after William had obliged him with a further groat. He took it and led the three across town to an old stone stairway leading down into the bowels of some ancient hall. With that, the rascal then hurried away!'

'To the nearest tavern, no doubt!' Frances jested.

Bessie then continued to relate how the three had proceeded down the stairs. Their echoing footsteps descending the steep void soon alerted a bailiff who was on duty there. The three quickly explained the reason for their presence.

'It was then that the bailiff spoke of burying that particular body. He had said to William that, if this turned out to be their missing man, then it was fortunate that they had come to identify him when they had. 'You see...' Bessie explained to Frances, 'they had already planned to bury him, in a pauper's pit, first thing the following morning.'

The bailiff had then led the men to a low Norman-arched doorway, where his cold arthritic fingers unhurriedly fumbled with a huge jangle of keys before he could turn the lock. Gilbert had described to Mary Brewster how it had felt like an age as he had waited there for the room to be opened up. Impatience almost made him snatch the keys from the poor man and throw open the door himself just so he could be inside and to see with his own eyes that the body within was not Thomas! However, once the fellow had opened he declined to enter himself, saying instead that he would trust the three as gentlemen 'not to molest the dead' and that he would be back at his post 'if needed'.

'The bailiff did, though, have the good grace at least to warn them to first cover their mouths and nostrils before they went in. Once inside, they soon realised why! The air was alive with blowflies, attracted by the putrid, sickly sweet smell of human decomposition!'

'Urgh!' Frances cringed and screwed up her face.'

'It was foul enough even to make hardened Stephen Hopkins heave.' Bessie added. 'Apparently, not even the death-like chill of this cold crypt was not enough to halt the bodies from rapidly 'ripening' in the heat of that summer.'

'That must have been so awful...'

'From the light daring in from a small slit of a window set high above, the three were clearly able to discern the contours of four corpses. All were laid out beneath grubby sheets on a narrow, stone ledge that ran the breadth of that cellar. The bailiff had said that the second one in line was that of the unknown murder victim found brained in the street. The one that he suspected might be Thomas. Both William and Gilbert stood with kerchiefs pressed hard against their faces trying to summon up the strength to uncover it. Finally, Hopkins stepped in. He being a lesser acquaintance of Thomas volunteered to lift off the sheet. He confirmed their worst fear. It was Thomas.'

'It was? You keep saying that Bessie but how could it have been? He is alive!'

'I know! I know! But it was Thomas! There was no mistake! He was lying dead on a slab in front of two of his closest friends!'

'But I don't understand...'

'Then let me carry on with the rest of the story...'

It was only then that the awful 'truth' had struck home leaving Gilbert's upright demeanour to sink as he steadied himself against a wall at the shock of it all. The others were equally stunned and enraged yet it appeared to have affected Gilbert Winslow the worst of all.

'His pain was absolute.' Bessie said. 'He was beside himself with grief and came to me later, quite inconsolable at Thomas's loss.'

'He sounds a good man...'

Bessie agreed that he was.

'Thomas was laid out naked. Apart, that is, for a cloth at draped across his loins for decency's sake. The bailiff had taken the rest of his clothes to help pay towards his burial. They said that Thomas's face was dreadfully swollen. That his expression was fixed and deathly grey in pallor betwixt the patches of black and blue bruising. There was bruising the length and breadth of his body. His eyes were firmly shut with the lashes clumped together by a sticky residue, obviously overlooked when some tender mercy had thought to wash his face clean, fit to meet his maker... That his hair was heavily matted with thick, dried blood. All in all they said Thomas was the most pitiful of sights.'

Bessie hardly got these words out as she broke down and cried. Lady Frances reached held her in her slender arms and kissed her gently on the cheek.
'Come on, Bessie... No more...'

Difficult as it was, Bessie was determined to carry on with the tale. She needed to let it all out. She needed someone else to hear her out to help lay any lingering ghost of a doubt she may still have hiding within her soul.
'It was Gilbert,' Bessie dried her tears, composed herself once more and continued. 'Gilbert who raised the question of how they were going to tell me. He was worried about what it would do to me if I knew of the frenzied injuries they had seen inflicted upon my husband's body? But William said that they were not going to tell. He wanted to spare me that torment. He was afraid that if I knew, then it would destroy me. Besides, he argued that no man would want his wife to have to see them like that! So, to protect me, they decided that they would return to the Mayflower and tell me that Thomas had died from a single blow and that he was already buried. The three then bade their private farewell to Thomas, Hopkins replaced the cloth over his body and they made their way back to the bailiff to confirm the identity of the body. William then spoke briefly about funeral arrangements and explained why no one would be attending. However, he handed over the rest of his purse, insisting that the bailiff was to buy Thomas a shroud and coffin and then implored him to treat the corpse with all due reverence and honour.

With that, they apparently made their way back to the Mayflower. That's when Mary and the other women came to me. When they had, I felt like my life was over. I so wanted to die as well. Then I begged them to take me to him. But they said it was too late.'

'And yet they were still convinced that this man was Thomas?'

'Yes, because it was Thomas!'

'Yet how can this be? How can a man be dead and then be alive again? 'Tis the devil's work!' Lady Frances exclaimed.

'Or could it not equally be God's?' Bessie said philosophically. 'Who knows? The only thing that Thomas could add for certain, was being told later by the bailiff that, just as he was about to be buried, someone realised that he was still alive!'

Frances still found this difficult to comprehend and now understood why her friend had been reluctant to tell her earlier.

'It does not bear thinking about what might have happened if they had not!' She said sympathetically.

'Do you know the one thing that had me the most deeply troubled, Frances? Even to this day?'

Frances nodded that she did not.

'It is that when Thomas and I were eventually reunited, we went over all this later and discussed it in the most minute of detail. Yet, he could listen to my account, even joke about his, yet still be distanced from the pain and distress it had inflicted on me believing he was dead. It was as if it had all happened to some strangers and not to himself and me. It bothered me so much, Frances, that a growing doubt niggled away inside until in the end I began to question if this man was really my Thomas after all?'

'That must have been so awful...'

'Frances...' Bessie's haunted eyes searched out those of her dearest confidant and confessed, 'There is worse.... Afterwards, in New Plimoth...I remarried, thinking he was dead...'

'Remarried? Oh! ...' The ramifications quickly

sank in. 'Then you committed bigamy?'

'In the sight of man...I did. Yet the marriage was one of contract only...we had both agreed to that. He had lost his wife and was in desperate need for a mother to care for his baby son. I was alone and widowed and needed a roof over my head. Yet, had I slept under the same roof as this man and not wed I would have been the target for malicious gossipers and risk a flogging or worse should their lies be believed... Therefore, we married in name only and not in deed. The union was never consummated...'

Frances was in shock. Though understandable, considering the circumstances and duress under which it had come about, it was still a serious crime...'

'Could you not have the marriage annulled?' She asked.

'Perhaps if all this had happened in England... Maybe so. Yet out there...out there Frances, it is not England. Out there, if this had even come to light my life, and others could have been made intolerable. I could have been sent home to an unsympathetic church court and hung. Not on the evidence, nor circumstance but instead simply out of malice for my being a Separatist...'

'So? How was this dilemma resolved?'

'It was all kept secret... Only William Bradford and a few others realised quickly what had happened when Thomas suddenly arrived at the settlement. William had him intercepted before it became common knowledge that he was there and still alive. I was gravely ill at the time... So... So they faked my death and we slipped away into a new life and I reverted to my real name...'

'Then in God's eyes you are blameless in all this, Bessie.' Frances said lovingly. 'And in my eyes too, my dearest friend...'

Bessie was so overjoyed with relief. She could not have borne the loss of this very special friendship.

'Thank you, Frances. You may never know how much these words of yours mean to my heart...'

'It must have been so difficult for you both to

come to terms with all that had happened?'

'Yes. It was. Then... When Thomas finally came in search of me... I had not seen him for over two years. It was such a shock. Everything was different... He had changed. It was as if he were a stranger. He was a stranger and yet I had no choice but to go with him because he was my legal husband. No matter what I may have wanted...how much I had grown accustomed to my new life...my new world...I had no say! Men decided my future life around a table. And I was passed over to this stranger like a chattel passing through owner's hands and then expected to go quietly into his bed at night as if nothing had happened. I can tell you Frances, it was a most awful experience.'

'I can imagine.' Frances quietly sighed out the words like a woman who really knew what Bessie meant. 'When I married, I had hardly met my husband but a handful of times. And then, never without a chaperone. Then, on our wedding night I found myself in a strange household with an unknown maid undressing me in preparation for my marriage bed. When my husband came in to me, I did not know either what I should do or say... Nor where I should look, although my mother in law had warned me briefly what to expect. He climbed upon me, lifted up my nightgown and told me that he intended to be gentle with me and that he sincerely desired that I would not come to consider this part of our marriage as being a burden to me. With that, he went about his business upon me. Then, the next thing I knew he was climbing off me again, thanking me then turning over to snuff out the bedside candles.'

'Oh Frances, I am so sorry I was not here to prepare you for married life...'

'It is all right, Bessie. He was always gentle and I did indeed come not to regard this part of our contract as a burden. In truth, I have come to feel affection towards him...and he I. So, as you see, I am very happy in my own way and I do think that this marriage agrees with me. And what of you, Bessie? You and Thomas do not look like an estranged couple to me. Besides, am I not right in my understanding that you two have been blessed with children!'

'No. You are keenly observant as ever! We are no longer strangers. In fact, we are very much in love...'

'Good! I am so very relieved to hear it! I could not bear to think of you being unhappy! Goodness,' Frances exclaimed on hearing three bells chime. 'Is that the time already! We had best go up to see my father before he is fussing for his afternoon nap!'

Bessie and Frances made their way up by the tower staircase to the East Wing apartments. On entering the bedchamber, they found Sir William's youngest daughter, fourteen year old Mildred, dutifully sitting beside him reading aloud. It immediately put Bessie in mind of herself when she was a young maid and she would sit and read to Lady Rose when her eyes had begun to fail with old age.

Mildred broke off, rose quickly up and threw her arms about Bessie in a loving embrace.

'Oh, it's you! It's really you!' She cried excitedly.

'Yes! It is really me!' she said hugging the young girl tightly.

'Willoughby told me that you were coming today but I just could not believe it until you came through that door! It is so wonderful to see you!'

'Yes. It is good to see you...' Sir William added his sentiment. 'Very good to see you indeed, my dear.'

'Thank you Sir William. I am pleased to see you again too.'

The old man turned towards his daughter and smiled weakly.

'Mildred, please be so good as to go and fetch me up another beaker full of that hot herbal infusion, my dear. 'Tis so soothing on an old man's throat.'

'Oh Father,' Mildred whined, reluctantly letting go of Bessie, 'but I want to stay here and talk with Mistress Dorothy...'

'I am certain, Mistress Dorothy would prefer it if you were to call her Bessie...and I am certain that she will have plenty of time to chatter with you before she has to leave. My herbal... please?'

'What if I come and help you, little sister!' Frances encouraged. Mildred agreed and so the two of them went off together.

'She has grown so much these past few years. I hardly recognised her!' Bessie remarked.

'Yes, she certainly has!' Sir William said proudly, 'and she has a certain look of my mother about her... if not more than a little of her spirit too.'

Bessie smiled in agreement.

'I was so sorry, Sir, to hear of Lady Elizabeth's passing.'

'Yes, it was very hard for all of us to bear. Especially Mildred. She was so young to have lost her mother. Elizabeth was much younger than me...so full of life. I never expected to be the one to be widowed. Yet, God takes us as he sees fit and we may never know his reasoning in the order of our coming and going... Enough of this sad talk of the past. What about you? What of the New World? I want to hear all about it.'

Bessie sat and talked with Sir William for more than an hour about her adventures in America. He sat and listened wide-eyed, like a child to a fairy story. Though his life was surely playing out, in his eye there was still that tell-tale Hickman twinkle at the proffering up of new knowledge.

After that day, Bessie often called in to visit with him. During the following year, she seized every opportunity of accompanying Thomas into Gainsborough whenever he had cause to do business there. Bessie would thoughtfully divide her time between chatting at Sir William's bedside and keeping young Mildred company by walking with her in the grounds or sitting chatting in the garden room on days that were more inclement.

Sir William let it be known that he had gained such comfort from Bessie's visits. She was one of the few people left he could still talk with about the old days at The Hall. His closest friends, his trusted steward, his wife and even long-time family servants were either mostly dead or too young to remember. Especially to remember his mother, Lady Rose.

Bessie often mulled over her conversations with Sir William on the ride back to Stowe. Living an extraordinarily long life must hold many advantages, she concluded, yet equally as many sorrows. On the one hand, it must be a comfort to live to see your children grow and blossom into adults and bear the fruit of children of their own. Yet, what of the sorrows? To watch as your peers die out, one by one, or to see a young wife pass away before you. Or much worse, children too. So, at what pain do some humans stay ripening on the tree of life far beyond others that are lost in June? Or that crop with which you passed summer by, until they fell from a bright September sky. 'Tis lonely to be a shrivelled remnant of a once plump, former blushed self. To still be alive and yet decayed. Still clinging to the bare bow when the cold December wind makes moan through the rest of the empty tree. All things considered, excessive old age was a burden that Bessie hoped she might be spared.

By that following summer of 1625, Sir William had become very much frailer still and although confined to his great, carved bed was still as interested as ever in life. The news of the death of King James a few months earlier had not come as unexpected. He had been old and in poor health for quite sometime himself. However, the royal announcement that reached Gainsborough Hall that June, was.

'My mother would certainly have something to say about this!' Sir William commented warily on the news of the royal marriage.
Bessie recalled the old lady fondly and readily conceded that yes, she certainly would have.

The new sovereign, Charles, had married the fifteen-year-old daughter of the King of France. Her name was Henrietta Maria and she was a Catholic, leaving many in the country now fearing this was but one step away from a return back to Rome. Sir William, like many others, received this news with great sorrow in his heart and a shivering trepidation boring deep into his protestant soul.

'Twas like hearing that the nightmare my mother lived through under Bloody Queen Mary was about to happen all over again!' He said mournfully. 'How can a son set out to so cruelly usurp all his father has striven to conserve? How can a monarch lead his subjects towards such inevitable conflict of conscience?'

Bessie understood that Sir William was referring to the precious status quo within the realm in which King James had kept the Catholic faith underground and in check and thus the still fledgling protestant country stable, despite the failed Catholic gunpowder plot to assassinate him.

'How can such an animosity have been nurtured and grown up? Charles surely appreciated how his father James feared the Catholics? Many more times over than he feared Puritans! He understood full well how England is like but one blade's edge balanced upon another and that the skill was to keep it all in kilter. And how with one, minute tilt the whole Kingdom could fall into a terminal chaos. King James had the wisdom to understand that, however much he may have disliked the country he had inherited, it had wandered too far down the Protestant road to be hauled back, kicking and screaming, to its Catholic Mother. He also knew the shortcomings of his Anglican Church, yet feared harsh reform of it. Any change in any direction brought on too quickly might have caused irreparable instability. Maybe he would have conceded to reform over time, else why had he not engaged in a massive purge of we Puritans with fire, like Queen Mary did with her dissidents. Or even Elizabeth? No! Change cannot be forced! More acceptable is the change that comes by degrees, so gradually that no man straight way even notices that it is happening.'

'Then why did your mother and you help our Separatist congregations?'

'Because the Bishops and the King left you no other way out. You were our brothers and sisters in

Christ. More petulant, more impatient siblings but wanting reform and purity in worship just the same as we did. We did not want to see you martyred, which was where we feared you were being led. Nor did we want the consequence of your actions undoing all of our work. Better, by far that we aided and abetted you to flee the country where you might bide your time, as we, in safety. We of my mother's generation and mine were happy to sew and nurture the tiny seeds that would start to change the church by stealth. Like God's rain weathering a stone newly hewn by man. Softening and remoulding it back to a more pleasing state to His eye. We are like a child growing slowly within its mother. The seed is unseen and at first virtually unnoticed. Like that of this much overdue reformation, it will develop secretly, hidden safely away from prying eyes. Later the Mother may take on subtle changes and even herself become aware that something deep within her is beginning to stir and yet the spirit may move her to know that this something is good and instinctively that she should protect its identity. Inch by inch, day by day, this embryo continues to grow ever stronger in body and flesh. By the time it begins to outwardly show, it will be too advanced for evil to try to abort. For it will be fully formed and of substance and unstoppable as it counts down the days until its inevitable outing into the world. Perhaps King James died hoping that his heir might understand this? Yet, barely is his cadaver settled in the dust when Charles has upped and married with a Catholic! He has at one stroke unpicked the seams that hold this country together and that have taken his father twenty-two long years on the English throne to securely stitch. I tell you, it is as if there is a curse upon this royal line whenever a spare son usurps the position of a dead Prince of Wales. Had the King's eldest son lived, I am certain he would not so lightly have cast off his father's mantle.'

Bessie appreciated Sir William's argument but also saw that it was flawed. However, she kept her own council. This was an old man's time to say his piece and who was she to deny him that?

'Yet, is not sometimes the father to blame?' Bessie asked thinking well to her husband's own past predicament.

'Maybe so...' the old man reconsidered. 'King James was, after all, a deeply troubled man. Who would not be, growing up in the protestant faith knowing that your Catholic mother was first vilified and then executed by her cousin the Queen of England? And then to inherit that same English throne? To become King to a country who had long considered your existing kingdom as an enemy state? No wonder he was dogged by the same paranoia as his predecessor, fearing assassins coming for him at every turn?'

'Then I should suspect that it is at least one thing the new King shall not have fear of Catholic assassins.'

'Mayhap he won't! But if he was of a mind to try to lead the country back to Catholicism, then he may well need to keep a wary watch on Protestant blades aimed at his back. Think on. He has avowed that he does not intend to convert to Catholicism himself, yet he allows his wife the freedom to practise the religion. Moreover she is to have complete control over any offspring's upbringing until they are almost adult. In effect, there is nothing lying between this Catholic Queen and her indoctrinating the next King of England into the Catholic faith...'

'Therefore,' Bessie suddenly realised the enormity of this new King's actions, 'come the time that Charles dies, we as a country will have no constitutional defence against a rightful heir ascending to the throne who also happens to be Catholic. A Catholic head of the Church of England!'

'Yes, Bessie. Bright Bessie! You have it in one! This can only be a cataclysmic event below the horizon waiting to break forth at some dreadful point in the future. It is as certain as night follows day. I am glad that my life is coming to a close, Bessie' Sir William sighed feebly. 'I would not want to live to see that storm rage that I feel is coming. I can sense it, like smelling rain on the wind before the thunderclouds open. The end of life as we know it, is about to be swept away...I fear.'

'Please Sir William, no more talk of dying.' Bessie gently pleaded trying to steer his troubled thoughts away from such doom. 'You must wait to see your grandchildren born.'

'Oh, they will come! Of that, I am certain! I will not live to see them, though...'

Bessie came away from Gainsborough with her own conclusions as to what lay behind this latest event. For she had heard William Brewster talking to others as they had met at The Hall all those years before. How he had quoted what King James had said during the Hampton Court Conference, which had been convened to deal with the growing number of dissidents, not long before the Separatist congregations had fled to Holland. The King had told his Anglican bishops that, since the age of ten he had disliked the opinions of the Puritans, and that, although he had lived amongst them, he was not one of them. Of how he had later told a hostile House of Commons that the Puritans could not be tolerated in any well governed commonwealth; that the Roman Catholic Church was the mother of the Church of England; and that despite her infirmities and corruptions, he was prepared to meet her halfway. If James had so hated the Puritans, what better a revenge could he have planned with his son than to convert the country back to Catholicism, no matter what he may have promised on ascending the English throne. After all, was he not too as equally capable of playing the waiting game? Even if it meant from beyond the grave?

That meeting was to have been one of the last, such visits Bessie would make to Sir William. Come September he passed peacefully away in his sleep. His wish had been fulfilled. He would not see the bleak changes yet to come.

'He wanted you to have this...' As they walked away from the funeral, Willoughby handed a soft velvety pouch to Bessie containing something hard like dried peas.

'What is this?' She asked.

'Look for yourself.'

Bessie loosened the drawstring and tipped the contents out into her hand.

'But this is your mother's pearl necklace! This should go to your wife or your sisters!'

'No. 'Twas not my mother's.' He countered. 'It belonged to Lady Agnes. Father's first wife. And he insisted!'

'Insist or not. Still...I cannot take it!'

'That is exactly what my father said you would say. He told me that you could not take it in the past... and that you had always been too honest. From since you were a very young maid and newly employed by my family, he came to trust you implicitly. So, on his deathbed he insisted that it was only fitting that you took these now! Take them, Dear Bessie, it was his final wish...'

Bessie did as Willoughby asked and received them with more than a hint of bewilderment in her teary eyes. How could Sir William have known, Bessie pondered? How could he have possibly known that she and Comfort had once found that same pearl rope spilling out from a secret compartment in the intricately carved head of his great bed as they had once gone about their duties as mere girls. Though it was worth a lifetime's wages to those poor young maidservants, yet the two had immediately put the pearls safely back inside.

Chapter Nine

'It lies not in our power to love or hate,
for will in us is over-ruled by fate'
- Marlowe

It looked exactly the same. Even though Bessie had not stood in that now empty lane outside the ancient church for more than twenty years, it was as if time had ceased to flow from the day she was forced into exile from home. Yet clearly time had passed, neatly marked out by a still-humped row of new graves.

She slipped through the gate and closing it securely behind, began to weave her way between them to the poorer, shadier part of the churchyard. A large newly fleeced, devil-eyed ewe raised its head mid-graze and stared intently as the wide-brimmed stranger approached. Suddenly Bessie stopped, aware now that every other member of the flock was suddenly stood motionless and checking on her progress. It felt odd. Sheep here had never minded her here in the past. Slowly she started forward again and the ewe bleated out a warning, turned tail and swiftly cantered away. Silently, like ghosts, the rest were quickly spirited away in her wake and off to a distance of perceived safety, towards the far end of the church.

Bessie soon found the spot. Although the mound of grass had now levelled over time and the wooden marker was long since decayed away, she knew this was her father's grave. As she knelt upon the ground with head bowed, she reached out to him in fond remembrance.

'I have missed you, father,' she said softly. 'I am so sorry that I have been gone for such a long, long time...'

'That's alright, child...' she heard him murmur on the autumn breeze. 'I missed you too. What kept you from me, my lovely?'

'Life, father. Life kept me away...'

'Aye, Bessie.' She could feel his kiss upon her face in the dappled sunlight. 'Life has a habit of doing that.. Still, you are here with your old father now...'

'Yes father. I am with you now...'

'I do that too...' A strange woman's voice suddenly broke in. 'I come here too to talk to the dead. I like to think that they at least can hear me...'

The overly plump intruder was very light on her feet. Bessie had not heard her approach and jumped up with a start.

'I am so sorry...' the woman apologised. 'I did not mean to interrupt you...'

She looked hard at Bessie. Then a spark of recognition ignited. 'I know you, don't I? You... you are Bessie...aren't you?'

Bessie felt herself squirm within her own skin. She felt dirty. Ashamed. Yet, what should she do? Deny it? Say she was someone else then turn and walk briskly away? Before she could do any of these, the woman stretched out her hand and took a hold of Bessie's.

'It's all right, duck.' She said with a kindly smile. 'Don't you recognise me? It's me, Humility. You must remember me, surely! I know I am as big as a house now and as grey as the vicar's mare but that is all that has changed! We were once friends...before... don't you remember?'

'Yes... I remember you well...' Bessie stumbled for words 'I apologise...my...er... thoughts were elsewhere...'

'I understand. You have not been back since... Since my wedding and all that trouble...' Humility smiled desperate to put Bessie at ease with her. It failed miserably. Bessie did not feel in the least bit eased. On the contrary, she felt as if she were standing before this woman naked. Humility surely knew all about her and what had happened with Elias and about the rape and her stepfather Nathan. What had the village thought when it had all come out in the trial during her absence? When they had learnt that Nathan had encouraged Elias to rape Bessie in order to force her into an unwanted marriage? And for what? Just so that Nathan might get the fine cow that he had coveted in return as a dowry? Had the catty village gossipers lapped up all of the dirty details with relish? Had some even mewed that perhaps Bessie had brought it upon herself? She did not want to know. She just wanted to get away from that place again and leave all that hurt buried there firmly in the past.

'I must go now... I am sorry...' She mumbled making to walk away.

'No Bessie! Please don't go.' A solace hand swiftly reached out for hers, 'not on my account. Stay!' Humility pleaded 'I...I have missed you. I often wondered what happened to you. Where you had gone to...If you were alright. I am so sorry I did not know! Many here were so shocked when they found out... So genuinely sorry that none of we women folk had stopped to try to help you...'

'Thank you...thank you...' Bessie cried with bitter relief.

'Elias confessed, you know?' Humility replied with tears of her own. 'He repented it all...publicly.. and was hung for it according to the law... He made amends by paying for what he did...but Nathan?' Humility pouted and shook her head in sorrow. 'Nathan denied any involvement at all in it. He twisted and squirmed his way out of every accusation levelled at him in court. He may have fooled the magistrates but not us. The village women wanted to lynch him. They reckoned he was every bit as guilty as Elias but had got away with it. Made a mockery of the law into the bargain! He got his comeuppance, though, in the end,' she sighed deeply. 'He died a slow, horrible natural death with not a hand raised up to help ease his suffering. And when he was brought up here for his burial most of the village women turned out to block Little Lane so the bearers could not carry his coffin in through the gate. Instead, our lads seized it and tipped his bloating body out onto the road. Then they dragged him over to a hastily dug pit outside the churchyard walls and threw him in, face down. Your mother...the vicar...they all just turned their backs and walked away leaving the others to it as they backfilled the dirt with their boots on top of him. Not fit they said...not fit to be buried with decent folk. Not decent folk like you and I...'

You and I...decent folk. Bessie took so such comfort from those five simple words.

'I came to visit my father...' Bessie began to explain as she dried her tears.

'Yes...I guessed as much. I remember the day that he was buried here. How you huddled-up beside your mother, just a-crying and a-crying. And how she stood so still and silent. I used to come and find you... afterwards...you know? ...To try to make the hurt go away. Do you remember?'

Bessie did not. Not until that moment when, suddenly it all began to flood back in a stream of vivid images.

'Yes... I do remember... You used to come and cuddle up beside me at the grave here and try to make me play games to forget. You were always kind to me, even if I pushed you away at times.'

'Will you push me away now Bessie?' Humility asked.

'No... I won't push you away...'

Humility smiled in obvious delight.

'You say you come here to talk too?' Bessie ventured. 'Are your parents dead now then too?'

'No. They are both still living. Though much frailer now, of course, what with age... I come here to talk to my little ones. They are all buried just over there,' she said pointing to the sunnier slope.

'Little ones?... You mean your children?'

'Yes. My children.'

'I'm so sorry Humility. I did not know...'

'It's all right, Bessie. How could you have? You have been away so long...'

'Do you want to talk about them?'

'Yes. I would like that. There's very little talking been done in the past. I suppose that's why I come here. I need to talk to someone about them but the living have so little time...'

'Then tell me. They say that I am a good listener.'

'Not much to tell really. I have birthed seven children and yet not one of them has survived. I guess that I was cursed never to be blessed as a mother... although I never really gave up hope that I might live to see at least one of my offspring grow into adulthood.'

'Then the baby you were expecting when you married...'

'Died...'twas born dead. Strangled with its own cord bound tight about its neck. A little boy it was too. So chubby and perfect when he finally slipped out that I could not understand how he could not be alive... He was born...Then they just took him away. I saw him but for a moment or two but the midwives never even, let me hold him. Not after all those months of carrying him and a-singing to him inside me. They just took him away and that was that. Some spiteful hags in the village said it was my entire fault for lying with its father before I was wed and for not being whipped for it. That it was a punishment from God in return for all my sinful ways. Afterwards, my husband's family turned cold towards me. Even colder when one by one our other babies came and died...'

'All seven, born dead?'

'No. Not all. I had a little girl after that and she lived for a year. Then, when I was with child again, we were all struck down with the fever. Not only did I lose her but also the little sister to her that I was carrying. Later on...it was tiny twin boys who lived but an hour or two. I had another daughter though and another a son. She lived to be six or more and, Jake, died falling from a horse at fifteen. Now they are all gone and my husband too. After Jake, his heart just gave out.'

'Humility! How could you survive such loss?' Bessie was choked again to tears on hearing of these dreadful, tragic events.

'I do not know, to be honest,' she replied. 'I have often heard my family say that I am made of stern stuff yet there were times when I went abed at sunset and I

171

prayed not to wake up to another day. I soon learned early on not to dare love the children growing inside me too much for the heartbreak that was certain to follow. Yet, I had little Mary for comfort and in good health for years, praying that I would see her into her womanhood. And Jake... I had him until almost a man. Each minute I have lived through with the two of them made the loss of the others somehow easier to bear. Then, when they too were gone, I started to come here to remember them all and to be with my babes again for a few moments in some small way. I do suppose it will not be long until I join them... Yet what of you Bessie?' Humility's brave smile led Bessie away from her own grief. 'Are you married?' She asked. 'Did you have children?'

'Yes, I am married,' she replied. 'Yet only these past four years. And I have a baby. A son named James and a foundling baby daughter that we named Hope.'

'A baby boy and so lately come! Is he close by with you now? Is he with your mother?'

'My mother? No... I have not seen my mother... yet. I rode out only with my husband. He is at Bishop's Bridge on a matter of business so I rode on here by myself.'

'Not seen your mother yet? Do you intend to?'

'I do not know if I have the will to. It has been so long that I do not even know if I can...'

'I understand. After all that has happened... yet... she is your mother...'

'I know. I must sound like a dreadful daughter but in truth there was little love lost between us before I went away. In truth, I had half expected to come here and to learn that she had died. Now? Now I fear that our bridges are too far broken to try to mend. There lies a chasm betwixt us that I fear might never be crossed. Yet, I would not want to think of her suffering in her old age.'

'Judd takes good care of her...but you are right to worry. They are both old. It must be getting so hard for Judd to keep on labouring yet if he has to give up then they will lose the cottage.'

Bessie thought for a moment. Had she remained in The New World and then learned that her mother was in need, then might she not then have been minded to send the old woman some portion of her wealth as a duty? That way, Bessie could have let her mother know that at least she was still alive and well and prospering instead of her never knowing what had happened to her only child while, at the same time, be allowed a sharing of some of her own good fortune.

'Your in-laws own that cottage, do they not?' Bessie asked.

'Yes. They own all them ones down that lane. Why?'

'Might they be persuaded to sell?'

'Yes. Very easily so. Why? Do you want to buy it from them?'

'Yes. I very much think that I do. If I can persuade the money from my husband, then could you be persuaded to lie for me? To tell them that I sent money from America to do this thing and perhaps a sum besides for replacing livestock or such. That way I might do my duty by my mother yet not risk opening up any festering wounds...'

*   *   *

November rain hammered down the windows of Blackthorn Farm like iron nails being driven against an anvil. 'Twas a night as such even the Devil would not want to venture out in. And yet, a devil abroad there was.

A violent pounding of fist against wet wooden door disturbed the quiet evening that Thomas and his wife were spending in the parlour.

'Who on God's good earth can be calling on us at this time?' Thomas exclaimed.

'I do not know!' Bessie replied. 'But it must be important for someone to have ventured out in this!'

'I best go!' Thomas warned Bessie. 'You stay well back, darling, when I open up in case it is nothing of good!'

He went into his study and quickly snatched up his old sword from out of its band, behind the door. It had not been unsheathed in anger since their Jamestown days. He sincerely hoped he would not need to use it now.

The hammering persisted on the door as a now agitated Thomas made his way up the hallway to open it, with the blade ready in his hand. Bessie stood halfway back, veiled in the shadows and out of sight. Only the flickering glow from the log fire spilling out from the parlour lent light to the scene.

Thomas slowly drew across the heavy bolts and lifted up the cumbersome latch. Immediately the hammering ceased. He opened up the door but a crack and shouted against the wail of the wind.

'Who is it? What do you want?'

'Sir Thomas...I want to see Sir Thomas!'

Thomas did not recognise the voice that shouted back and so was reluctant to open up further.

'Aye, but maybe Sir Thomas does not want to see you, stranger!' He said.

'I am no stranger to him,' the voice replied. 'Tell him Mister Rech from Jamestown wants to speak with him!'

Rech? This had to be the last person Thomas expected to see.

'Sir Thomas?' Thomas opened the door up a little more. Rech tilted his head slightly, sending a torrent of rainwater gushing from the brim of his black hat and cascading down over his already soaking shoulders.

'Rech? What are you doing here?'

'I am here on business. Please be so kind as to let me in,' he pleaded. 'I am soaked to the skin.'

'I know of no business you can conceivably have with me.' Thomas was in no hurry to do so. He had never liked Rech particularly nor he him, as far as he could recall. Thomas therefore found it rather suspicious that this man should now be standing here at his door demanding an audience. Yet, this farmstead prided itself in its Christian hospitality and after all, the weather outside was atrocious.

'Let me enter, Sir. Then I can explain,' Rech persisted.

Uneasily Thomas let him in. Rech followed his lead, slithering past Bessie like a snake and on into the parlour.

'Very pleasant,' he said. 'Yet not as grand as I imagined your home would be. That is, not after I had learnt that you had received a knighthood.'

Bessie could not help but notice that under his coat, Rech's clothes appeared threadbare and his boots split open with wear. He had obviously had a high fall from favour since leaving the ship in Kent.

'And where did you hear that?' Thomas got the nasty feeling that perhaps Rech had already undertaken a great deal of delving into his private affairs.

'Quite by chance,' Rech snapped back, 'from an ex-clerk at the Virginia Company office, to be precise. You see, once I had, though, I just had to come here to look you up.'

Bessie too perceived that something unpleasant was about to unfold so wondered if her husband might not prefer her to take her leave.

'Shall I go up to your mother, Thomas...?' Bessie asked.

'No! Stay! There is nothing to be said that you may not hear...' Thomas turned a cold eye towards the other man. 'You say you have been looking for me Rech? Why?' He demanded.

'To offer you my services,' he replied peevishly. 'Now you are a man of position with an estate to deal with I am certain you have the need of a trustworthy steward, like me. A man...shall we say...to help share the burden of the day to day running of it and... shall we also say...a share of the profits?'

Thomas rightly detected the overtures of a blackmailer plying his trade.

'What makes you think I would have need of your miserable services.' He said icily. 'I already have an excellent man to help manage the farm and he does not demand a share of anything other than a fair wage from me in return!'

'To silence my curiosity.' Rech mewed cattily.

'Your curiosity?' Thomas laughed in his adversary's weak-chinned face.

'Yes. Curiosity. I mean to say...one moment you are man of no importance dying in the colony...then next? Next, you are miraculously 'cured' and further more in receipt of a knighthood from the King for no obvious reason that I can ascertain. Which poses the question as to why?'

'And what business is this of yours?'

'I have made it my business,' Rech sneered triumphantly. 'With so many people losing so much in Virginia...there you are.. at the very same time... suddenly ennobled! Well, it makes one wonder why? What, I asked myself, could this lowly, nobody artist have done to receive such a rich reward? And I know many others who would dearly like to know why too.'

'I ask again? What business is this of yours, Rech?'

'I will tell you what business it is of mine, Sir Thomas. While you have gained a knighthood and favour, I Sir have lost everything! My father is all but ruined and blames me for sending word back from Virginia urging him to invest. I am dismissed from my family like a servant without a penny. I am left in disgrace and penury as a result of the collapse of the Virginia Company. Even my own pittance of an inheritance, left to me by my natural father, I had put into shares. Now I am penniless. Forced to employ what talents I have at my disposal in order to survive each day. Yet you? You have profited from my abject misery! Why is that?'

Thomas refused to be drawn.

'I think I have the answer.' Rech goaded. 'I think you were sending evidence to the King's commission to support the disbanding of the Virginia Company. You were nothing but a low common spy and I think that is what you received favour for...'

'Poppycock!' Thomas shouted. 'Everyone knows I was engaged for the very opposite purpose and served the Virginia Company well. My drawings proved popular with the King, which is all. Luck shined on me. Nothing more. As for my health? I am blessed indeed by a recovery, which I mark down entirely to the more conducive surroundings of England as opposed to that mosquito-infested hole called Jamestown. Now...if that is all, I bid you good night, Sir!' He said manhandling Rech towards the front door.

Rech fought back with one more volley of taunts as he resisted being ejected back into the night.

'And what about the child?' He snarled. 'Are you so willing to risk losing that natural-born brat of yours? I know all about her, you see. Those others might have been fooled but I was not! I have eyes. I have seen her up close for myself. She is a natural...and you have no right to have her here and I will see to it that she is taken away!'

'You will do no such thing...' Thomas grabbed him by his scrawny throat and hurled him against the passage wall. 'Go whining to the King...that's if a worm like you can get to him... Even if you could...what do you think he will do? You are a nothing Rech! Nothing but a snivelling malcontent of the Virginia Company which he despised so much that he had it destroyed. Do you really think that he would remove our child from us? For what purpose? To appease a miserable, blackmailing wretch like you? Go! Get out of this house and go back into whichever black hole you crawled out of!' With that, Thomas roughly threw Rech back out into the storm and slammed the door shut.

He hammered on the door shouting and cursing that he would see to it that Thomas would live to regret that night. Rech swore he would have his revenge.

'Do you think he will go to the authorities?' The thought of losing her beautiful daughter filled Bessie's heart with pain.

'No. I think it was nought but hot air and bravado from a very desperate man.'

'But would it not have been better to humour him. To pay him off even? Just to be certain.'

'No, Bessie. You do give a man like that an inch. Once you do, then he perceives it as weakness or fear on your part and then he thinks he has a hold on you for life. Besides, how could I ever sleep easy again at night, knowing that someone like that was privy to all the little intimacies of my life? Just waiting, hoping to come up with something else with which to blackmail me? No! 'Tis better to call his bluff now. I am certain he will now go away and give the matter up. I do not believe we will hear from him further...ever!'

Chapter Ten

'The Eagle Suffers Little Birds To Sing...'
- William Shakespeare

Over the year or two since Thomas and Bessie had returned, they had soon came to realise that the England they had come home to was fast changing to the one that they had left behind before travelling to the New World. For one, the Puritan movement within the Church and throughout the country had grown from strength to strength and now boldly voiced its views throughout the realm. No longer were those who wanted radical reform of the Church of England willing to whisper their ideas from the safety of the shadows. Now, they were more likely to stand up in the churches in their villages and even in Parliament to preach their demands. Nor were they afraid to clothe themselves in the garb of their simplistic pious views like stoics from an ancient age. No frivolity in garments for them, no dancing or other wasteful worldly pursuits. God was their focus as was purity in all things and behaviour. The world was a corrupt place in which they avowed to remain an uncorrupted force and an example to those fallen away.

After all her involvement with Lady Rose and belonging to the Separatist congregation, one might have expected Bessie to feel some kindred bond towards them. She did not. On the contrary both Thomas and she found this continuing Puritan evolution sinister, to say the least. Instead of taking on a mantle of saintliness, conversely Bessie saw them now like spiteful crows making ready for to raid the songbird's nest.

When Charles took over the throne, a rift between King and government soon began to open up like an infected, festering wound. On his regular business trips down to the City of London, Thomas also experienced this Puritan voice now vocal in people of power. He soon came to observe that certain Members of Parliament openly expressed their latent dislike for the new King's obvious penchant for popishly elaborate religious rituals, which they blamed largely on his marriage to his French Catholic Queen. Others, not of the Puritan persuasion and with no obvious religious axe to grind, were equally vocal in ridiculing the King for his continued interference in costly wars in Europe and in particular over his choice of political advisors. However, the majority shared in one deep-seated suspicion that the Sovereign might be open to persuasion to return the realm back to the old Roman religion. As a result, a deep feeling of uncertainty and fear began to permeate through every layer of society. From the peddler on the street corner to the Lords of the Manor, all were filled with such an un-easiness that had not been felt since the dying days of young King Edward, the ill-fated son of King Henry VIII. The present monarch, in his arrogance did little to quell such worries. Quite the reverse as by the year 1629 he had simply decided it easier to shut down Parliament altogether than to listen or reason with it and so opted to rule alone instead.

However uncertain the politics of the country or how shifting the sands on which it was governed now balanced, these years and the following decade would prove the sweetest of all for Thomas. Free of obligation to politics, Thomas enjoyed running his estate and indulging in the company of his wife and two growing children. Sweet years too for his wife Bessie, as the their love for one another grew stronger with each passing year as they settled into middle-age together in happiness and prosperity, especially with the income from the family's plantation holdings in Virginia.

Young James grew from a quiet, bright infant into an intelligent, studious boy and at fifteen was sent off to Oxford University to study Law. Meanwhile, Hope grew from a precocious and overtly adventurous little girl into a breathtakingly beautiful young woman. With her dark eyes and exotic looks she soon ambushed the heart of many a young man who saw her, yet she steadfastly refused the advances of any. At first, James appeared oblivious to his adopted sister's charms but by the time he was approaching his final year at University, and after many long absences from home, a deep understanding was fast developing between them.

However, by early 1640 after ten long years without Parliament, elsewhere in the country discontent was rapidly swelling up like a pustule fit for erupting into an all-consuming infection.

The first reason being that the King now too had male offspring who were fast approaching manhood, making ready for the day one would inherit the throne.

The other was that without Parliament to grant him money, the King had been forced over time to find other ways to raise funds, mostly by implementing ill-liked taxes and extraordinary measures which many regarded as not only unjust but as downright unlawful. One such man who was opposed to these was Baron Francis Willoughby of Parham, brother of the late Lady Elizabeth Hickman and so uncle to Willoughby Hickman, who had been named in honour of this maternal family. Little could the friends and relatives now gathered at Gainsborough Hall have known that Parham would soon feature heavily in the turmoil set to befall Bessie's and Thomas's home county of Lincolnshire.

From the walls of the dark wood-panelled dining room, Lady Rose and Sir William looked down intently at the small clutch of family and friends. It was a pleasant finale to the pleasurable day that Bessie and her husband had just spent at Gainsborough Hall. It did her heart good to see Willoughby so happy and contented as he entertained his guests. She also knew that much of this was down to the influence of his loving wife, Bridget. Marriage and fatherhood obviously suited him well.

Having consumed their fill of a course comprising of Scotch collops, Dutch pudding, brawn, boiled onions, carrots and a novelty dish of potatoes, followed by syllabub and gingerbread, the small dinner party soon settled down to chew over the juicy morsels of gossip Parham had already served up from his recent visit to London. There was a lot to digest, not the least being what the outcome of it could mean for them all. King Charles, Parham reported, had finally seen fit to recall Parliament.

'They do quite shame themselves in their derision of the sovereign!' Parham remarked. 'Most aspire to be gentlemen yet many are not. Take one Member of Parliament called Cromwell, for example, he's but a loud warty mouthpiece! He calls himself a gentleman yet he does not handle himself as such, nor does he attempt to curtail his rough tongue in His Majesty's hearing. He is but a farmer sat in Parliament!'

'Bearing is not the be all and end all, is it? Remember Captain Smith was also but a farmer's son...' Thomas joined the dinner table conversation.

'Come to that, so are you Sir Thomas!' Willoughby teased.

'Maybe so, but I should hope that those who know me would say that I conduct myself with dignity...' Thomas retorted with a hearty laugh.

'Which is something I have heard none accuse Cromwell of!' Parham scoffed. 'Nor would I make my Sovereign grovel when he comes to Parliament to make a reasonable request as their King. Instead Cromwell and his cronies set out to bate him like a bear... They would give him money.. all the money he asked for...but only if he agrees to their programme of radical reforms.'

'And will he?' Thomas asked.

'I do not think so. His patience visibly grows thinner by the session. Some of the days I have spent in the House you could slice the atmosphere and butter it for supper!'

'Is it really that bad?' Willoughby asked his uncle.

'Yes. And no one seems to have the vision to see beyond this impasse. That, I find to be the most worrying aspect. We may all be like blind men edging slowly towards an abyss.'

'Then there is all this rumour that we may find ourselves in a civil war?' Bessie enquired grimly. 'Surely it will not come to that?'

'Surely I fear that it must!' Parham answered. 'If the dogs will but keep baiting the bear then, I am afraid, he must surely snap and turn upon them. The problem is, who shall end up with the worst mauling?'

'So, hypothetically, should this dreadful talk of a possible Civil War became a reality, am I to understand that you as a noble would fall his side, Uncle Frances?' Parham's reply came as a surprise.

'No, most certainly not, Willoughby! I am a Puritan, besides which I have found myself opposed to his Majesty often enough these past few years. Especially when it has come to the levying of ship money and fighting the Scots! I may not care much for the likes of Cromwell, but all in all, I think Parliament is right to try to rein in this wayward sovereign a little. 'Tis just their brutish manners and method of employ I cannot condone.'

'Then what of you, Thomas?' Willoughby posed the difficult question. 'You were once part of the Separatist congregation here in Gainsborough and all but harried out of the country by King James. Yet, you returned and received a knighthood from him. So, if King Charles called on you to join with a Royalist Army, would you join with him? Or take up arms with like-minded Puritan reformists?'

'Do not forget, the same might be asked of you too, Willoughby. Your family is Puritan yet King James knighted your father also... However, in answer to your question, I think that I might. I am not a political animal, like Francis, as you know. Yet, even if I were, I would find it hard to go against the rule of the land, which states that the King is our Sovereign Lord, and anointed as such by God. Therefore, if he be such a bad King then he will answer for it in Heaven. Therefore, I do not see what right I have to question God's given order? As for siding with Puritans? Your Father and Grandmother were saints to our congregation when we were in great peril. We might have all perished without their interventions! However, when the Puritan Council itself met it did not choose to side with us when we stood up to the demands of the Anglican Church to conform. We wanted many of the same reforms as its members. We were even applauded for our stance by them. Yet, instead of standing up with us to be counted, they chose instead to slip back into the shadows and to let us be persecuted out of the country. Therefore, I do not see why I should stand with them now!'

'Strong words, my friend. But casting aside any religious differences that there may have been in the past and considering that now we Puritans are standing up to be counted, as you put it; what if the monarch in question is a tyrant? Or a murderous madman who is intent on needlessly sacrificing loyal subjects to death on a whim. Or one like Bloody Queen Mary? Do you stand by and watch your country suffer?' Parham asked.

'Yes. I think we must.' Thomas argued. 'We might not bow down to their demands if they clash with those of our conscience but to take up arms against them is treason. All that stand must fall in time and I believe God in his own way ultimately passes judgment on the tyrant. After all, look at the protracted and painful end that bloodied Queen met. No, I believe negotiation must ever be the only weapon raised against this our Sovereign and the resolute belief that reason will win out in the end.'

'What of you, Willoughby? Will you fight alongside your Puritan uncle?' Bessie asked.

Willoughby looked up towards the twin portraits of Lady Rose and Sir William hanging on the wall. He did not need much time to consider his answer.

'I hope I would do that which my father and grandmother would council, if only they were here. I would not allow my soul to be enslaved by my Sovereign but neither would I openly oppose him. Nor would I jeopardise my family for mere consideration of my position, property or above all - money. I would render unto Caesar that which is Caesar's. However, I agree with your husband as I do with my uncle, up to a point.

Yet, it is a point beyond which I would not tread on either side of the argument. If civil war came, and I earnestly pray that it does not, then I for one would try to defer from taking sides. I would not join with the Royalist faction nor would I join with Parliament's. I would not wish to take up arms against my fellow man but would quite prefer instead to hold my estate as neutral territory.'

'And if a wounded soldier of Parliament came bleeding to your doorstep?' Parham asked.

'Then I would see that his wounds were tended to.'

'Would that not then be seen as treason by the King?'

'I would vehemently argue not so!' Willoughby calmly replied. 'For does not the Bible command us to love our enemies? And doth not the commandments of our God take precedence over all else? Come to that... do they also not say 'thou shalt not kill?'

'And yet name me one sovereign who has not done so? Maybe not in direct deed, I grant you, but who hath commanded killings to be done at their behest...' Parham argued.

'So 'tis as many arguments begin...all about money or God?' Bridget broke in with a smile. 'Then it appears that we must all agree to disagree...and as my husband said earlier...earnestly pray that it does indeed not come to war or else it appears that we, like many other friends and family, may find ourselves divided and upon opposite sides...'

'And say we go to war and the Royalists win out. What then of the Parliamentarians who took up arms against their King?' Bessie's question took away any levity from the discussion.

'Then they may all well be hung, drawn and burnt as traitors, My Love...' Thomas pointed out the dread likelihood. 'For is that not the prescribed consequence of treason?'

'Surely not! Surely the King would not stand by and execute half the country?' Young Bridget was quite shocked by the prospect.

'No...' Willoughby assured his wife. 'I am certain the King would not vent his anger against the common man led astray by the persuasion of his lord. I do however expect that he would seek retribution against those in command of this rebel revolt. They, I am certain, will receive harsh justice and the most severe punishment.'

'And if the supposed conflict should go the other way?' Bessie posed the equally distasteful proposition.

'Then he must bow to Parliament.' Parham replied.

'And how precisely does one make a King bow?' Bessie pressed further.

'By negotiation, by reasoning...'
Bessie seemed to have hit a raw nerve.

'And let's say, Frances...the King chooses not to recognise the authority of Parliament over himself? What then?'

Parham seemed reluctant to answer her question.

'Yes, what then?' Willoughby too was eager to hear his uncle's answer.

'Then...' he said solemnly 'we declare the King a traitor to the state and....'

'Execute him?' Bessie had pushed Parham into admitting to the extreme. She, unlike some others, had followed the argument through to what she feared might be its unnatural conclusion.

'At a last resort, yes. The King would face execution.'

Bridget gasped in disbelief.

'Would that not be the best course of action for the Parliamentarians to take in any case?'

Parham seemed more than irritated that a mere woman might have concluded this action so far in advance of events. He shrugged his shoulders and pretended not to understand.

'If Parliament's army were to lose a civil war then the King would have its leaders executed for treason. If Parliament's army wins and the King agrees to negotiate a peace, what is there then to stop him from bringing them all to trial at a later date for treason.' Bessie pressed.

Parham still did not answer.

'I suspect nothing...' Willoughby concluded. 'Nothing at all.'

'Then the only real option for Parliament would be to kill the King and replace him with the Prince of Wales?' Bessie observed.

'Not necessarily...' Thomas replied. 'There is one other option...to declare England a republic. A republic like ancient Greece or Rome.'

'A republic! Now there is a thought!' Parham rallied. 'Though I do not believe there is any real intention of' replacing the King with a republic...it is just hoped that the mere threat of it might be enough to make him see reason. I know how Parliament works! Believe me!'

However, Bessie did not believe Parham. It was obviously an appealing scenario and one that Bessie could not believe he had not already considered at length, no matter how surprised his expression was now.

'By replacing one King with a house of five-hundred, do you really believe things will alter for the better? Do you think tyranny will be less tyrannical? Injustice less unfair?' Thomas said coldly. 'I, for one, have already had experience of living in a petty republic in the New World. One where a council of little kings has replaced the rule of one big king. Each one with his own agenda, each one forcing their will on their subjects and mostly to their own end. I earnestly pray that it is put to an end there and shall never happen here!'

The room fell silent and expressions pained as if all the rich food had caused an outbreak of indigestion.

'Enough of this gloomy talk!' Bridget tried to revive the earlier lightness. 'Let us walk Bessie, and look at the changes I intend to make to the apartments.'

Bessie smiled and rose to her feet and let Bridget lead her out into the corridor while the men folk stayed quietly behind. Thomas helped himself to more brandywine while the others charged up their tobacco pipes.

Parham stood by the open fire warming his back on the flames.

'She is no dullard, Thomas, that wife of yours,' Parham remarked. 'Yet, be warned! Intelligence in a woman is a dangerous thing. And that woman of yours is wilful with it.'

'She has had a good example, Francis!' Willoughby joked as he lit a taper from the fire and handed it to his uncle. 'She was a protégé of my grandmother's, didn't you know!'

'Ah! Well then. There you have it!' Parham retorted looking straight up into the steely eye of Lady Rose's portrait. 'Maybe 'tis best that you never cross her, Thomas!'

With that, the tension broke sending laughter echoing out down the hallway to catch the ladies up.

'That sounds better.' Bridget said as they turned towards the tower suites. 'At least they are laughing together again.'

'Yes,' Bessie replied. 'They should enjoy laughter and each other's company while they may. I fear time for laughter might be close running short...'

'You are right, of course. None of us know what may happen tomorrow. Even without all this talk of war.'

'I was so sorry to hear of Mildred's death.' Bessie said sombrely. 'We were both so sad to hear the news.'

'Willoughby was quite distraught. She was always the baby of his family. To not yet be thirty and gone. It makes you realise, does it not, how fleeting our time here on earth can be and how we must treasure each new day that arrives for we are never to know who will next take their leave...'

After their tour of the apartments, Bridget showed Bessie to her room for the night and bade her a good night's rest. It was already late as Bessie started to undress, expecting Thomas to come soon to retire to bed. She was not vexed though when he did not but was instead pleased that he was enjoying the company of other men. The tenseness of the times had not lent themselves too much socialising of late. Besides, she was quite enjoying sleeping in the same tower bedroom that she had once shared with young Lady Frances. It was so cosy and welcoming, slipping into the canopied bed, snuggling up under the fine crimson eiderdown to sip the creamy sack-posset brought up by a maid as a nightcap. So cosy, in fact, that she soon fell blissfully asleep...

*   *   *

Bessie and Thomas returned to Stowe with much on their minds to discuss.

'Are you not afraid of taking up arms in a civil war, Thomas?'

'Twill be only like going hunting when we were in America.' he casually replied.

'Hunting was killing out of necessity for the pot. This will be warfare, Thomas! What will you bring home for the pot from that? A man's soul drenched in his widows tears? An orphaned babe like Hope?'

'You make too much of this! Besides, it will never come to anything like that!'

'You think not? Were the men who did that to Hope's mother not also gentlemen? Not so very different from the men you will find yourself mixing with as a Royalist?'

'No! They were different! They were affected by the wicked malignancy endemic to that place. Behaviour like that would not happen here.'

'You are a fool Thomas if you really believe that is true. They were but men with their blood got up just the once too often. The same could happen here easily...' Thomas would not at once answer for fear he might lose his temper. He could feel his head beginning to throb.

'So...you really do mean to take up sides with the King?' Bessie continued.

'Why, yes! Did I not make myself clear last

night?' Thomas snapped.

'Yes, but that was said in company as hypothetically or 'mayhap'. What one says in polite company does not necessarily mean the same as what one truly intends.'

'Well, when I said it, I meant it Bessie...'

'But what about the estate Thomas? What about your family...and me?'

'You will be fine. My mother managed the estate alone until I returned so I am certain you can too. After all, Ned will be here. He will look after things.'

'There was not the possibility of a civil war going on about her when your mother was alive.'

'Bessie. Stop! What do you want me to say to you? That I will not go to support my King if asked? For if that is so, then you will carry on wanting. I will not be found shilly-shallying like Willoughby. My world is black and white not shades of grey as in his. I shall go with the King if called upon and you shall do your duty to me as my wife...and look to our interests in my stead.'

'But why Thomas? Why support the King over Parliament and our Puritan friends?'

'Because that way lies treason, Bessie! To take up arms against your sovereign is punishable by death. So, win or lose Parliament is hung! And I for one would rather keep my life and my estates intact!'

'What choice do I have in this? I am only a woman. Choices in matters of such gravity are the privilege of men. As you are so quick to point out, 'tis but a woman's duty to obey her men folk. But heed you this Thomas. Behind every honoured man there may be a woman permitted perhaps to bask in the reflected light of his glory. Yet, behind every condemned man stands an equally condemned woman. I might not take up arms against Parliament yet I will be dealt with as if I had. Heaven forbid, but any punitive action taken against you will be metered out to your family and me too. It has always been the way of it!'

'Punitive action? You talk as if the King is but a

mere commoner! He is sovereign master of this realm! What power do you think these Parliamentarians really hold? Only that which the sovereign allows them! He has proved this repeatedly by dismissing Parliament at a stroke. And yet, you talk as if the dog can whistle to the master! Yes! The King has taken certain advantages in raising the taxes that parliament denied him. Perhaps maybe he has even stretched the laws of the land to do this. Yet, what at the end of the day can Parliament do?'

'They can remove the King.'

'Remove the King! As I have said to you before. There is no question of Parliament doing away with the Sovereign over a few extra taxes.'

'What of King John and the Magna Carta? The nobles of this land came close to removing the King then, did they not?'

'I think not. 'Twas a show of strength. An empty threat, if you like, to rein the monarch in and to amend his ways in law. That is all and it achieved its aim. And that is all I think will happen again. At worse the King might be minded to comply with a similar petition that will then come into our law.'

'What if this is not simply about admonishing a wayward King? What if this is about Republicanism? What if these rebels are malcontents, unwilling to rap the King over the knuckles then to return quietly to their seats in Parliament? What if they are set upon a course to abolish the monarchy altogether and this talk of reformation of our churches is but a guise? What then of all you who have followed the King? Will you not also be seen as obstacles to this end? Obstacles to be removed from the equation along with the sovereign?'

'Bessie, why do you not listen to Parham and me? These hysterical fears of yours will not come to pass! Trust me. All will be well!'

Bessie wanted to trust him. Yet, only a fool is to place their trust in someone who has no control over that which they presume to promise to deliver. However much Bessie might not want her husband to go, she also knew in all good faith that she would not dare stand betwixt him and his conscience. Whatever it was he chose ultimately to do, then as a dutiful wife she would abide by his wishes and try to make his choices easier for all to bear. Yet she knew also, if pressed, then she too had a duty to follow her conscience and her God. No matter what her husband bid.

*   *   *

'Father!'

Thomas was overjoyed yet surprised to hear his son's voice.

'James! When did you get back from Oxford?'

'I came up yesterday but as you and mother were away and I was so exhausted by the journey, I chose to sleep in this morning. Father...I need to talk to you. It's important.'

'Don't tell me you plan to give up your studies?'

'No. No, Father. That is the last thing I would do. It's about Hope...'

'Hope?'

'Yes, Father. I have discussed this, at length with our most respected tutors in both Divinity and Law and see no impediment to my marrying with Hope. Even though we are so obviously of different blood, they say we are one in Christ and therefore can see no just cause or impediment as to why we should not marry. Except of course...your permission father. Hope has made it plain that she will never marry without both yours and mother's blessing.'

'Hope? Marriage? This is a bit sudden, isn't it? And you are not even come of age yet?'

'I know father, but, I beg you. I love her now and I have done for ages. Nothing is going to change that...'

Thomas naturally looked towards his wife for guidance only to find that she was already smiling knowingly.

'I see...' he said sternly turning his back on his son as he walked towards the window. He stopped by it, deep in thought as he looked out at his estate stretching away into the distance.

James turned towards his mother and was

about to speak to his father again when she gestured him to wait a moment. Bessie knew her husband well.

'This, of course will be all yours one day, James,' Thomas finally spoke. 'You are my only son and sons automatically inherit their father's lands. Yet, there is also my land in the New World and there is Hope. I have often wondered what would become of her after I am gone and how I might bequeath to her and not some greedy husband, that land as her birthright. I suppose if you did marry Hope, then all my worries would be at an end because my grandchild would inherit both. Yet you two are still so very young...'

James's head drooped in disappointed only to quickly rise as he caught his father's closing words.

'Very well,' he said 'I suggest that we compromise and set the wedding date for your twentieth birthdays.'

'Oh Father!' James ran over and hugged Thomas. 'You do not know how happy you have made me!'

'I do, James,' he replied, 'I do.'

Chapter Eleven

'The true beginning of our end...'
- William Shakespeare

August 22nd – 1642

The unthinkable happened. At the height of a summer boiling with tension, King Charles I set up his standard at Nottingham and formally declared war. True to his word, Parham rejected his King's summons to join the Royalist Army and instead took command of a horse regiment under the Parliamentary commander, the Earl of Essex. By the following January he was made commander-in-chief of Lincolnshire.

Equally true to his word, Thomas rode away to join the Royalist cause despite Bessie's desperate pleas. Though both sides still hoped that outright war could be averted, or at least decided on the outcome of just one decisive battle, it was not to be. Soon the English Civil War had begun and up and down the country, friend soon found themselves facing friend, across opposite sides of the battlefield.

*   *   *

Thomas returned home briefly from his garrison in nearby Newark. Winter was upon the land and therefore not the season of choice for campaigning. James also was home, having been summoned by his father to take a temporary leave from his studies.

'I am here by special dispensation,' is all Thomas would admit.

'Special dispensation for what?' Bessie quizzed.

'For Christmas.'

'But our family does not normally celebrate Christmas. And besides, if special dispensation for one then why not for all to be with their families that do!'

'Not all have a wedding to go to.'

'A wedding? What wedding?'

'Yes. A wedding! With our country on the cusp of war I would like to celebrate Christmas by seeing my children wed.'

'But James has no intention of going to war as you have heard him pledge.'

'That may be so. But I am. I am pledged to go to war and some of us are therefore bound to die. Who may say that I will not be one amongst many never to see Christmas again? If I must die, then I would like to go with an easy mind that my estate here is settled. And that cannot be until James and Hope are married.'

So it was, that the banns were posted and Hope and James would duly become man and wife.

*   *   *

There had been a hard frost the night before. It was a bright morning but a cold one with the mud sloshed roads now firmed up enough to make for an easier passing. Never the less, Bessie was reluctant to risk the carriage so instead had Ned saddle up her grey mare, Filly, so she might more easily accompany her husband into town.

The ride was pleasant and a rare opportunity for husband and wife to enjoy each other's company once more in an everyday pursuit. They soon reached the sandy warrens where Gainsborough lads could often be seen rabbiting with their dogs and ferrets. As they made their way along the road into town beside the marshy strand by the river, Bessie was surprised to come across newly completed bulwarks thrown up around the south approach to the town and even more so then to be stopped and questioned by armed militia men. It was quite unnerving for she had not encountered men so blatantly bearing arms since the pair had lived in Jamestown.

'Good day Sir.' A willowy man of good bearing advanced upon the couple.

'Good day to you too.' Thomas replied. Looking about and gesturing with his gauntleted hand he asked, 'And pray what is all this wood and works about, my dear fellow?'

'You do not know? Then I must beg to ask from whence you are come and what be your business here with the town, Sir?'

'I am come from my farm in Stowe with my wife to buy ribbons and lace for our daughter's wedding gown.' Thomas answered calmly.

'From so near and yet you did not know?'

'Has been a wet autumn Sir and the filthy roads not fit for riding so we have kept much to ourselves about our village of late. So? What is the reason for these works? To keep us villagers out or to keep you Townies in?' He quipped.

The militiaman relaxed and smiled broadly.

'Maybe so! The people of Gainsborough have decided not to declare for King or for Parliament. Instead, we wish to remain an open town. As such, we feel duty bound to throw up these defences to see off any rovers that might threaten our freedom. However, I do not somehow think that you and your good lady wife fit that description. So, you are free to go upon your way,' he said seemingly satisfied.

Thomas and his wife rode on passing by a small company of men practicing arms nearby. Once out of their hearing, Bessie dared asked.

'You knew they were there, didn't you?' She had studied his face well.

'Yes. I had heard rumour but I needed to see it with my own eyes. 'Tis no secret to me that Gainsborough has declared itself neither for King nor Parliament. However, at the end of the day, that decision may be taken out of the hands of the townspeople.'

'Then you are not only here to see our children wed as you would have us suppose, but to spy once more for the King. I could feel you counting their weapons Thomas!'

'Gathering intelligence, Bessie. Not spying. Simply gathering information that might lead to my living that little bit longer. Our forces straddle both here and North divided from each other by water. The Parliamentarians and their Eastern Alliance lie to the east. A garrison of Roundheads in the town could wreak havoc with our lines of communication to the North Country.'

'So you are planning to take the town forcibly for yourselves?'

'My Love, make no bones about it. For if we did, we do no less than the Parliamentarians will. Are you so naïve to think that they will come meekly to the checkpoint and ask 'pray let us in?' Better by far we do this with as little loss as possible than wage full bloody battle over it.'

'It would not come to that, would it?'

'Madam, I assure you it could. If they were to get a firm foothold here then there would be very little to stop them from taking control of the whole county. If we do, then we would harass their Eastern Alliance mercilessly and press our presence here to the fullest advantage. Either way, Gainsborough is of strategic importance to both sides and I fear it cannot escape that consequence, no matter how they choose to declare themselves.'

Bessie was stunned to hear Thomas address her as Madam. 'Twas not her husband talking but the verbal swagger of a lapdog gone feral after a few short months away from its leash with the pack animals. How could he talk so coolly about making attack on their Puritan friends in the town? Besides, had he not always been the one expounding to her that it would never come to real warfare. That instead, this civil war would prove no more than a brief show of arms followed by Parliament backing down. Yet, since being garrisoned at Newark his talk had changed most sinister. His attitude, which now seemed to relegate her views as subordinate to any other, was hard to accept. 'Twas as if she were to be but a bystander with no say in what part she should play in this war? Had he forgotten Jamestown and the horrors of the warfare he had witnessed there with the naturals? Or was he still under the illusion that somehow fighting amongst his own people might magically prove less painful. She was at a loss to understand this change come about in her man and not certain how to respond to it.

They continued into town with a head full of

dread scenarios for Bessie to carry about the market. Thomas's powerful words kept burrowing through her brain as she scoured the market trying to keep her thoughts upon her daughter's wedding needs and away from what conflict the future might hold. As she tried to shop around, Bessie watched the ruddy-faced townspeople about their everyday business and wondered if they realised how easily their mundane lives might soon be shattered. Least among them, her own.

No sooner had James and Hope wed than Thomas was away once more with an undignified haste. Like an old dog on the scent of something exciting. James tarried for a week or two more before making his way back to University at Oxford. The parting this time proved even harder for Hope to endure than before. For this time she was bidding farewell not to her brother, but to her husband and lover too.

*   *   *

Winter was dying at last. Everywhere green March shoots were breaking forth to herald the resurrection of the countryside. Around St. Mary's, the Lenten lilies were fat with yellow buds fit to burst open. A scattering of perfect, white, new lambs gambolled at the heavy fleeced sides of their mothers up and down the pasture. Bessie's cherished hens were back in lay a-plenty and the milk from the cows tasted creamier by the day. 'Twas as if nothing was amiss in God's green country yet soon all was about to change.

Bessie was in the dairy churning butter as Ned came hurrying into the house to tell her that Gainsborough had been taken by a Royalist detachment.

'Word just passed through the village! They do say that they surrounded the town at daybreak this morning, demanding that it should instantly surrender to the King. The townspeople panicked and did so without any further resistance or argument.'

'Oh my goodness. Then it is really begun. The war is coming to us!' Bessie cried.

It was a small comfort to hear that the town had

fallen so easily. At least if Thomas was there then he was unlikely to have come to any harm. Yet, what of his assertion that the town was far too valuable for either side to hand lightly to the other? With the town of Newark garrisoned by Royalists, Gainsborough now afforded the only other good crossing point over the Trent open for Parliament to take for their advantage. What of the Eastern Association, which was known to be growing in strength daily? Would not the Roundheads be itching to both take the town and defend its eastward positions, she thought?

*　　*　　*

Thomas took up a billet in Silver Street. He had been amongst the strong party sent out from the Newark garrison to capture Gainsborough town. His intelligence gathering had proved most useful to the Royalist cause that day.

It felt odd to him to be in a town he knew so intimately as one of its 'conquerors.' A town barely six miles from his home in Stowe yet now beyond a far greater divide. After all the years under the yoke of marriage and responsibility, he had forgotten how much he had missed living day to day among the company of other men. It was like being a footloose bachelor again in the newfound arms of a mistress, the army. She was a spell binding harlot and as many a mistress does, she beguiled her gentlemen into forgoing the tried and tested comfort of their wives, in return for the lurid thrill of the chase and the excitement of embarking upon adventures new with one's peers. 'Twas betrayal indeed fit to wreck many a marriage and to sorely put to trial many more - Thomas and Bessie's for one.

Morale amongst this Royalist Gainsborough garrison was high and their cavalry officers, matched by their cavalier attitude, strutted about the town as bold as painted cockerels. It was not an attitude set to endear their cause to the townspeople. In fact, friction between the two began to build quite quickly. Mistrust was especially felt towards the common soldiers suddenly thrust upon the townsfolk. Only a few years before, King Charles had quartered three troops of guards in and around the town during his war with the Scots to the north. During their stay, there had often been trouble and a rash of crimes committed by some of their lowly number. Not the least of them being the rape of a young woman.

Old feelings of resentment lay like poppy seeds in the Gainsborough ground. It only needed the disturbance of this one upheaval to bring them forth from out of their dormancy to spring up anew in unexpected places. Old scores ripe to be settled under the guise of patriotism began to be settled. Ordinary families, often their only 'crime' was being known as Puritan sympathizers, were systematically harried and some even ordered out of the town for refusing to swear an oath of allegiance to the King. Even the Lord of the Manor found himself under gentle pressure to show for the Royalist cause.

'So you still will not come over to the side of the King?'

Despite Thomas's pleadings on behalf of the Earl of Kingston, the new town commander, Willoughby Hickman refused to be swayed from his previous stance to take up arms against Parliament.

'It was the decision of the people of this town to remain neutral,' he reminded Thomas, 'and one I hoped your commander might deem fit to recognise.'

'Yet those very same townspeople buckled like hay stalks and surrendered Gainsborough up to us!'

'In ignorance and fear, indeed they did. For when the dogs snarl, they put the rabbits to flight. However, tell your commander this from me, that I am neither ignorant nor fearful! You may march in here like a pack of hounds but do not think you will have the run of it all for good! Meantime, we God-fearing people of Gainsborough do still protest most strongly that we be acknowledged as neutrals in your dealings with both Parliament and us. For by going against our wishes and garrisoning yourselves amongst our town folk you put us all at a peril not of our making.'

Thomas had expected no less from his friend and so instead moved on to question of supplies for the army.

'And our commander's requisitions?'

'Again, I know that if I do not comply with his 'requests', then your commander is likely to take what I have anyway. I know this as his officers have already done so amongst the families they have forced themselves upon. We will hold up a tally and when all this madness is over, we shall bring it to our King to account for it all. Meanwhile, tell Kingston that I will make food and supplies available for his disposal. For God commands us to love our enemies as our neighbours. For in truth, are they now not proving to be one and the same? Besides, did not the Bard, as you are so fond of quoting, not say that 'the robbed who smiles steals something from the thief?'

So, it was that for the time being at least Willoughby Hickman and Gainsborough were spared the sack of the present victors.

While garrisoned at Gainsborough, Thomas took part in a number of daring raids. In league with the Newark forces, they freely ranged the local countryside and harried nearby towns. Attacks upon Market Rasen and Louth were just two such goading thorn pricks in the Eastern Alliance's iron sides, working their way under the skin and fast beginning to more than niggle. It was time for these to be grasped by their Royalist's shafts and pulled out and cast aside on the ground, one by bleeding one.

*   *   *

July 1643

Bessie threw open the widow to the blessed cool night air. She was flushed hot. So very hot and so bone-achingly tired. As she made her way back into her lonely bed she could hear a cockerel already beginning to crow outside. She felt cheated. Cheated of sleep and cheated, in her middle age, out of her husband by this callous King. What cared he of her and the countless other wives suddenly stranded in their lives without their menfolk? What was it to him if they never came home again but a temporary gap in his ranks or a drop in revenue by way of his lost taxes? Yet to her and thousands like her, their future happiness, their future survival lay in his majesty's none too careful hands. She thought back to the last time she took communion at the church. How she passed by the brass plaque on the cold stone wall as she waited to take up her place at the rail with the other weep-weary women. How she had read the sad epitaph to Amy Burgh and her family etched in finest script upon the dulling metal. Amy too was now at rest beneath the cold flagstones of the floor. Safely asleep beside the remains of her long-dead husband. Yet, although her son John's name too was inscribed upon that commemorative for the whole world to read, his body was missing from the grave.

Bessie remembered how it had been on that day, many years before and barely a year into her friendship with Amy. How she had dropped everything to dash to Stowe Hall to be at her side on hearing the dreadful news. What do you say to a mother who has just lost her child? To lose a child to the vagaries of life, to a myriad of waiting infections vying to snuff out tiny lives, is pain enough to bear. Yet, to have come through all that, having seen her precious little one through such dangers and reared him up into manhood, what do you then say to the mother who has then to see her son sacrificed in a futile game of war? 'Tis the children that are missing that you notice the most,' Bessie remembered Thomas's mother saying to her once. 'The silence of their absence is deafening,' she had said, 'enough to drown out the throng of their remaining siblings.'

There is nothing on this earth to compare to a true mother's love or to the grief of a mother for a child she has lost.

'Oh Amy! I came as soon as I could!' Bessie had run all the way to Stowe Hall to try to console her friend. Amy Burgh had looked up from Bessie's warm embrace with such a haunted look. Her eyes were swollen and red as were her lips too, as if in the grip of a terrible cold on that bright January morning.

'My John has been dead for quite some time, yet how could I not know?' she cried. 'All the while we were making merry at Christmas and chattering about looking forward to his return, his body was already rotting in some stinking French pit.'

Amy snatched up the letter, officially informing her of Colonel-General Sir Richard Burgh's courageous death.

'I should be proud, it says here... Proud that my son died a noble and valiant soldier whilst in the service of His Majesty...'
With that, she broke down in tears once more as Bessie did her best to comfort her grieving friend.

'A valiant and noble soldier?' Bessie cursed under her breath. 'More like a pawn given up by his King on a whim!'

Then, as time passed by the dreadful truth slowly seeped out. Charles had been meddling in games of kingship once more. This time with Louis, King of France. Advised by his Catholic Cardinal Richelieu, Louis had rekindled the flames of religious war in his country once more by declaring war on its Huguenots. This provided Charles with an excellent opportunity to gain the support of his own wavering English Protestants by mounting an expedition to the town of La Rochelle to liberate the now besieged Huguenots within. For this, he needed to capture the Isle of Rhé, which controlled the approaches of La Rochelle.

However, at a crucial point some months into the valiant campaign, with the English desperately short of supplies, King Charles suddenly diverted away the precious funds set aside for the urgent relief of the expedition. He instead had decided to use the money to buy artworks for the royal collection that had unexpectedly come onto the market. As a result, thousands of noble and valiant soldiers like John Burgh were sacrificed in vain on that foreign land, never to return home to their loved ones. What a curse to be a soldier's mother and to see your precious man-child put to death so easy.

Now the King was about playing with loyal lives once more, casting them aside like lost pieces in his game. He was gambling with all of their futures now and for what purpose? For this regal eagle to puff out his chest to prove what a great bird he was? While all about the little birds sing in fear.

Bessie slipped back into sleep, only to wake in the morning like a cup already half drained. She made her way down to the kitchen and lit the fire ready to start over a new day's chores. Chores that seemed never to be completed now Thomas and so many of the men folk were away fighting.

Ned popped his head around the kitchen door to bid his mistress a cheery 'good morning' before making his way across the yard to the tool shed to fetch out his scythe. Bessie quietly thanked God that Ned was not among those gone away for she did not how she would have managed without this family's faithful old retainer. He was a good man. A simple man yet nobody's easy fool. He could always be relied upon for good common sense thinking, though he slurred his words though a lazy drawl.

As Bessie set about mixing the dough for yet another day's bread, Hope soon wearily joined her by the fire to take in an herbal before setting out into the yard to tackle a mountain of washing. The evening before Hope had cleared out huge bucketsful of wood ash from out of the kitchen hearth and tipped them into a great close-weaved filter basket above a vast to make lye water ready for dissolving grease and grime from the linen.

Now it was morning, she piled all the washing into the lye water vat and left it to soak for a while before she went off to feed the hungry chickens and collect up their precious eggs.

'I am about to leave my dough to prove, Hope. Shall I come and give you hand?' Bessie said wiping the flour from her hands.

Hope was relieved to hear these words.

The two set about paddling the linen in the sunshine with battledores to pound out the dirt. They laughed and chatted to make light of the chore yet still it was utterly exhausting. It was the one odious task about the farm that proved every much as burdensome even when shared with another woman.

While her mother returned to the kitchen to knock back the dough and to shape it into loaves, Hope started to ring out the bed sheets and set them out to dry. Soon Bessie returned, just in time to help spread out the load over the hedgerow to dry. Poor Hope's hands were chapped painfully red by the harsh lye water. They bled from tiny new cracks between her young fingers so Bessie stopped and picked some heads of lavender to make up a soothing hand lotion.

As Bessie made her way back along the paddock side, Filly whinnied gently and raised her head momentarily in a gentle nod of recognition as she grazed on the lush new grass. Then, slowly flicking her long grey tail, she plodded over to the fence and began to fondly nuzzle with her mistress's waiting hand. Bessie teased out her mane with her fingers and gently stroked the horse's velvety nose before turning to make her way back up to the farmhouse. Filly's dappled grey head hung sadly over the rail watching as Bessie then walked away. It was as if she was wondering when, if ever, her mistress and she might find time for riding out together again. The pasture, though green, proved poor compensation for company.

Bessie was starting to cook up some breakfast when Hope suddenly rushed into the house to fetch the laundry basket.

'My, my but you are in a flurry!' Bessie remarked with one eye on the weather outside. 'That linen cannot possibly be dry already?'

'No mother! It is not,' she said breathlessly. 'But I can hear thunder in the distance so the rain cannot be far away.'

'Rain? Surely not! 'Twas a clear blue sky not five minutes since!'

Bessie went outside into the yard to see for herself. Sure enough, it was a beautifully fine July day without a hint of cloud in the firmament. Yet, as she turned to speak to Hope, she too heard the low rumble in the distance. She heard it and in a flash thought back to Jamestown.

'That is not thunder, Hope. I recognise it. It is cannon fire! Run quickly and find Ned.'

Hope immediately did as her mother said while Bessie ran upstairs to see if she could see anything from out of her bedroom window. She heard the boom again and shielding her eyes from the sun with her hand, she saw a pall of black smoke rising up in the distance.

Hope came running back into the courtyard below with Ned and his son Titus too.

'You hear it, Lady Elizabeth?' He shouted up to her.

'Yes,' she replied, 'It is cannon fire. And I can see smoke, Ned. Lots of black smoke coming up from Gainsborough way.'

'God, have mercy, Mistress! God have mercy on us all – it must be a battle going on.'

'Oh Ned! Do you think Sir Thomas is there?'

'Well it takes two sides to make a fight, Mistress! And if them Parliamentarians are there then so must be the Royalists too.'

'Cannons fire alone does not make that sort of smoke, I am certain. Something must be on fire. Something big!' Bessie exclaimed.

Then an awful thought occurred.

'You don't think it could be Gainsborough Hall, do you Mistress?'

'Oh Lord!' Bessie felt sick at the thought. Almost as much as to think that her Thomas might be in the thick of the fighting. What if he was? What if the Royalists were routed? What would then halt the Roundheads from swarming that way?

'Stay there Ned! I am coming straight down.'

Bessie said.

Bessie went to the casket hidden under the bed and dragged it out. Almost everything they had of value was in it, her pearls, money and deeds. She tried to pick it up and carry it but it was too heavy. So, she dragged it out onto the landing and called down to Hope to help her bring it down the stairs. She trusted Ned in most things but was simply obeying her husband's orders. He warned her that should she suspect that the enemy might be coming that way then she should bury the casket out back of the house where no one else would see. Especially none of the servants. The two women left it hidden beneath some linen under the kitchen table and then went back outside to the men.

'What shall I do Mistress? Do you want me to ride into town to see for ourselves what's going on?'

'Won't that be too dangerous Ned?'

'Only if we are foolish enough to get too close. And that we are not! I can get some of the lads in from out of the fields to come wait up here with you. As protection. If you wish?'

'Do you think we will need protecting?'

'I really do not know Mistress. I have never been in this position before!'

Hope suddenly rose up her apron to her face and began to cry in terror. Bessie hugged her tightly.

'It is all right, my darling. It will be all right. If it is soldiers then they are far from here. Ned will go see and come back. If we think something bad is coming this way then we will simply run out into the hedgerows and hide. Just like you used to do when you were a child.'

As indeed Hope had as a little girl. She had once fashioned herself a hideout, deep inside the bushes by scrambling her way in and weaving all the branches together like a willow-work basket then fallen asleep inside. Several frantic hours had passed by before her worried parents and a search party had happened upon her.

Hope lightened a little and dried her eyes. She

knew her mother was right. Bessie would make certain nothing bad would ever happen to her.

'Yes Ned. If you are certain of your safety, please then go and look. But before you do, please send word out around the estate so the workers can prepare themselves, just in case.'

When Bessie was certain that Ned had gone, she strode off towards the tool shed. She soon returned carrying a stout spade in one hand and some sackcloth in the other.

'Go back inside Hope and bring me the silver candlesticks. Fetch anything else you can think of that is valuable too. We will wrap it in this sacking and bury it and the chest near to the May tree yonder. No one will notice us digging there!'

Within minutes the task was done. All that remained now was for the two women to wait.

Several days more of smoke and cannon fire way off in the distance passed by. Ominously, neither Ned nor Titus had returned. Rumour circulated about Stowe that there was a bloody battle in the town. However, none had dared venture near for fear of coming betwixt the two fluid lines of fire. Bessie began to fear for faithful Ned and his son. She felt an awful guilt well up inside her because she had encouraged them to go. Albeit at their own request, she had selfishly known inside that she was willing them on to do so, just so she might have word of her husband. If Ned and his son had lost their lives through this, then it was all her fault. She had encouraged them to leave the safety of their home and family to do her bidding. How could she ever face Ned's family after that if the two did not return alive?

Thankfully, Bessie was to be spared that grim task as the two returned the following day.

'Was it The Hall on fire Ned?' Bessie was so impatient to know that she started her questions before poor Ned could get down off his horse.

'No, Lady Elizabeth. The Hall is safe! In fact that's where we have been holed up these days past!'

'Then pray tell me what's happening...'

'Twas cannon fire, all right! Lots of them!' Ned reported excitedly. His eyes were wide inside his grimy old face as he told her all about the events in Gainsborough. 'First the Parliamentarians had taken the town by complete surprise! Their General Willoughby of Parham marched in as bold as you like and just seized the town with barely a scuffle. But it weren't to be for long, Mistress! The Royalist forces came back to try to drive him out again. Then more Parliamentarians came to Parham's aid...cavalry too ... with an Oliver Cromwell at their lead.'

Frances and Cromwell - side by side! That seemed strangely ironic to Bessie.

'Well, both sides are desperate to hold onto the town,' Ned continued, 'what with the port and the river crossing and all making it a gateway to the North...'

'And so whose was that cannon fire we could hear?'

'Royalist. Ca'ndish came first with his men but then the Earl of Newcastle followed on down and took great satisfaction in playing his cannon over the town from the top of the hillside above. He brought with him a massive force and is driving the Parliamentarians back out of town. They in retreat, them cowardly Roundheads!'

'And Sir Thomas? Is there any news of the master?'

'Yes, Mistress. I have seen him with my own eyes!'

'And is he well?'

'Yes, Mistress. He is unharmed and bade me to tell you the same and how you are not to fret for him. He was at The Hall, the north edge of town when the Roundheads arrived so he was able to escape by horse and get word to Ca'ndish. He says that he will write to you as soon as he can and that you are not to be afeared. I also heard him saying to the steward there how he was of the opinion that the war would now be short lived and how he was looking forward to being home again shortly.'

'So the Hickmans are safe too?'

'Yes, though it was madness all the time Titus and us were there. The Hall was full of wounded from both sides and townspeople caught up betwixt the two as they battled. Hickman's kitchens have been baking bread around the clock to try to feed the multitude of frightened people sheltering under his roof. And all at his own expense mind...'

'That was very kind of him...'

'Clever too if you ask me.'

'Clever?'

'Yes, Lady Elizabeth. Clever! Hickman must have realised from the start that his old pile could not withstand but one cannon strike before caving in like a house of straw. Nor one spark before burning to the ground like tinder. I think it was a well thought out strategy to take the stance he did. Letting it be known from the start that he would throw open his doors to the dying and wounded from both sides and administer to them equally. After all, who is going to open fire on such a saint? Especially if some of your own men are helpless inside?'

Bessie had not thought of that before and had to concede that it was as clever a tactic as any Lady Rose might have employed.

Bessie insisted Ned return to his family that night and not keep a watch from the barn as usual. It was the least consideration she could offer Ned's wife after all the worry she had been forced to endure during his absence.

Night was fast falling. As Bessie sat by the kitchen table picking over a trugful of raspberries, something pale streaked across the periphery of her vision. She jumped up and ran across to the window to look out.

'What is it Mother?'

'Nothing...it's nothing. Just a trick of the light I expect,' she said scanning the lengthening shadows of the courtyard. Whatever it was, if anything, there was no sight of it now so; she went back to stirring the mutton stew in the cauldron slung over the fire.

'Shall I go and fetch some more wood?' Hope volunteered.

'No, you take over here and I will go out for it. I could do with a breath of fresh air.'

Bessie grabbed her shawl from the chair back and wrapped it around her shoulders before stepping outside. There was a definite chill in the air that evening even for July. She had travelled not half the distance to the wood store when suddenly a great number of horses galloped into the courtyard. They were hot and sweaty and snorting great plumes of misty breath. Their Roundhead riders, fully armed, looked wild and hunted. Perhaps they were but a detachment lost or separated from their main party. Whichever, Bessie soon found herself surrounded yet boldly stood her ground and refused to be intimidated.

One man dismounted, obviously an officer of sorts. He removed his helmet and made his way over to her. He was stockily built and very plain, bordering perhaps on ugliness some might say. In all, an unexceptional looking man apart from his eyes. Those piercing eyes held fast their gaze upon Bessie like limpets. Even the clothing beneath his armour, as she would later see, was simply adorned and unpretentious as well as being somewhat soiled. Though someone, somewhere must have loved this man, for one sleeve of his red coat had been carefully darned. Unless of course he had sewn it himself. Perhaps he was a tailor by trade?

'Good Evening to you, Good Wife.' He politely greeted, yet his manner seemed brusque to say the least. 'Is your Master at home?'

Bessie's simple dress and apron must have belied her position.

'I am Mistress here!' Bessie replied curtly for she did not care for his manner. 'And no, my husband is not here. He is away...'

'I beg your pardon, Mistress. Only I had been led to expect a gentleman's household and not that of a yeoman farmer. All to the better, though! For back home I am a farmer too.'

Bessie neither denied nor confirmed his assertion.

'We need shelter for the night, Mistress...these barns and outhouses will suffice...' he pointed across the courtyard, 'and food for my horses and for my men. I am empowered by Parliament to commandeer all that I might for our needs but I trust I shall not need to enforce that...'

'No sir, you will not.' Better, Bessie thought to play the willing host rather than to give these Roundheads the excuse to make away with whatever else she had. She had been warned before that should matters come to this to expect looting.

Suddenly, some unseen commotion broke out from amongst the Roundheads at the rear as a man was jostled and manhandle through their ranks and forward to the officer. It was a shaken looking Ned, come to his Mistress's aid.

'Do not hurt him!' Bessie pleaded, 'He means no harm. He is but our headman, acting in my husband's stead for when he is away on business. He is only doing his duty in trying to protect me!'

The officer gestured for the old man to be left alone.

'Tis all right, Ned,' A cool-headed Bessie subtly prompted her man. 'These gentlemen are staying with us for the night. Perhaps you can help to assist them with their needs?'

Ned nodded readily like any respectful servant yet Bessie could read the concern for her in the dear man's eye.

'As I was saying,' Bessie continued, 'there is plenty of hay and feed in the stables. Ned will show your men where. As for food? I will see what my daughter and I can provide for your men but 'tis a goodly number of mouths to feed at such short notice. I have plenty of cheese and half a large ham. And a good many eggs too that we can boil but I fear there is only a little bread to go about. I have a pot of mutton stew ready for my daughter and myself that I might gladly share with you and any officers that you see fit to come dine in the house.'

'That is most generous and shall come as a veritable feast. If you hand over the vittles to my lieutenant he can pass them out about the others. That way I shall keep my men out of your way and away from the house as much as possible. I can assure you, there will be no looting. As for dining with you? I would be delighted to. Mutton stew is one of my favourites at home and I have not been home for a long time now'.

'So 'tis just you then? Very well then.' She said. 'I will show you through to the parlour where you might make yourself comfortable whilst I see to the preparations.'

Bessie called Hope down to the kitchen to help her prepare the food ready for the Roundheads. When all was done, Hope disappeared back up to her room with her supper.

'Shall I lock myself in, Mother?' she asked.

'No. Their officer has given me his word that we shall not be interfered with and I think we can trust him to honour that. Even so, should you hear anything happen to the contrary down here, then lock yourself in and scream out from the window for Ned.'

Bessie returned to the parlour to ask her guest to come into the dining room. As she entered she found the officer thumbing through the pages of one of their books he had helped himself to from the shelf. It appeared to be one he found of extreme interest.

'Tis a strange book for a yeoman farmer?' He said holding it up while marking his place with his thumb. 'A volume by Captain John Smith? I have read all of his books. Does your husband have an interest in the military?'

'He has an interest in the New World.'

'Indeed? Has he been there?'

'Yes. We both have. In fact he was commissioned to make drawings there for Captain Smith.'

'You? You have been to the New World? When?'

'In sixteen twenty. I sailed to New Plimoth aboard The Mayflower.'

'The Mayflower? So, you were one of the survivors?' He seemed amazed. 'That must have been a dreadful time for you in the colonies. Were you hoping to make your fortune there?'

'No, Sir. We were with the Separatists...'

The officer's stance softened, as did his tone.

'Then you have my admiration, dear Lady...' he said kindly. 'My admiration for the courage of your conviction.'

He stayed and chatted quite courteously with Bessie as they shared supper together in the dining room. Hope remained mostly out of sight upstairs. Exhausted by the day and polite conversation, Bessie then began to clear away the supper plates into the kitchen. The Roundhead surprised her by helping, then he lingered while she stacked the crockery ready for washing in the morning. It was as if he did not intend to let her out of his sight.

'If you will excuse me now,' she finally said, ''tis almost dark and I must away to my bed.'

'Then if you might kindly show me to mine...'

'Yours Sir? I am afraid I have no room spare for you!' She exclaimed. 'Besides, what rumour would spread abroad amongst your men? That their commander spent the night in a house with two un-chaperoned women? I have my reputation to think of as you do yours!'

'Quite rightly so! I humbly beg your pardon.' He seemed embarrassed. 'You are, of course right and I had not meant to cause you offence.' He said picking up his helmet from the kitchen table. 'I bid you goodnight and goodbye, Mistress and I thank you for your Christian hospitality. My men and I shall be gone before daybreak.' With that, he left and Bessie soundly bolted the door shut behind him.

She lit a candle from the last embers of the fire and made her way up the creaking stairs to her bedroom. She stopped to look in on Hope. She was sound asleep.

Silently she made her way across the darkened landing and into her own bedroom. She got undressed and into her nightgown and made her way over to the bed. After kneeling down to say her prayers, Bessie snuffed out the candle and slipped between the sheets.

Suddenly a hand reached out from the blackness and clamped about her mouth.

'Shhhhhhhhh!' A man's voice whispered in command. 'Do not make a sound!'

Bessie's heart pounded. The man then loosened his grip a little, trusting her to stay quiet. In the darkness, Bessie reached out towards him chancing her hand against the hard steel shaft of his musket, already primed and ready for action.

'Is there anyone else in the house?' He asked.

'No, Thomas!' She exclaimed in hushed tones. 'But you know that there are Roundheads camped here, don't you? They are all in the out buildings and I have the doors downstairs locked and bolted against them? How on earth did you get in?'

'Yes, I know they are here!' He said making safe his firearm. 'I guessed some were retreating this way and I needed to be certain that you were safe! I must have beaten them here by just minutes. I wasn't sure that I had though. That's why I came in unannounced. Besides which, if I had let you know I was here, then you would have had to lie to them if asked about my whereabouts. I did not want to put you in any more danger by risking you being tripped up by a lie. I know how badly you do that!'

'You must be hungry?'

'Yes, I am starved... And stiff'

'Stiff?'

'Yes, I have been hiding under the bed in case they decided to search the rooms or worse...Then I heard the back door slam too and you start to make your way up here. Then to have to lay here and listen to the rustle of your skirts as you let them slip to the

216

floor... well... 'tis enough to make any man stiff!'

'Thomas!' She wondered what had gotten into her husband. For a man nearing his sixtieth year he was acting like a spring tup.

'Can a man be glad to see his own wife?' He whispered as he let his hands wander across her matronly frame.

'Hush! Stop this silliness or we will wake Hope up else! Let me go fetch you some food!'

Bessie slipped silently downstairs in the dark and gathered some bread and left over stew from the kitchen. By the light of the big bright moon now shafting in from the windows, she fumbled for a mug full of last autumn's home-pressed cider. Then she crept back upstairs to her bedroom with it. Thomas was already stripped to his shirt and under the blankets. His boots and breeches were carelessly strewn across the floor making her passage to bed more difficult. In the dark, she half tripped but luckily, Thomas almost snatching it out of her hands saved the meal.

'I am ravenous!' He said tucking in heartily. 'This is a meal fit for a King!'

'Why? Do they not feed you in this army of yours?' She said curling up beside him on the bed.

'Some. But no-one cooks like my own Bessie!' He quickly cleaned his bowl, threw it down on the floor beside him and took up the cider and gulped down a large mouthful.

'Or makes cider and beer like you. My but I am a lucky man to come home to a woman of your ilk!'

'How long are you here for?'

'That very much depends on our company down there,' he said nodding towards the courtyard below. 'But my guess is that they will want to be out of here before first light. Before our men have a scent of them again!' He took another drink and drained the mug dry. Then he dropped that to the floor too.

Bessie was certain he would wake Hope up and cause her alarm though it was clearly the last thought on his mind right then.

'Anyway, I am going nowhere fast until they do! So...let's not waste anytime' he said pulling her down onto the bed and prising open her thighs.

His hands were rough and callous as they rubbed across her still soft skin and he smelt of stale sweat and horses. His cider lips were quickly pressed so tightly to hers that she felt that she was being smothered. As he ripped open his shirt and cast it aside, she felt the hard contours of his chest and stomach start to writhe against her body. The middle-aged paunch he had sported for so long was now gone, replaced by a much honed down physique more akin to how he was when much younger. Roughly, he grappled with her nightdress as he drew her knees up and aside to make his entry easier. All the while his open mouth pressed hard against her lips as if to silence any residual resistance. Then he rode her hard and fast like a stallion, all the way home. Within a minute or two, he was done, dismounted and rolled over onto his back. All this without so much as a word, other than the long low inaudible groan as he had ejaculated deep and longingly inside her with some great relief. Bessie felt confused.

Soon Thomas was sound asleep while she lay silently wakeful beside him, perturbed by her husband's reinvigorated lovemaking. Though she had found it unexpectedly enjoyable, Thomas's whole demeanour had descended into something quite different from that of the husband she thought she had known these past decades. She lay in the moonlight watching Thomas at sleep there beside her and wondered what the future would hold for them. Wondering when he got up to leave, as she knew he must, if they would ever lie there together again. Maybe this was the explanation for his eagerness to make love to her. Maybe he too had asked himself that very same question and taken his pleasure with her while he still may.

Bessie realised that their marriage was fast becoming like the sea passing over the shore. Each time they were parted, it was never quite the same on Thomas's return as it had been on Thomas's leaving.

Their relationship was turning into sands in shift, as wave after wave of conflicting emotion washed over them. Dashing their feelings this way and that until both were in danger of no longer recognising each other. Yet through all, Bessie's unfailing sense of duty towards her husband stood resolute. She may no longer have understood him or at times liked his stance, yet she remained constant in her love for him and in the belief that once this awful conflict was at an end, then they might find happiness in each other's arms once more.

Bessie eventually fell into a deep sleep and roused from it again to find Thomas crouched low beside the window peering out into the dawning light. The sound filtering in of metal striking against cobble and the jangle of bits and stirrups were sure signs that the Roundheads were preparing to ride out.

'I could easily hit him from here.' Thomas whispered, training his musket upon the unguarded back of a now mounted Roundhead. Just one shot and he would be dog meat! Such a pretty quarry to bag yet with you and Hope's safety to consider, I have no choice but to let it pass by.'

'Whom are you talking about?'

'Him! Their commander there!' Thomas pointed his target out, 'I could kill him easily but then they would storm the house and kill me in revenge. Still, it is a pity. Cromwell standing within musket shot and I have to bide my time and watch him ride away.'

'Cromwell? Where?'

Bessie scrambled over beside her husband to look out at the object of his obvious loathing. It was the same officer that Bessie had entertained to supper the night before. She could hardly believe it was true.

The two watched intently as a silent file of infantrymen suddenly filled the lane. Then the cavalrymen fell in behind them and rode off, heading towards the direction of Lincoln. Within moments the yard was quiet once more, as the sun slowly began to rise.

'You have to go too, don't you?'

'Aye! Very soon I must.' Thomas replied. 'I need to report back the Roundheads position though I expect I will shortly run into my men already on their way in this direction.'

Bessie watched helplessly as her husband pulled on his breeches and thigh high riding boots, put on his sword and take up his musket once more.

'Shall I wake Hope? I know she would want to see you.'

'No, Bessie. 'Tis hard enough to have to take my leave of you as it is, without a crying daughter too. Let her sleep. And when she wakes give her the biggest kiss from me and tell her that her father loves and misses her.'

Bessie followed Thomas down to the stable. He went to saddle his horse but Bessie could see it was still exhausted and lame in one leg.

'You cannot ride that poor beast. You will kill him! What happened to your own one?'

'Dead, I am afraid and this is the only horse I have! Horses are in very short supply just now on both sides. I am surprised they didn't steal yours!'

'Then you take her!'

'What?'

'Take Filly.'

'But she is yours. I cannot...'

'Yes you can! She is strong and surefooted, as you well know. And all she does is pine all day to be out riding. Take her. I want you to have her. That way it will be as if a part of me is with you too.'

Reluctantly Thomas took Filly from the paddock and threw his beaten saddle across her. Soon he and the horse were ready to go.

'I will be back again as soon as I can. We have these rebels on the run. We will drive them all the way back to London in defeat and then I expect we may all be home for Christmas and this folly put to an end for good!'

However, Thomas's optimism that the war would soon be over was ill-founded. In October a great

Parliamentarian army of some six thousand men, under Manchester, Fairfax and Cromwell marched north from Boston to wreak their revenge upon the Royalist County.

*   *   *

'It's a dead barn owl!' Hope watched Bessie lift the poor limp creature from out of the trough.

'It has broken its neck, poor thing!' Her mother said breaking off from chopping up firewood. 'Flown down and crashed into the ice. Most likely lured to its death by the moon last night. It was so bright I could swear it was day when I looked out late.'

'Were you not sleeping again, Mother?'

'Not well. No need for you to fret though! 'Tis nothing but bone ache. It comes to us all with age and this cold plays upon my body merrily this time of year!' She rallied swinging her axe cracking into another upended log and splitting it through.

'Should we not call James home from Oxford to help us out more?'

'We should do no such thing! He came for the harvest and that was more than well enough! James must finish his studies Hope! Then you shall both be set for the future. It is what your father wishes. And more importantly – what I wish for him. Besides, what is there for me to do this time of year apart from fetch wood?'

'We could sit and sew at baby linens.' Hope smiled.

'You? You are not already with child?'

'Yes.' Hope replied sheepishly. 'I very much think that I am!'

'Oh, my!' Bessie said excitedly. 'When?'

'I have not seen the curse for two months now... so Midsummer I should think.'

'Oh Hope!' She said hugging her daughter. 'Here we be at almost Christmastide with all this talk of a baby coming! And now this? 'Tis such wonderful news my darling. Wonderful news!'

Christmas was indeed near, just a few days away

in fact. That is why the arrival of bloodied men in the village and the rumble of cannon fire in the distance hit home with even more horror. Royalist infantry swarmed down the narrow lanes of Stowe in chaos snatching up what supplies they could as they scurried through with the enemy in hot pursuit. A ragbag straggle of battle ravaged men fleeing for their lives.

Bessie hurried out with all the bread she had in the house, broke it up and handed it out amongst the beaten rabble as they hurriedly passed by the farm gates. As grateful souls snatched it from her hands, she asked if any knew of her husband. Some replied that they did but in the confusion could not say if Thomas was dead or alive. By all accounts, there were many dead in Gainsborough town and many captured too.

Later, when the Royalists had passed through, angry Parliamentarians looking to summarily punish any found aiding and abetting their enemy in retreat suddenly besieged Blackthorn Farm. They raided the outhouses and looted the barn. Bessie ran out and screamed hysterically at the soldiers who were snapping the necks of her chickens and starting to make off with them. Suddenly a cavalryman rode into the yard and shouted at his men to desist and saying that this was a farmstead that had sheltered their beloved Cromwell in the past and so was to be left unmolested. The soldiers immediately dropped their booty and made off to the next unlucky homestead caught in their path.

Bessie dropped to her knees in the feather strewn yard and wailed. What had happened to her husband? Why was he not among those passing by?

*   *   *

A few agonising weeks later the letter arrived. Bessie immediately recognised Thomas's fine hand, though it appeared a little less neat and a lot more hurried than it used to be in the past. Yet, that was quite understandable considering the circumstance.

'I did not stop. I did not want you, my family, to see my like that. Before it was different. Then we were the ones routing the enemy and chasing them down.

This time it is they who put us to flight. We were running in defeat through our neighbourhood. Like foxes being run to ground by those wretched dogs. Besides, what if I had stopped. What if I had come into the farm for one last fleeting embrace with my wife and they had followed? I have seen it with my own eyes what they do...what even we do to collaborators. When you have stood by and watched a comrade you ate breakfast with cut in half by a cannon ball by lunchtime, or ridden through the streets with an inferno all about you and musket fire and sword stroke, all aimed with the one intent of ending your life, you too would want to strike back at the heart of the enemy. And if you find their loved ones in your path, better still to vent your anger upon them too'.

When I came home before, it was hot in pursuit of the retreating Roundheads. I had come to you little realising the death and destruction that lay behind me in Gainsborough that day. It was not until my return that the bloody enormity of the truth sank in. Brave Cavendish was lost, shot in the head then run through by a sword as he lay on the ground so that within two hours he was bled out despite our best efforts. Roundheads too lay slaughtered in number yet, as I looked about, it was those innocent townspeople who had suffered the most. The guilt and shame of it all must lie squarely with our two armies. First, we came in and made demands upon then, knowing how they begged to remain neutral. Then The Parliamentarians came and destroyed many buildings in routing our men, especially with fire. Though not in possession, they too took from the townsfolk to provision themselves before being rooted out by our Earl of Newcastle, who then in turn took great pleasure in playing his cannon upon the town for good effect and with ordinance and mortar, again setting fire to parts of the town. Yet still the townspeople refused to obey and the military treated them with scorn and ignored their pitiful pleadings. Now Parliament has returned in force to attack the town by cannon from their boats in the river so we are driven out once more. Again the town is a fire and its innocent people needlessly slain amid rumour that the rebels aim to slight its strongest buildings and raze the town so that there will be nothing left for the future to be put again to our advantage. Yet, neither side stopping to consider that these were family homes and livelihoods being wantonly destroyed. Not castle strongholds or fortresses. Yet they care not whom they caught up in their crossfire. Women, children, it made no difference to either commander. As I escaped, Gainsborough was burning with many of our men surrendering to the enemy. Puritan or not, I fear that even Willoughby Hickman may have lost The Hall. More so, if word were about that he was lately elevated to Baron by way of recompense for such losses already endured'.

'I am not a proud man any longer, Bessie. Indeed, I am humbled when I think of you and your wise words warning me it would come to this. Yet, would I listen? So blind in my self-righteous indignation that a woman might hold a firmer grasp upon the realities of what was about to unfold than I dared imagined. I so wanted to be right. Yet, as things played out, I was not. You were right, my Bessie. You were always right. So, now I beg your forgiveness'.

'No soldier chooses to campaign in winter and none really expects to. Yet, I tell you, these Parliamentarians get a plan into their heads and they ride with it, no matter the season or the difficulty. They seem to have a determination that many on our side would relish to have imparted to our own men. This Cromwell of theirs is a cunning fox and to give him full due, quite brilliant at times. And with Meldrum, this time showed true determination to oust us from our garrison at Gainsborough for good.

I am here once more on the road with my Sovereign's Army in the cruel depth of winter when I curse that I could so easily be sat in front of a roaring log fire in my home with you. Now? Now I am obliged to see this bloody thing through to its conclusion knowing that there can be no coming home for me again until this war is won or my broken dead body is hopefully returned. I am sorry. So very sorry, my lovely for all I have put you through. I love you more than I can say and ever will – Thomas.'

Chapter Twelve

'... And he smelleth the battle afar off, the thunder
of the captains, And the shouting.'
- Old Testament, Job

After two long years of seemingly futile battles,
the country was wearying of Civil War. The conflict
had only served to tear the country asunder, setting
friend against friend and often family members against
one another. Each side of the schism claiming God to
be on their side. Each side indulging in unholy acts
of barbarism. As the fickle pendulum of 'success'
continued to swing wildly betwixt the armies yet still
there seemed no end in sight...

*   *   *

The roof shook as a giant thunderclap boomed
overhead and ricocheted through the house. The dark
Eastertide sky had suddenly blackened and erupted in
sending a shattering of heavy hail down, scattering its
away across the bare yard like a ripple of fallen glass
beads.

'Did you hear that?'

'Yes and you shouldn't be hurtling around the
place like that in your condition!'

'The thunder was so loud! Do you remember
what Grandma would say when she was alive whenever
it thundered when I was little? That I was not to take
heed of it as it was only the angels up in heaven moving
God's furniture about.'

Bessie smiled. She did remember. She missed the dear
old soul.

'Tis hard to plant out betwixt these heavy
showers,' Bessie said wearily, 'and with such a long
drawn out winter behind us, we are already sorely
behind on the spring sowings'. Bessie made her way
across to the deep kitchen window sill where she had
set her precious potatoes to chit. 'Still, if it clears up
enough later I might at least get these planted out in
the garden, if not they shall have to wait till Monday to

be fitted in amongst the heap of chores I already have for then!'

The weather did clear to herald a bright afternoon when Bessie indeed managed to plant her potatoes. It was a crop she was proud to admit she always had success with where others still often failed. Maybe it was the fact that she could appreciate the difference in climate betwixt their native habitat of the Americas and cooler damp of England better than nearby farmers did. She had mastered timing their planning and knew to protect the lush young shoots from lingering May frosts by earthing them up well as they grew. It was becoming an ever more useful crop to the farm and one that rarely was pillaged.

As afternoon quickly ran out, Bessie sat on a bench by her garden at the end of a newly planted row and considered this job well done. Birds chattered in profusion as the dying sun flickered through the pale green strands of the newly clothed willow beyond the courtyard wall. The melancholy 'wha-whoo-whoo, wha-whoo-whoo' of a collard dove calling for its mate, cooed loud above the warble of blackbirds and thrushes singing somewhere off in the bare branches of the sycamores. They were yet to bud, and bore only a slow climb of green ivy to cover up their spring nakedness.

Bessie rose up stiffly to go into the house. The May bush might have been out in flower but a stab of icy winter's chill still lingered on in Bessie's heart as she faced the prospect of yet another coming summer without her husband by her side. It was so hard now managing without him. Indeed, without the other labourers who had gone away to fight. Bessie had made it clear in her management of the estate that she would make no distinction between their tied labourers regarding which side they had chosen to go and fight for. Instead, she assured all the women and children left behind would be found work fit to their purpose around the estate and that none would go hungry under her care. It was a far more generous stance than many other landowners had taken. There again, Bessie had worked on the land as a peasant and knew all the hardships that losing the man of the household entailed. She opened her heart to her tenants and let them in, which made them love and respect her in return. How could they not? A titled lady who would hitch up her skirts and work the fields alongside them. Often stooped low with sickle or arched high with a hoe in her hand she was at an age far beyond the first flush of youth yet still working on from daybreak to dusk regardless.

As spring slowly turned to summer, news from Thomas began to dry up like the little beck that trickled close by to the house. As the fruits on the apple trees began to swell, so now had Hope. By the time James had briefly returned from Oxford for haymaking, Hope had given birth to their baby son.

*   *   *

Bessie broke the seal and opened the letter immediately. Once read, she could almost smell her husband's scent on the parchment as she held it to her face and kissed it. Then she placed the open letter close to her breast and thanked God for the news within it. It had been almost two months since she last received word from Thomas. Two months of hearing gossip of fierce clashes between the two warring factions and snippets of news rippling back along the line through the network of Royalist families in the county. Each, like her, had husbands, brothers or fathers away fighting with the King. Each like her, not knowing from day to day and to hour if their loved ones had survived the latest onslaught.

'A letter? From James?' Hope was sitting in the parlour, nursing baby Thomas in her arms and spied it as her mother made her way in.

'No. It's from your Father, though there is word of James. Here,' she said immediately proffering it up. 'Would you like to read it for yourself?'

'I have only just started to suckle him,' she sighed looking down at her tiny new son, 'and I think he will howl if I were to distract him now.'

The new baby was proving to be a difficult feeder.

'No mind,' Bessie smiled. 'I shall read it to you instead.'

Bessie sat down on the ornately carved settle, drew up a cushion into the small of her arthritic back and began to read the letters content aloud.

'Oxford ~ First Day of November, in the year of our Lord, 1644.

Dearest Bessie,

I hope that this letter finds you in good spirits, my love and that by the grace of God, in good health also.

I am sorry it has been so long since last I wrote but we have been in such a game of cat and mouse this past season with those wretched rebels during which, we have had a good run of getting the better of those rag-bag traitors. However, our most recent encounter almost ended in disaster. We found ourselves in such a situation that, were it to have gone against us, it could quite easily have put an end to our Army at a stroke and led to the King's surrender to Cromwell. Yet, I believe none other than God Almighty Himself delivered us up from the evil of that ugly warty-faced toad of a Devil's familiar.

We were camped at Newbury, in the county of Berkshire when we were taken by surprise. The Parliamentarian intelligence had found us and before we knew it the Roundhead hoard was in spitting distance of us up on Clay Hill to the east. We knew we were too badly outnumbered to face them out on the field so, instead decided to make our stand at Donnington Castle and defend ourselves as best we could against the attack which we knew must surely fall upon us the following morning.

Poor Filly had been lame and not then yet fully recovered. So, I left her in safety and being a sound shot, proceeded to dig myself in with the King's Musketeers. We took up defensive positions as best we could. Some like myself, made good advantage of the moat while others where dotted about the still blooming rose gardens. I remember thinking clearly, that it would have been a beautiful setting for anything other than slaughter.

I tell you; sitting out that night in the cold October air, I heard not one word of complaint pass the lips of any of my brothers in arms. Though we were preparing to defend ourselves against impossible odds, I witnessed not one faint heart amongst them.

Numbers are not everything, many reasoned. For were we not the more superior in valour and experience? We were seasoned veterans each worth at least three of their sorry men.

We were men of nobility, courage and honour and what were the Parliamentarians? Nought but a rebel rabble of farm workers and peasants in the command of traitors to the Crown who would be executed when justice prevails and the King is victorious? Then there was the King himself. I tell you, Bessie; in his shining plate armour, he looks so positively Christ like stepping out to face his opponents. It is a sight to truly inspire.

On top of all this, though it may be strange for you a woman to comprehend, we felt lucky. Yet, to temper this, there was also a streak of realism amongst our ranks. Some of our numbers set about supper, defiantly eating the best of their rations, determined that at least, should they fall, then they would do so in the knowledge that the enemy were not going to get the chance to choke on their particular spoils. Others, like me wrote letters to loved ones in the hope that if killed, then our comrades would see them home to our families. I still have mine safely in my pocket, Praise the Lord.

Morning came and we readied our weapons and waited. We waited dry mouthed knowing that any moment the enemy would attack from the east. The waiting, that was the part of it we found almost intolerable to bear. I grew increasingly restless. We were all restless. We just wanted to get on with it and to die if we must.

Then by noon, the terrible realisation had hit. Cromwell had split his army and somehow managed to march his men through the night, in a great arcing sweep behind us and were now taking up their position to our west. We thought we were done for. How in Heaven's name could we hope to survive an attack on two flanks? We had to admire him though, for pulling it off! We knowing very well ourselves how daring it was to move infantry by night and all the dangers that involved. The regulation sixteen feet long pikes are difficult to carry at the best of times as they hit overhead trees or can send their bearers piling into the ground, risking injury to comrades all around them. I know many of our own pike man risk heavy fines by sawing off the bottom few feet of their staffs just to try making them more manageable yet even then they hurt the neck, shoulders and arms terribly to be carried any great distance. Besides that, marching with pikes and packs, powder and guns is exhausting, so no wonder their army had made no move until this late in the day. Still, why should have Cromwell hurried himself in making ready to spring his trap? 'Twas not as if we were going to be able to get away. We were caught up like a neck in their noose.

Then, at three of the clock, we heard one of their great cannons fire. It must have been a signal from one half of the Roundhead Army to the other to let battle commence because within moments the rebel forces began to advance. First came their pike men who charged forward under a hail of our cannon fire and musket shots. The air was soon thick with acrid smoke and the smell of sulphur so strong in our nostrils 'twas as if the bowels of Hell had spewed out upon the earth. Watching their men horribly cut down gave me bad recollections. 'Tis no less awful to see bodies mutilated by cannon fire than it is by tomahawk. Yet, more unsettling than seeing their ranks falling in front of our eyes, was to witness them push on towards us regardless. They even marched on over the remains of their own shattered dead with the crack of bone being crushed beneath the heels of their boots. We fired on, reloaded and fired again repeatedly. Still they fell, yet still they came on until infantry was fighting infantry, hand to hand. I was forced to turn my spent weapon and so use it to club the oncoming enemy. Then I unsheathed my sword to strike out. I knew then it would be a fight to the death.

We put up the most impressive defence of any army ever assembled. Despite presumably being attacked from both sides yet, we amazed ourselves by continuing to hold out despite some heavy casualties. Still, the battle raged on yet still our forces refused to collapse. Then we came to realise that something was obviously going awry with the Roundheads' plan and prayed to God for that failure to continue. To our utter relief, our prayers were answered as night fell and the battle abruptly ceased as Cromwell's Army withdrew.

Then we began to understand why we had miraculously survived. Our lookout aloft reported that the commander upon the eastern flank had failed to move his army. It could be the only reason for this ingenious, simultaneous two-pronged attack to have failed! It seems incredulous to think that they had not heard the signal, nor sent out reconnaissance to see the state of obvious play. Our King, himself put forward the reason. He addressed we officers, saying how he thought that the commanders, be they commoners or more likely Lords, had come to their senses in realising the gross illegitimacy of their chosen cause and the grave consequences for the country should they allow their Sovereign to be defeated by common rebels. In short, that they had had some sort of divine revelation from on high demanding that they put a stop to this madness by thwarting Cromwell's plans for Charles ruination.

In any eventuality, one thing was patently clear. Come the new day, should Cromwell bring his two forces to order and fall upon us again, we would not be able to resist them much further. So, under the cover of darkness, we attempted to make our escape from out of the castle and to try to make our way back to safer territory. Incredibly, we met no opposition or hindrance at all. We did, however grow increasingly suspicious as we then reached the only bridge lying between freedom and us. It was the perfect spot for the enemy to swoop down upon us in ambush. Yet, as we cautiously began to cross over, it soon became clear that it had been left completely unguarded. And so we made our escape, thank God!

The King plans to winter us here, back at Oxford and to profit from the time by recruiting new men and training them up to be combat ready by spring. I have met up with James here and all is well with him, though he is angry that all study has been suspended for the time being as many of the students have signed up and the quads have been turned over for daily exercise. We have talked long and hard, him and I, both expressing our views freely upon the rights and wrongs of the current conflict. I know Hope and you will draw comfort that he still resolutely refuses to take either side in this civil War and asks that at the Winter break, if you might please, send Ned down with the cart to collect James and his belongings and transport him back home till this war be done. If it be possible, please send with Ned a new pair of hose, for mine are wholly darned beyond redemption. I would also be grateful for a cheese to carry in my saddlebag for when rations are wanting. I will try to hold on for him here.

James is grown into such a fine man now. Though I am disappointed that he does not feel that he can join in his father's stance in this matter, I am none the less proud of his steadfastness of conviction and consider him no lesser my son for doing so.

Well, my lovely. That is all I have to say for now, apart from that I love both you and my daughter and I will return, God willing, soon. ~Thomas.'

'James is coming home!' Hope exclaimed excitedly. Then she realised. There had been no mention of the baby in the letter.

'Perhaps the letters crossed,' Bessie tried to reason, 'or maybe it was a simple oversight on Thomas's part. You know what sieve-brains men can be like.'

Even so, Hope was still left feeling a little

disappointed that no mention was made of her new born son.

*   *   *

Surely, the King had intelligence? Surely, his spies had hotfooted it back to Oxford to report about the sweeping changes that Cromwell had made to the Parliamentarian Army? Not only had they also spent the winter in military training but Cromwell had completely reformed his troops into a New Model Army, complete with full uniform, new weapons and most importantly, new commanders. By Parliament's blessing the 'old guard' consisting of Members of Parliament and the ennobled had been swept aside to make way for new officers, promoted on grounds of ability and not favour. There could be no doubt from then on, as to where the Army's leaders true allegiances lay and therefore no shameful repeat of the battle at Newbury.

If reports of all this had been presented to the King, then nothing had swayed Charles Stewart to make any changes to his, other than to appoint his much favoured nephew in overall command of the Royalist troops.

'He is a fearsome man of courage and I have every confidence in him...' the King trumpeted. He was so confident in fact that he wrote home to his queen telling her that 'things had never looked so good!'

Thomas was not alone in questioning this wisdom. He feared that the King's confidence might better be served placed within several differing baskets. Rupert's forces might have been successful in the past but a few muttered that some victories of his had come about despite his presence and not entirely because of it.

By April, the last of winter was rapidly retreating and by early May both sides were restless to be on the move once more.

'So this is farewell for now, my lad,' Thomas gripped his son briefly in a manly hug. 'We have just received our orders to depart.'

'Where are you heading for, father?'

'North, James... well some of us are. Despite grave misgivings, the King has decided to split his forces. Half will head for the West Country while he with the rest will strike north towards home to rally support and reign in more recruits. I may even get to see your mother again shortly! But don't you go telling her that I said so son,' Thomas warned with a frown. 'No point in going rising up her hopes if only to have them dashed by the King leading us on somewhere else instead. Give her a kiss though. Ned should be here any day now to fetch you. I will draw comfort at least from knowing that you are back home to look after her. But don't you go telling her that, either! For I dare say she would straight way protest that she be well enough capable of looking after herself!'

'I will, Father.'

James hesitated, as if there was something else he had on his mind to say but not yet certain, perhaps, if he had truly the conviction to do so. Thomas sensed it, but did not push the matter. If his son had need to tell him something, he was certain that he would find the words to do so without his father harrying him into it. If it was important enough, then it would out, he reasoned, if not – then it was something of little consequence. To the end, Thomas was determined not to be like his own father, always coercing, always bullying to get his child to bend to his own will.

'Oh, and give my love to your sister as well...' he added

'And your grandson too?'

'Grandson? You mean?' Thomas had no idea. He knew Bessie wrote to him regularly but with no guarantees that any of her letters would get through the Royalist network of contacts that struggled to pass on such letters as best they could.

'Yes, father. Hope has had a baby boy... we have named him after you...'

'A grandson? Well, I'll be...'

'Grandfather...' James quipped 'You will be Grandfather Thomas - old man!'

With that, they hugged once more and parted.

The Royalist forces, with both The King and Prince Rupert at its lead, arrived at Market Harborough in Northamptonshire. They had not an inkling of where the Parliaments army might be. Imagine his men's horror when intelligence arrived that Lieutenant General Cromwell, in command of his New Model Cavalry and Fairfax with the New Model Army, were only about sixteen miles away and with a force of over thirteen thousand men. King Charles immediately called a council of war.

'I propose to turn and engage the rebel army...' Charles said calmly with a saintly countenance.

Thomas was stunned. Had the King taken finally leave of his senses? How could he hope to take on the full strength of the Roundheads with only one half of his army? Better, by far, Thomas reasoned, to continue north with all haste to try strengthening their depleted ranks and send for the rest of his troops before trying to tackle the rebels face on while still outnumbered.

'Sire! I beseech you,' Prince Rupert urged his uncle 'Take caution!'

A sentiment echoed by many others. However the King would not be swayed.

'They are still but a rabble of shoemakers and dray men,' he countered. 'Dress them up as you may! They are still no match for seasoned gentleman soldiers!'

For the first time Thomas seriously questioned both his sovereign's intentions and his own conscience. This was not a man acting under divine guidance so much as blind arrogance. While the enemy command might ultimately flinch away from actually harming the person of their King, they were nonetheless going to be intent on the wholesale slaughter of his followers.

'Does he really understand what he is asking of us?' Thomas argued inside. 'If he did, then he held their loyalist lives very cheap to risk throwing them away so easy...'

Thomas left the council with grave misgivings.

On the Saturday of the fourteenth of June, in

the year of our Lord sixteen hundred and forty five, the two armies met near the village of Naseby. From opposite hilltops, Christ and Antichrist prepared for Armageddon in the valley below while a disillusioned Thomas no longer knew the difference between the two. The tipping point in this war had been reached...

*   *   *

Thomas lay shivering in the ditch with his boots full of stinking water.

'I shouldn't be here at my age!' He cursed to himself, 'I should be at home in front of a fire dandling my grandson on my knee. Not out here like this – dying! God! Please. Not alone out here like this!'

His back was soaked through where it had lain exposed to the heavy dew and the shroud of smothering thick mist now up to the top of the bank edge above him.

'It must be nearing morning,' he thought aloud to himself, though he could not tell for certain.

He was right about one thing though. This was no place for a man to be lying low like an injured animal hiding from a pack of baying hounds. Especially not for a man of his advancing years.

Thomas summoned up all his strength and with his good arm reached up and tried to grab a hold of a clump of sedge to haul himself up above the grassy parapet. It was useless. It just slipped through his fingers like a handful of cold grease. Besides, even he had managed to hold onto it, the effort would have proved futile. The left hand side of Thomas's body was all but useless. There was no way he could have clawed his way back up the bank.

He glanced down at the raggedy arm of his bloodied blue jacket. He could see through the shredded sleeve to the red-edged shirt slit below and to the flesh sliced open. It looked more like raw chicken meat or something Bessie might prepare in the kitchen rather than human flesh. The wound was still oozing a copious amount of blood and now that the initial shock of his injuries had worn off, the pain from this and his broken

238

bones was almost unbearable. Thomas reluctantly resigned himself to the fact that this place he had sought out unwittingly for safety was now probably going to end up as his grave. There was nothing more he could do other than to wait for blood loss and the elements to finish him off.

As he awaited his fate how he wished he had a pen and some paper to write one last letter to his wife. To tell her that he loved her and not to grieve too long for his passing. One last explanation to his family of how he had met his end and why? Instead of idly writing the words in his head, he soon found himself dictating them out aloud.

'Oh my dearest Bessie... We found ourselves severely routed with our men retreating from the conflict down that which we took to be the main road. 'Twas thickly hedged on both sides and so impossible to see much ahead. We that were on horseback held off until the very last but seeing all was lost, were also forced to flee on the heels of the sorry remnant of our brave infantry. From behind, Cromwell's Cavalry was harrying us on. Only, as we got to the end of the road we found that it led into a large enclosed churchyard surrounded by high hedges. We had stupidly let ourselves be herded like sheep into a pen waiting for the slaughter man to mark us out, one by one, for dispatch. Some of our fellows made a run for the church to claim sanctuary but I saw the bastard Puritan minister hurry inside and bar the huge oak door against us. There was no choice for those on foot, no other choice than to fight on, hand to hand amongst the tombstones. It was utter carnage. The dead falling upon the dead of life's lesser conflicts.

I, and those few other lucky enough to still be a-horse, desperately scoured the perimeter to try to find some way out. Then, by fluke, I noticed a small hillock where our horses might make use of the advantage to jump out. I went first, barely spanning it as Filly's hooves clipped it. Others quickly followed my lead but not all of them made it over for I saw at least one fail and he hit the ground with a sickening crack and did not get up again. Our infantrymen tried to break through it or scale it but those who succeeded got little further than slaughter in the field beyond. After that, we riders dared not look back. We just galloped away, blindly on with the Roundheads in hot pursuit. How they must have laughed to themselves as we tore up the countryside until we jumped one final hedgerow only to find to our utter despair that we were back on that same bloody killing field from whence we had fled.

I tell you Bessie, my love. There is no glory to be had in this war. No glory in King and Country if it means a man doing as I have seen done, to his brother man...'

Thomas suddenly fell silent as bitter tears ran down his battered cheek and he began to all but choke on self-pity.

Meanwhile, on the battlefield Parliament's men continued to mop up the spent Royalist army as Thomas and the others reluctantly re-joined the fray, galloping across corpses with the Roundheads closing in from behind. Then, a downed enemy pike man must have seen Thomas riding towards him. For, with one last defiant gesture, he thrust up his broken weapon into Filly's chest just as she galloped across him. The beast managed to stumble on a few yards, with the shattered pike shaft firmly embedded, before finally crumpling to the ground. As she did, Thomas's lower leg was trapped underneath her as she rapidly began to bleed out. As Thomas lay defenceless on the ground trying to struggle free from Filly's corpse, a sword wielding Roundhead charged at him dealing a slicing blow as he rode past, followed through by a crack to the head as the enemy's mount clipped him with its hoof. Thomas had barely escaped having his arm cleaved through yet felt little pain as he slumped back heavily onto the ground and into a warm pool of blood then, oblivion.

When he came too, the battle was well and truly over. Enemy soldiers were already scavenging the field in search of fallen comrades amongst the bodies scattered in profusion. From the intermittent screams abruptly cut short, he surmised that they must also be about dispatching those fallen royalists not yet completely dead. Thomas stayed low and still as they worked their way towards him only closing his eyes at the very last moment. As he did so, he prayed that he might live to open them again. Thomas was helpless to defend himself. All he could do was to hold his breath and volunteer not so much as a flicker as he laid feigning death half hidden by his horse. His recollection of events then became hazy as waves of nausea and light-headedness ebbed and flowed over him though nothing could wash away smell of death all about him. That would remain with him until the last, as would the voices he now heard at close quarters.

'What about this one here?' He had heard one rebel shout across to another. 'He looks about your size.'

'He may be that but if you think I am wading through all that shit only to find that I can't get to the other boot then you are sorely mistaken...'

'Never mind the boots...he might have valuables hidden about him.'

'Then if he has, he can take them to Hell with him as far as I am concerned. But mark me; should you get seen by an officer, then that's the end of you. If you want to wade through that blood and guts for a few coins or a ring then end up in front of a firing squad then go ahead and help yourself...'

The man thought better of it.

It seemed an eternity that Thomas was forced to lie there feigning death until the last of the soldiers had drifted away back to re-join and regroup with their comrades.

Thomas remembered then kicking at the rump of Filly's corpse with the bloodied boot of his free leg. He kicked and kicked in a Herculean effort to try to inch it off his foot, somehow he succeeded enough to drag it clear. Though he could not see, his ankle was hideously swollen inside his boot and as Thomas tried to stand and to make it bear weight, he only then realised that it must be broken.

This killing field was no place for him to remain. The Roundheads were gone but that did not mean that they would not be back - or that others would not come. Corpse robbers would no doubt be already on their way, eager to pick over the dead. He had seen them before after many a previous battle. Had it been enemy soldiers, though distasteful, as it may have seemed, Thomas could pardon, even understand the victors walking the battlefield picking up spoils from their enemy. After all, they had won through after taking the same chances and facing the same odds of dying as those corpses they then plundered. If anyone had any right to these, then it was fellow soldiers, no matter from which side, but the others, the bold-faced cowardly hearted jackdaws that suddenly spilled out from the towns or villages nearby at the close of battle to steal what they could from the corpses, were vermin. A soldier might strip the boots from a fallen man because he had sore need of them for himself - for his survival. These others would strip a corpse naked just for the miserable price of the clothes. Then there were the various followers of the army. Mostly consisting of other family members, male and female, or old retainers who often tramped the length and breadth of the country shadowing their loved ones. As the armies prepared for battle, they would seek shelter close by to await news of the outcome. At the end of many such a day as this, Thomas had seen them too, walking the field of dead looking for their missing menfolk, cheek by jowl with the heartless looters, often fighting over the same body as one sought to dignify and comfort in death while the other to humiliate and rob. It was one of the more unpleasant aspects of this uncivil war that Thomas was grateful for his wife not to learn about.

He knew he was vulnerable out in the open as he was, not only from being discovered but also from the elements when night eventually began to close in. So, when he saw an opportunity, he dragged his broken body away from the scene of carnage and across to ditch beside a narrow track. Thomas rolled down the bank then he must have passed out for the night.

As he now lay in the mist of that would-be grave, he listened intensely for the sound of others. He could hear nothing. No thunder of hooves, no firing of muskets. No more screaming from the dying and wounded. No shouts. No strains of squabbling over the spoils of death. It was a new day, a silent day.

Chapter Thirteen

' ...Nor should life rest on a single hope...'
- William Shakespeare

Bessie dashed out to meet the covered cart as it trundled across the courtyard. Ned looked drawn and tired as he brought the horse to an abrupt halt and tied off the reins.

'In the back, My Lady. In the back!' He cried jumping down.

As his mistress started to throw off the covering, Ned was already by her side.

'Tis not a pretty sight now, is it Lady Elizabeth?' He said revealing the lifeless body beneath, 'but a least I've brought Sir Thomas home to you!'

Bessie was horrified. Thomas's right eye was swollen shut with the black and blue indent of a horseshoe clearly visible on his broken cheek. His half-fastened jacket was filthy and the left sleeve ominously empty while further down his left leg, though splinted, looked hideously twisted at the foot.

'Titus! Titus!' she called across the yard to where she had only just seen the lad go into the tool shed. He immediately appeared at the door. 'Get help! It's the master! We will get him inside!'

As Titus ran off, Ned quickly drew Bessie aside and frantically whispered something out of Thomas's hearing.

'It's alright, Bess...' Perhaps recognising her familiar voice and realising that he was home at last, Thomas began to rouse. Bessie heard and quickly leaned in close to him and the good eye flickered open, 'I am home now, my darling...' he murmured.

They got him inside and onto the kitchen table where Bessie was relieved to find Thomas had not lost his arm as she had first dreaded but that instead, Ned had set it in a sling on his chest for the rough journey. The flesh adjacent to the wound was swollen, red and hot to the touch. The cut itself was oozing pus and full of foul debris. As she expected, it was badly infected though thankfully there was no sign of gangrene in evidence. Bessie knew that she could attend to the outward affliction, but was very aware that the fever also in evidence could prove fatal in itself. As for the ankle? Bessie suspected that it was badly broken and that perhaps the bone was already knitting together crookedly.

'Darling, shall I try find a doctor for this?' She asked him. 'I am afraid that I might hurt you by trying to reset this?'

'No. Don't do that. He may bring a Roundhead with him...' Thomas gasped. 'Besides...I would rather put my trust in you to heal me than any so-called doctor... Do what you must...my darling...and with my blessings...'

'But I cannot promise you that it will be as good as new...' She was not certain if Thomas understood how bad his injuries were.

'No heed...my dearest...' His eye was beginning to close again and his words became increasingly drawn and slurred. 'If it heals crooked...and I am hobbled... then it only means I can...never wander off...from you again... And I am...in agreement with that...I just thank God...that James had more sense...than me to go off to war...'

Ned looked at his Mistress and she back at him with neither daring to say a word. Bessie already knew that when Ned had gone to fetch her son from Oxford, James had declined to come home with him. Instead, he had explained to the old retainer that after a radical change of heart, he had decided to join with the Royalists and follow his father into battle that day. Ned had been on the killing fields looking for the young master when he came across and recognised Thomas's dead horse. He had noticed the drag marks leading away to the ditch and discovered his master's body lying wounded. Ned never did find neither hair nor sight of James. All the family could do now, was to cling on to the belief that somehow he had survived and got away with the King. For the time being though, Bessie had decided, it was better not to tell her husband about James. For despite his lucidness, she realised Thomas was gravely ill. There was no point in adding to his misery now.

'Then fetch Hope from the nursery, Titus. Tell her to bring me a fresh draw of cold water from the well and fetch it straight in here with as much spent sheet as she can find from the linen chest for compresses and bandaging. While you...you get to the pantry and fetch some Brandywine to help your master with the pain...'

Titus obeyed and after Ned had managed to persuade Thomas to down the best part of a large beaker full to render the poor man well and truly stupefied, Bessie began the grisly task of trying to treat his wounds.

'Ned. I will need you to assist me with this splint.' Ned nodded.

'Darling,' Bessie turned to Thomas. 'I am going to unwrap your ankle and try to get the swelling down as much as I can with a cold compress so I can much better work out the lie of it. Then, Ned and I will reset it and I will swaddle it up as gently as I can so it might set more naturally.'

Thomas was barely able to make any reply so his wife proceeded to remove the grubby improvised dressings. She had been right. Beneath the blackened bruising, the break in the bone could be seen through the skin. It was badly displaced.

'Oh! Mother!' Hope had prepared the compresses and fetched it over to be greeted by the sight of her father's wounds.

'What can you do with that?' Ned asked grimly.

'Very little I am afraid.' Bessie replied. 'I could try to realign it; re-break the mending bone then reset it more naturally but I am afraid that the shock could well kill him. The best we can do now for him is to bring down the swelling then to re-splint it as best we may. Whatever, I think the leg will cripple.'

'Maybe so Lady Elizabeth, but at least the master

will be alive.'

That indeed would be much to be thankful for.

'Let's roll him onto his right side,' Bessie suggested. 'I need to get a better look at this arm. Besides, this is a better position for him to be in, now that he is in and out of consciousness. Less likelihood of him gagging or choking should the brandy make him vomit.'

Titus and Ned gently tilted Thomas's limp body over onto his side and supported him there while Bessie carefully inspected the wound. It desperately needed incising to clean away as much of the infected material as possible within.

'Hope. Go into the dairy and fetch me out my boning knife and a cheese wire.'

A blue bottle attracted by the putrid dressing lazily bumbled its way into the consultation and landed on the wound. Ned quickly flicked it away. A half-remembered conversation replayed in Bessie's mind.

'Wait! ...Titus... You go instead and fetch the things from the dairy for me! Hope...' she said turning to her daughter, 'you have a much gentler touch! I have a task better suited to you!'

Hope was to be surprised by her mother's request. She was to take a pad of fresh linen smeared with a dab of honey, a small spoon and an embroidery needle and to go out into the herb garden where she and Bessie had found a fallen blackbird a few days earlier. Bessie had picked it up and laid it under the hedge. Hope knew exactly where and so was able to find it. When she did, it was full of thin hungry maggots, as Bessie had suggested it would be. Hope scooped up as many of the wriggling creatures as she could with the spoon and popped them into her apron pocket. Then she looked about for Friday's raw fish head that she had discarded on the compost heap. It was now covered with a fine deposit of long pearly white flyblow. Diligently, Hope painstakingly teased them off with the needle and secured them safely onto the honeyed linen pad then quickly returned indoors to her waiting mother.

Meanwhile Bessie had prepared the sword wound with a Brandywine wash before taking a deep breath and making an incision along its length with the razor sharp knife. Thomas cried out and tried to rise but then quickly slumped back as thick puss exuded out from the cut relieving some of the painful pressure. She then took up the cheese wire and ran it gently along the wounded surface to clean away as much debris as she could then, gently she set about the delicate task of cutting away as much dead matter as she dare with her tiny needlework scissors. By the time she was through and had cleaned the wound again with brandy, there was quite a deep void left behind.

Bessie took the maggots from Hope's apron pocket and slipped them into it along with a peppering of finely powdered cinnamon. Then she took up the linen pad and placed it, honey-side down, onto the wound to cover it. Then Bessie gently redressed the arm with a loosely woven linen bandage so that plenty of air could get in to her army of squirming helpers. She had remembered Captain John Smith remarking to her and Thomas that he believed he owed his life to the maggots in his own dreadful wound for eating away the infection within and thus allowing it to heal. With luck, Bessie was hopeful that it might also just work for Thomas as well.

'Tell me more about Oxford, Ned.'

Thomas was safely at rest by then up in his own bed at last. Hope was in the nursery with the baby and so Bessie and Ned were sat alone in the kitchen sharing a simple supper of bread and cheese. It had been a long and eventful day and now, as the long light evening stretched ahead, came the first opportunity for Bessie to closely question her old retainer about her son's failure to come home and of how Ned had retrieved her wounded husband.

'Well...I gets there Mistress, to Oxford and I goes in search of the young master. Only...the place is virtually deserted apart from some very elderly looking academics. They tells me that all the students is gone away...that most classes are dismissed for the rest of the year. Many of the students have returned home but that the most have been persuaded by the King and Prince Rupert to enlist in their army to fight the royalist cause.'

'King or no King! That man has no right to go into our universities to entice our young men away to die for the sake of his ego!' Bessie seethed with resentment. 'What about us? He has a baby son here and a young wife pining after him. James had already made his intentions clear that he would never join in with the war. What right has that man to come along and coerce him to do otherwise?'

'I dunno, Mistress. Maybe it wasn't the King...'

'What do you mean by that?'

'Well, I did hear how James's father had met with him only shortly before. Apparently, Sir Thomas then departed with the main army after making his farewells and that it was only then that Master James suddenly saddles up his horse and sets out after him. I don't think it was entirely the King's words that swayed him but more like sentiments for your husband drove him to do it.'

'I just cannot for the life of me fathom it... Thomas wrote and from the tone of his letter, he was certain that James would not... I wish I only knew what possessed him to do it. Have you any idea where he is now...'

Ned seemed reluctant to answer.

'Ned, tell me everything that happened when you found my husband. Tell everything you saw Ned...'

'I canst Lady Elizabeth...some of it was just too dreadful to tell.'

'Believe me Ned, in the Americas I experienced dreadful. I ate, drank and slept it... so please...tell me all.'

Uneasily, he agreed.

'I followed the main roads in search of the army. It wasn't difficult. So many men moving together can hardly ever be kept a secret. I met up with others on the road too, those following their loved ones so as to be at hand should the worst happen...'

'I understand. Thomas wrote to me about these followers in one of his letters a long time ago.'

'Well...as we neared Market Harborough, word came back along the road that the King and his army had suddenly turned back upon lesser roads to face the Parliamentarian Army gathered near a small village of Naseby. And.. that they were planning to do battle...'

'Then?'

'Well, I stops overnight in the town with the others. It's the nearest we durst get without being tangled up in the battle itself. It's what the followers usually did, they told me. Though some of the more feckless ones, if you ask me, did make it their habit to follow the army right to the edge of the battlefield. Quality women, with their servants as well, who might have been expected to have more sense! Anyhow, I stays in the town all the next day waiting to hear word of what's going on. We hears whispers of gossip but nothing really substantial from Naseby...Not until late on...then we hears that there has indeed been a terrible fearsome battle and that the Royalist Army, outnumbered from the start, was in defeat. Well, I don't know what rightly to do next for the best. So...I stays put.'

Ned stopped for a moment to wet his lips with a mouthful of small ale before carrying on.

'Then, just before it starts turning dusky, word gets round that there are prisoners being led up the road and into town. Royalist survivors that have been rounded up and are being escorted into the church as a makeshift prison. I goes with some others and we slip amongst the townsfolk all lining the street to gawk at the prisoners being led in. I thinks to myself, well at least I will see if either of the masters is amongst them. I tell you, it was a pitiful sight. Enough to make a blind man weep. There they came, bedraggled and bloody, some barely able to walk save the efforts of their comrades. Only walking wounded mind! Either there weren't none badly wounded or they simply did not make it off the battlefield. I looked mistress. I looked into the eyes of every Royalist man brought in but neither Master Thomas nor Master James was amongst them.'

'Oh Ned, so how did you find Master Thomas?'

'At first light, next morning, I takes the cart and I follow the way down to Naseby. I am not alone as one or two others have the same mission...to seek out their loved ones. We know we are getting there for the number of bodies strewn along our route increase. It was awful to see. Wounded men obviously cut down in retreat by the Roundheads. They must have been in a bloody frenzy with the devil himself in charge because we found women amongst the dead...followers...hacked about and many with their noses slit. Can you imagine that? That God fearing English men could inflict such horrors on defenceless women just for the hell of it?'

Bessie shuddered yet she knew it was true because just such God fearing English men had mutilated Hope's mother. And none could have been more defenceless than a heavily pregnant woman.

'None of the bodies I come across are the masters, so I carries on following the others till we reach an open plain between two hills and it is covered...absolutely covered in dead bodies. Like Hell has opened up and spewed all its tortured dead out onto the landscape. I don't ever want to see anything like it again afore I die! Not if I live to be a hundred!'

Ned needed another swig of Dutch courage.

'I walks over that entire field mistress, weaving in and out amongst the dead looking for them. It was like being in one enormous abattoir. Just bloody carcass after bloody carcass. For that's what they were for the most part. No longer human...just so much, disjointed, slaughtered meat. Hour after hour, body after body I walked through them until I grew hardened to the site of what dreadful injuries a human body can be inflicted with and yet still remain just about recognisable. Then, just as I was about to turn about and leave I sees a horse lying dead. It's a dappled grey and her markings stand out instantly. I know that it is your Filly, Mistress, so I runs over to her. There are bodies all about but none of them is him. Then...then I sees drag marks in the mud and grass and a trail of blood leading away and across to a ditch. I follow it and there I find him, lying in the bottom and unable to get himself out again. I climbs down fearing the worst for he is in such a bloody mess and when I gets to him...well he is as cold as a frosty land...'

'Thank God you did, Ned. He would never have had survived...he may not still but at least if he is to die, it will be at home and amongst his family and friends. For that, I will never be able to repay you...'

Over the weeks and months that followed, Thomas's physical recovery was slow and incomplete. Thankfully, due to Bessie's nursing skills, the infection in his arm healed, as did the flesh all but for a tell-tale dent of a scar. However, Thomas could never raise it up much like he could easily before and the resultant weakness in it caused him much frustration. As for the break in his ankle, Thomas was left with a heavy limp, which meant that he often needed a stick, which badly hindered his mobility. His soldiering days were over, even if he were ever to find cause again.

Though there was no word yet from James, his family had not given up on his returning. For although the King was shortly captured and imprisoned there were believed to be still a large number of Royalists at large determined to set him free. They hoped to reform and to then face down the Roundhead Army in battle once more and drive them off the face of England forever.

For now, although the Parliamentarians were in power there was yet to be any real threat of a lasting peace breaking forth. Thus, whenever Cromwell's soldiers came to be garrisoned where previously Royalist feelings had run high, then there was always the likelihood of trouble flaring up.

*   *   *

Bessie struggled to succumb to sleep that night.

When she eventually did, for the first time in years she had found herself dreaming about her earlier life at Gainsborough Old Hall. She was young again and newly appointed as Lady Frances' nursemaid. The child had been put to sleep for her afternoon nap but Bessie was too wakeful to join her. Instead, she had crept across to the tower door, quietly lifted the latch and opened it. As she stepped through, she glanced down at the stone stairway spiralling away into the darkness below. Above, a shaft of light beckoned the girl's curiosity onwards and upward.

'Be careful!' She could hear Mistress Goode's warning words still. 'If you should have a need to use those stairs take care! For if it has been raining, the water drips down and can make them as lethal as stepping out onto black ice. I did hear tell how a serving lass, back in the days of the Old Lord Burghs, did fall down them and broke her neck!'

Bessie slowly closed the door behind her, silently letting the latch fall. Cautiously she climbed the stone steps all the way up to the top where they opened out onto a small sunlit platform free to the air. She looked down from her lofty perch. Below her, the leafy canopy of tall trees rustled in the same gentle breeze that tousled her hair with a mournful whisper. Down and beyond on a swathe of lush green she watched a young falconer training his bird of prey. His cadger, an older servant who was experienced at caring for falcons, stood beside the wooden cage. Inside the almost made bird, tethered by a long, thin creance was feaking its beak on his perch. The cadger untied the leash then lured the young falcon from off its block, on to his hand then struck the hood, opening the braces ready for removal. Now perched on the gloved hand, the young bird cowered for a moment shaking and quivering her wings briefly before rousing her feathers and settling down. At a prearranged signal, the hood was gently taken off. The handsome blonde master whistled loudly to call off the falcon from the cadgers fist and to fly to his own where it took stand, sharply set and keen.

He stroked his fine-feathered hobby, and then cast her off, sending her soaring, spiralling upwards into the blue and away. As the falcon disappeared from sight Bessie stood mesmerized by the young man's angular figure. Motionless, he stood amongst the green like a watchful statue cast in stone. One hand raised to his forehead, shielding his eyes from the bright autumn sunlight as he tracked the progress of his beauty. The hobby waited on, circling high above the falconer's head waiting for the cadgers boy to flush out some game from the church-side copse.

Then, from the corner of her eye, Bessie spotted but a trace of motion upon the firmament. It was a white dove. Unhurried in its flight and oblivious to any danger from the bird of prey above. A gentle dove at ease on this beautiful fall day.

The young falcon, impatient for an earthly quarry to be raised, had also spotted it. Suddenly the bird changed direction, making two or three sharp turns as it swooped from out of the dazzling sun. It stooped to foot the inke of its quarry. Bessie gasped aloud. Too late! The falcon struck the dove's neck with its foot and binded to it. Then the dove was gone from out of the blue. Snatched from the grace of the heavens by treacherous, cruel talons. Snatched and sent plummeting from on high to the depths of the earth and the grasp of death below.

Bessie suddenly awoke with a great sinking feeling in the pit of her stomach as an overwhelming feeling of great foreboding swept over her. Yet, in her half-sleep state she could not understand why, apart from an illogical premonition that something bad was about to befall her.

Bessie sat up and looked across the bed to her husband. He was sleeping soundly. She got up carefully, so as not to disturb him and quietly made her way across to the open window. There she stood, as she had done countless times before on such sleepless nights as this. Looking out, she tried opening up her mind and willing her heart to try to sense her son's presence, somewhere out there in the distant moon bathed horizon. And like countless times before – she felt nothing. She could no longer feel that invisible bond between them that they had shared for so many years. When a mother can sense her child stirring in another room without sight or sound to warn her. Or to suddenly stop what she is doing midstream only to run to the door to find him coming down the lane towards home. Or to simply look up and feel him thinking about her. Bessie had not felt any such thing now for so very long. Hope may still have been resolute in her sincere belief that James would return but Bessie? Bessie had long since resigned herself to never seeing her only son again. Deep in her heart, her mother instinct told her that her son was dead. Yet, for Hope's sake, she had kept her grief to herself and had cried her tears of mourning in private. Yet also, she had earnestly prayed to God each day that she should be proved wrong.

Bessie glanced back towards her sleeping Thomas and wondered if he felt the same as she. Had he too, reconciled himself to the fact that after so long without word that James must surely be dead? Or was he, like Hope, desperate to hold on to the dream that he might one day return. As a couple, they no longer even talked to each other directly about this one important thing. Indirectly, yes. In response to Hope raising the subject, they did talk about their son but the conversation was always interjected by, maybe, perhaps, if...in reference to him returning. Never alone and face-to-face did they express their belief to one another that it was futile. That after so long without a word that James must be gone. Did Thomas grieve in private too, Bessie wondered. Did he cry deep in regret that his only son chose to follow him into the Royalist cause, despite his own misgivings, taking up the cause of the father he adored? And at what cost, this son's adoration? That as a result he was to lose his life to it, while his father survived? If so then the pain Thomas bore must be so very great that Bessie wished he would share it with her so, at least they might find comfort together in his loss. Instead,

Thomas had become distant, turned in on himself and away from life though not overtly. His behaviour was subtly changed in a way that others may have not fully noticed but Bessie had. Openly he might share a joke with Ned or the others but then she would catch him far away somewhere else, deep in his thoughts and with such a sad, lost air about him. Yet, if she went to him, to offer words of comfort or a loving embrace he would just look into her eyes and say, 'I am alright, Bessie. I am all right!' When clearly he was far from ever being all right again. For his audience, Thomas was playing out the role of normality when inside Bessie feared he was falling apart. As if he was closing a door on his Bessie and locking himself into his own private grief. In effect, after more than twenty good years of marriage, Bessie had lost Thomas too on those bloody fields of conflict.

*   *   *

Bessie woke to find Thomas grappling to get his breeches on quickly.

'There's some sort of commotion going on down there,' he quickly explained nodding his head towards the yard below. 'It's Ned's young lad and there are several Parliamentarians. I had best get down and see what's going on,' he said trying his best to hurry away.

Bessie slid out of the bed and across to the window. She could see that three mounted Roundheads had got young Titus surrounded and were clearly intimidating him. There seemed to be hot words passing betwixt them and a lot of jostling going on as the lad tried to get out from the horses way. Bessie became quickly concerned by the erratic behaviour of one of the leading men's beasts. It looked highly-strung and overly nervous. It kept stepping quickly, from hoof to hoof and she could hear it whinnying loudly, a sure sign that the horse was frightened. As the fracas intensified, the mare repeatedly tried to rear up. Bessie could see the rider pulling tightly on the reign and his face snarling as he gripped his knees closer into the poor creature in order to stay on. Bessie became increasingly concerned that Titus might be about to be trampled. She backed away from the window a little and into the privacy of the shadows. Still watching, she let her blackwork embroidered shift fall to her feet then stepped out of it. Quickly she started to pull on her day dress and though still only half-laced, she ran down the stairs to follow her husband outside.

Thomas was now stood amongst the horsemen too. She could hear him, calmly trying to reason with the Roundheads. Their officer was angrily accusing Titus of attacking one of his men during a brawl outside a tavern in the town the night before. He had later died of his wounds. Meanwhile, Titus stood shouting back, just as angrily, vehemently denying that he had anything to do with the killing and steadfastly refusing to go with his accusers. The scene was fast turning nasty. The soldiers closed in and tried to herd the lad away with their horses, kicking at him and scoring his bare arms with their spurs. Suddenly, Titus had enough. He pulled out a knife from nowhere and plunged it into the nearest soldier's leg then made to run off. The Roundhead fell from his horse screaming in agony as his comrade quickly dismounted to go to his aid. The commander calmly took up his musket, cocked the hammer and aimed to shoot Titus in the back as he fled. As he was about to, his skittish mount reared up and tried to throw him off. Thomas instinctively grabbed hold of the horse's reigns with his one good arm but it had already thrown the officer off balance. Screaming loudly, the horse then half-reared again, circling back towards Thomas in the process. With Thomas still holding fast to the reigns, the commander was now turned face on to him. What followed might have been an accident or a deliberate act of retaliation. Whichever it was, for Bessie helplessly looking on, time faltered like sand dropping grain by grain through a glass as the wretched scene began to play out before her eyes.

The musket fired with a cloud of smoke. Bessie did not register its report. Only the sickening thud as it hit Thomas. His body juddered. Then he crumpled and slumped heavily to the ground. Blood and brain splattered over the soldier's red coat and face and then onto the dust dry ground like rain. The musket ball had blown near half of Thomas's head away.

Bessie screamed but nothing came out. She was rooted to the spot like a mute willowy tree swaying gently as the shock and horror of what had just happened slowly began to sink in.

Ned came running in from the field alerted by the gunshot. The old man went straight to his master's side but could immediately see that there was nothing to be done. Thomas was stone dead.

Ned screamed and cursed at the officer who in turn just wiped his face with the white kerchief he had fetched out from an inside and ignored the poor fellow as if he wasn't even there. What was he anyhow, but a worthless ranting old man? This fine Parliamentarian had better things to do now, like helping his injured man back up onto his horse before all three then headed off in pursuit of Titus. Maybe if the commander had known that Ned was his father, then he might have dispatched him too.

As they fled, Ned lurched across to Bessie and tried his best to persuade her to go back indoors.

'I will tend to the Master, Lady Elizabeth...' he told her gently. 'No wife should have to see her husband so...'

She meekly complied as he took up her hand and she let herself be led away like a sleepwalker from a bad dream. The shock of it all had been too much for her to resist.

Swiftly, more labourers ran in from the fields to see what had happened. They saw the master and the blood and hurried off to wrench one of the barn doors off its hinges. Then they used it to stretcher Thomas's corpse out of sight and away to desperately set about trying to clean it up. One lad thoughtfully fetched a spade and used dirt to cover up the tell-tale blood pooled on the ground in full sight of the bedroom window from which Bessie was now grimly watching down. When he was done, she turned slowly and walked back across the room to her bed where the indentation of Thomas's still warm contours remained in the mattress and his pillow. Bessie threw herself down upon it and began to weep uncontrollably. Soon an equally inconsolable Hope, ran into the room to join her mother in grief. Together the two began to cry out their pain, alone in each other's arms.

Meanwhile the preparations for the funeral were set in motion by drier eyes and steadier hands, though no heart was unmoved by the needless loss of such a good master. Household chores were anonymously undertaken, meals quietly cooked and baby Tom was lovingly cared for. The vicar was summoned and he came, giving what comfort he could to the bereaved. By late afternoon, farm labourers had the grave already dug out and a coffin made. All was prepared for Sir Thomas's funeral the next morning.

Come daybreak, Ned set out to walk the short distance to the churchyard to see for himself that all had been readied for his master's burial. It was a soft dawn with but a lingering mizzle of rain left over from the long, black clouds of the night before. Dutifully, he trudged onwards up the lane with a weary gait. Somewhere close by, a blackbird began to sing such a beautiful, cheery refrain. It was soon answered by another, and then joined by a veritable hedgerow choir that was heavenly enough to lift any soul. It fell on deaf ears. Ned's head was fixed on other thoughts. Not with those just of his grieving mistress and how he might spare her further pain, but also of his son. For as Bessie and her daughter had passed the night keeping a candlelit vigil besides Thomas's coffin, Ned had spent the hours waiting and watching too. Titus had failed to return home by nightfall leaving his father beside himself with worry.

Ned came to the church gate, lifted the latch, creaked it open and went through. All was peaceful and still. He looked up at the ancient tower high above, now bathed with gentle light. He stopped for a moment and almost felt God lean down to touch him. Unmoved, he walked on towards the family plot where Bessie had wanted Thomas laid to rest beside his late mother. Then, from the periphery of his field of vision, something all at once caught his attention. There, in the yew tree, strung up like butchered meat in the cold room, hung the body of his son.

There was no one there to shield Ned from the sight that no father should have to see. Of his son's loving face, horribly swollen and blackened as the last lingering breath of life was slowly choked out of him by the all too short drop, the indignity of this grown lad's breeches soiled by death's last humiliation. Ned was alone, as he frantically cut through the rope to bring down his boy into tender arms that scooped him up and cradled him close like he was still his father's best 'baby'.'

As Bessie and the others later walked in procession behind Thomas's coffin, they hardly registered the covered wagon tethered by the churchyard wall. Ned, nearby his mistress's side had said nothing. Only later, much later in the day, did word slowly filter back to her, long after Ned had taken his leave. How Titus had been discovered hanging in the churchyard and how, from the looks of the evidence, he had climbed up on a gravestone and placed the noose about his neck himself before swinging off to bring about his demise.

By now, it had also emerged that Titus had been telling the truth to the Roundheads. There were witnesses to prove that he had played no part in the killing of the soldier. He had been completely innocent. However, he deemed himself guilty for the death of Sir Thomas. Held himself solely to blame for the loss of his father's much loved Master. Had he not run, he must have reasoned, then Thomas would not have been shot.

When Bessie heard of this, she thought that it served no justice at all. The self-sacrifice of the one life did nothing to bring back even one lost moment of the other.

'It is all such a terrible waste...' Bessie was heard

to say, over and over, 'such a terrible waste of such a young life.'

*   *   *

Hope brought her mother up a bowl of broth.

'Try to eat a little, Mother.' Hope coaxed. 'It has been days now and you need to keep your strength up. Father would not want you to be like this...'

'I know. You are right. I must try to put away my grief and we must get on with our lives. For yours and young Tom's sake if for nothing else...'

Bessie took the young woman's hands lovingly in her own and looking into her dark eyes whispered,

'I am so sorry Hope...'

'Sorry? Sorry for what?'

'Sorry that I took you away from the New World... Away from the life you should have lived..'

'What life? I should have been dead had it not been for you and my father...'

'Yet we could have left you there...after. We could have tried, somehow to get you back to your own people, to raise you up instead of stealing you with us to this God forsaken Kingdom. You might have lived a happy life there...be happy now still instead of this...'

'I would not have wanted this other life you talk of.' Hope replied, 'I am home. I have my life here and I know no other. True...sometimes I dream...I have always dreamed of being in a great forest...of being like a deer running free through the trees or a great bird swooping out from the sky. But that is all I have ever had...dreams. My reality is here with you.'

'But what about your natural Mother? Do you not regret never knowing her? Not even her name?'

'No. Never, you...you are my mother... You always have been. You never treated me as if you were anything other... You were always there for me... You... father...and James...' with her husband's name, Hope broke down and cried.

Bessie did not want to be cruel. Yet it was time that she tried to persuade Hope to give up any clinging notion that James might somehow still be alive. Better for her to swim with the truth now than to be dragged under by the constant self-lie.

'Hope, I think it is now for the best that you should face the fact that James is dead...'

'What if he is not?' She countered. 'Maybe he is still alive and will come back to us...'

'No Hope,...the dead only come back once in a hundred lifetimes. He is gone, my darling and we have to accept that.'

Bessie could see it in her daughter's tear-filled eyes. She could see that deep down, Hope too knew that her husband was dead yet, must have clung on to her own grief until she could hear the actual words tumble from her mother's heart. It was almost as if it was a blessed relief. As if Hope had been waiting all this time for permission from her one surviving parent to abandon this futile belief and begin the process of grieving for her James's loss. For permission to let her husband go with his father and to patiently await a future reunion on some far off, distant plain.

'Then....what now, Mother?' Hope asked after tears finally began to lose their bitter sting. 'What do we do without them?'

'Now?' Bessie replied. 'We let go of our life. We let go! Then we spit on our hands and we grasp on to it once more with an even firmer grip. We go on Hope!' she urged. 'We go on...'

The End

Author's Notes

Within a month or two of the original publication of Mayflower Maid, in the autumn of 2005 I had the pleasure of travelling with my co-author, Roger Vorhauer, to see the Plimoth Plantation in New England. This neatly ordered reconstruction of how the original settlement is believed to have been, perches upon a gentle hillside overlooking the Atlantic Ocean, just as the modern town of Plymouth does today.

To my British-born eyes, the landscape looked very much like home. Although, as I strolled along the winding pathways, I found myself repeatedly stopping to ask my American friend the names of the trees, shrubs and even birds that I was encountering for the first time, none the less I could imagine the great comfort those early settlers from my homeland must have taken from these almost familiar surroundings. Even the climate and the maritime weather of New England is not so different to that of the British Isles.

I had, of course, already carefully studied William Bradford's journal of the early colony in his 'Of Plimoth Plantation' before settling down to write Mayflower Maid. Now though, I took the opportunity to sit with it, opened up across my lap, high on Burial Hill in Plymouth. Looking out across the perfect blue sea, I tried hard to recapture the thoughts of the many who came in 1620 and that now lay buried beneath my feet. Despite the dreadful death toll of that first cruel winter, and the ravages of several serious food shortages, I imagine those who survived for any length of time too came to feel very much at peace here. For the whole place seems to exude a certain calmness about it, of a town long inhabited and at ease with itself. As if the remnant of those from the Mayflower, now long passed over, were looking down too and sighing 'Yes. This was a place well founded.'

Within a few weeks, Roger and I had worked our way down the Eastern seaboard of America to Virginia and to the Chesapeake Bay. With the possibility of a sequel to Mayflower Maid very much on our mind, we went to visit the Jamestown Settlement, a very similar reconstruction to that of Plimoth Plantation. So visually alike, in fact that one could almost pick up the two replica early colonial towns and switch them over without either looking much out of place in its new local.

Each boasted a sturdy fort complete with cannons and each town was enclosed by a tall, wooden palisade for protection. Both were populated by a host of small cottages and buildings, visually very similar in features to my own 17th century home back in a tiny village in Lincolnshire. The only real, striking difference between the look of the two, that I could see, was that while those of Plimoth were mainly built of wood and planking, Jamestown had opted for the more traditional wattle and daub method of construction. As the latter usually required the liberal input of the by-products of cattle rearing, which neither colony had at their outset, perhaps even these differences are more marked by the reconstructions than perhaps would have been by the original two towns.

However, even though the Jamestown settlement was as equally clean and ordered as its colonial cousin in New England, I immediately felt less easy here in Virginia than I had back there. Even though it was by then late into the year, the air still felt uncomfortably heavy and humid to me and the infernal chatter of insects was completely alien to my senses.

The wooden walkway beside the moored up, pristine replicas of the original Jamestown vessels, the Susan Constant, the Godspeed and the Discovery, was neatly constructed with the James River beyond looking almost inviting in the bright sunlight. However, I knew from reading contemporary accounts from the time, that this well-groomed re-enactment of the early colony was far from the harsh realities of the actual place back then. In fact, some of the locale around Jamestown had been readily described by some observers, as worthy of being ranked alongside some of the most inhospitable and unhealthy areas for habitation to be found anywhere in Britain. The river, with its boggy banks, rotting vegetation and stands of stagnant water, were a lethal breeding ground of sickness and disease, especially for the dreaded ague, which the population frequently suffered from, just as they did back home in the drained fens and marshlands of England which also harboured mosquito type insects.

Although blessed with creeks and streams, just as the Plimoth settlement was, far from providing a copious reserve of sweet water, at Jamestown the supply was brackish and for the greater part downright dangerous to use for drinking water which led to problems in supply of this most basic of necessities. However, this water was perfectly fit for irrigating the rich fertile soil and to support the one crop which could be grown here that would prove to be worth a King's fortune.

Neither Roger or I claim to be anything other than passionately interested amateurs, on either Pilgrim Father or Jamestown history. Yet it appeared obvious to our way of thinking, that there was one real, over-riding fundamental difference between the two early settlements. One far more reaching than merely the differences in location, climate and disproportionate value placed upon the differing crops which could be grown in the two colonies.

Jamestown, from its inception appears to have been a purely commercial, money-making orientated venture and governed mostly by men of that same persuasion. Whilst also primarily a commercial adventure, in the minds of many aboard The Mayflower, the Plimoth colony also had a spiritual raison d'etre for coming into being and was mostly governed by men of equal persuasion. We have come to believe that this crucial difference in mind-set between the government of one town, centred upon the pursuit of mammon and that of the other one, primarily focused upon the following of God's teachings in all aspects, be it in life or commerce, led to the ultimate fall of the former and the survival of the latter. A consideration which might also have been responsible for the very different experiences of the two towns when dealing with their indigenous neighbours.

While both settlements also suffered, what contemporary writers have described as 'starving times' early on, there is some evidence to point towards the less nobly born of Jamestown dying in disproportionally higher numbers, than compared to those of the higher echelons of that society than say in Plimoth, where the colony appears to have been run more along the lines of a commune in those early days, with possibly a much fairer pooling and sharing out of finite resources. A close inspection of the detailed muster of Jamestown for 1625 (where the location and owners of every item of property, food and livestock can be inspected), makes very interesting reading and in our minds bears out these observations.

However, no hint of suspicion as to the inequitable hoarding or misappropriation of supplies or even mal-government of the colony of Jamestown should ever be allowed to detract from the sheer courage and fortitude of those early settlers. Today, where long-haul journeys across the globe are considered benign and common place, one might be forgiven for underestimating what a great undertaking these early trips to America were. Trips to an alien, hostile destination, where there was no ready shelter, no food stores nor any of your kind waiting to greet or support your arrival. No search and rescue party ready to come in and immediately snatch you away to safety should your situation turn critical. The closest scenario I can imagine in modern terms, to sending those first settlers to Virginia, would be like sending a party of politicians and store-keepers to colonise the moon.

Understanding why they came into being and the socio-economic situation back home in Britain at the time, is paramount in fully understanding the workings of these two colonies. Late Tudor England cities, despite the frequent ravages of plague, were none-the-less becoming over populated by both a surplus of employable youth and 'spares' to the heirs of rich, noble families who, at a time when the oldest son usually inherited absolutely everything, were desperate to seize any opportunity to make a fortune of their own. (Unfortunately most of the latter, having been brought up in the lap of comfort, often had little or no skills that could be used or adapted to help them survive on the virgin land as colonists).

At the same time, the English Crown had laid claim to vast tracts of territory in the New World, which in order to secure indefinitely, needed to be populated by English subjects. King James I (of a now united mainland Britain) understood this only too well and so initially gave his blessings to companies of merchant adventures willing to bear the great expense of the instigation of colonies in the New World on his behalf.

Such was the need, that at one point even prisoners were extended the opportunity of a pardon, in return for serving out a period of time as indentured men and even a blind eye was turned to the rounding up of stray children and youths from the bustling streets of the cities to also be pressed into service there. Life expectancy for these lower orders in Jamestown was particularly low and also borne out by the census records of the time.

In order to constantly attract new investors and more money to fund these foundling colonies, these merchant companies needed to be able to offer a handsome return on those investments. Initially, the vision had always been that rich mines of silver or gold would be discovered in Virginia, just as the Spanish had found in their New World territories. However, when it was not, a profit had to be found elsewhere, whether in clapboard, furs or such-like by the shipload in order to help finance further expansion, which was in no way as lucrative or glamorous as gold.

Yet, thanks to the intervention of a certain young girl native to that country, the art of cultivating a high quality tobacco crop, hither to the sole domain and jealously guarded monopoly of the Spanish, was soon mastered by John Rolfe and the other Virginia colonists which resulted in commodity every bit as valuable to the Jacobean merchants as gold. Indeed, had it not been for the perfection in the art of growing this increasingly profitable crop in Virginia then probably Jamestown, if not the entire colony, might have been abandoned completely as a venture ill-founded. Instead, tobacco and its huge profit did flourish and despite the miserable toll on the lives of those working the colony, the continuing influx of get-rich-quick minded adventurers, backed by greedy investors continued to fuel the hell-fires of Jamestown for many decades before it was given up completely.

So, whether by accident or design, it came to be that people were continually fed into Jamestown to satisfy that demand and until the English population could eventually grow to such numbers that they were then able to withstand hostile attack and totally subdue the native population or drive them out, allowing the colonists and the land devouring tobacco to spread out all across Virginia. In time the inhospitable nature of Jamestown no longer needed to be suffered as a first tentative foothold on the country. Jamestown out-served its usefulness and so as the colonists moved onwards and outwards, in 1699 the capital was relocated to Williamsburg and Jamestown ceased to be a metropolitan centre.

In writing both Mayflower Maid and Jamestown Woman, Roger and I have tried to give the reader a detailed insight into the ordinary lives of people on both sides of the Atlantic. Again we felt it was important, especially for our American readers, to have fed into the novel the background to events occurring in Britain at around the same period, to produce a fully rounded rendering of the times as one might hope for from an Anglo-American writing partnership.

So, having spun out our story, what of the key New World characters that have become woven into our novels, Mayflower Maid and Jamestown Woman, who were not figments of our imagination? How did they go on to fare in real life?

Of Jamestown itself, one of the most memorable characters for me was Lady Temperance Yeardley. She had originally come across on the Faulcon in 1609 and survived the dreadful food shortages of that time (that had reduced the colonists to eating rats or in some instances far worse, corpses). Having married Sir George in Virginia in 1618, born him three children and witnessed her husband become fabulously wealthy, she was to be widowed in 1627. Although she quickly remarried, she too died shortly afterwards.

Captain John Smith, apart from one abortive return trip to America, never went to sea again after his 1614 voyage to the North Virginia coast, which he named 'New England'. In his remaining years spent in and around London, he published some eight books relating to the New World. After an illness he died on June 21st, 1631 aged 51. He never married.

Thomas Rolfe was educated in England before eventually returning to Virginia. Touchingly, records from the time show that he approached the assembly in 1641 for permission to go into the Indian country to visit his late mother's sister.

Although a fictional character, the young servant boy, James (whom Bessie befriended in Jamestown), was based on a first-hand account of an actual young lad of the time. Having arrived after the massacre of 1622 (and writing a very similar letter home to his parents to that portrayed in the novel), his name is then missing from the Muster records of shortly after - so presumably he died.

Of the Plimoth colony, Dorothy/Bessie's contemporaries fared a little better. Mary Brewster, although already middle-aged by 1620, survived long enough to be re-united with her remaining children on their arrival in the New World. She died in 1627 aged around sixty while her husband, Elder William Brewster lived on to his eighties having survived over twenty-three years in and around Plymouth.

William Bradford remained Governor of Plimoth for most of his remaining life. He remarried, had more children and lived on into his sixties.

Stephen Hopkins and his wife lived on for around twenty years in Plimoth and had five more children together.

Frances Eaton, who had the dubious honour of being the first person committed to the town's stocks (which he had been commissioned to build), remarried and had three more children. His son Samuel survived to marry and have children of his own.

Dr. Samual Fuller died in the dreadful sickness of the summer of 1633, which coincided with the Pilgrim's first encounter of Cicada Septendecim, the seventeen-year locust. This 'sickness' was probably an outbreak of small pox.

The fate of the remaining Hickman family and others in England will play out in due course in the last book of this trilogy, Restoration Lady.

Of course, we have already mentioned William Bradford's account of the early New England colony in 'Of Plymouth Plantation 1620-1647' which is widely available, edited with an introduction and notes by Samuel Eliot Morison (IBSN 0-394-43895-7). Three other books which we can highly recommend are 'Jamestown Narratives - Eye Witness Accounts of the Virginia Colony,' edited and with commentary by Edward Wright Haile (ISBN 0-9664712-0-2), the splendid read 'Love and Hate in Jamestown' by David A. Price (ISBN 1-4000-3172-9) and 'Captain John Smith and the Founding of America' by John Haden and the Pupils of Willoughby and Partney Schools, published by Barny Books, 2005 (ISBN 1-903172-46-2).

Finally, the old adage that 'truth can often be stranger than fiction' holds true! While Roger and I were still researching for 'Jamestown Woman', his other family members were busily investigating their genealogy. So it was that Roger quite unexpectedly discovered that he is a direct descendant of Pocohantas through the Gay Family line.

Still utterly bemused by this unexpected coincidence, it was then brought to my attention that I too might share a Jamestown family connection through my Morris family lineage. I am at present proceeding with researching my genealogy, albeit with some trepidation lest I find out I am also related to Roger!

Sue Allan

Also by Sue Allan

The Mayflower Maid -

The first part of the New World Trilogy

400 years ago a group of like minded men and women fled England and religious persecution to start a new life on a new continent - America.
One woman's story begins here....

In the infant colony of Plymouth in 1623 a woman lies consumed with fever. In her delirium she insists her name is not the one everyone has come to know and love her by.

The story of Dorothy's tragic journey amongst the Pilgrim Fathers is a vivid and moving account of a pivotal moment in history. The story of how she became the Mayflower Maid is an unforgettable tale of love and loss set amidst the strife and religious bigotry of Seventeenth Century England.

Restoration Lady -

The third and final part of Sue Allan's New World Trilogy

The much anticipated finale to this wonderful story following events in post civil war England.

Stripped of her title and wealth Bessie faces revenge from past enemies, accusations of witchcraft and the catastrophes of the plague and Great Fire of London.

This concluding part of the New World Trilogy is gripping reading for all followers of Bessie - the Mayflower Maid.